Why The Birds Sing

Gregory P Robertson

Book 1 of
The Vertical Speed Chronicles

LARGE PRINT EDITION

Library of Congress Control Number: 2014956038

This story is conceived from the mind of the author. Names, characters, places and incidents are the product of the author's imagination. Any resemblance to actual persons living or dead, business establishments, events, or locales is entirely coincidental.

ISBN: 978-0-9906921-3-3
First edition 2014

For more information
about the author and the book, go to:
www.gregoryprobertson.com

Ralphster Magoo Publishing, LLC
Silver City, NM

This book is dedicated to all those people that faced that open door and stepped out to hear the birds sing.

Why
The Birds Sing

You are Attracted to a person's Body

You become Friends with a person's Mind

You fall in Love with a person's Soul

Chapter 1

Vicki leaned her body into the engine cavity of the old pickup truck until her hands touched the newly painted inner fender just as her feet came off the step stool. She stuck her legs straight out to balance her body above the loose wires that lay on the fender. As her practiced hands wrapped tape around the wires that ran from the front left headlight, her eyes scanned the empty cavity for other uncompleted items. The garage door clicked open.

"Are you out here Vicki?"

"I'm under the hood, Mom," Vicki said. She pushed herself upward and found the step stool with her feet. As she regained her footing, she moved her head around the open hood.

Her mother stood in the doorway with her father's arms around her waist. He rested his head on her shoulder. “We’re leaving for Adam’s baseball game,” her mother said. “Are you sure you don’t want to come?”

“Not this time. I want to get this finished so I can put the engine back in this weekend.”

Her father looked to the engine on the stand beside the truck. “Did you retighten the exhaust manifold bolts?”

“Yes. I tightened them to 75-foot pounds. I also put the new main jets in the carburetor.”

“Okay. I'll help you get it into position in the morning before I leave for the station. Adam can help you get the motor mount bolts in.”

“If I get it running on Sunday, can you go with me on the test drive so I can practice for the driver's test?”

Her father chuckled. “As long as you've been moving and parking trucks around the station, you won't have any problem with the driving part.”

“I know. But I just have to get my license. I'm tired of the jokes I get from riding that old boy's bicycle. I want to pass it on to Adam and start driving this."

"Ok. We'll go out if you get it finished."

"Are you going to be okay for dinner?" her mother said.

"I'll make a sandwich. I 'm going to study more for the written test as soon as I finish this up."

Her mother smiled. "You worry too much honey. You aced the learner's test and you'll ace this one too."

A long horn blast sounded from the driveway. Adam's restlessness showed. "Tell Adam I'll be there next week for the playoffs. I'll take his picture if he scores the winning run."

"Ok honey," her father said. "We won't be late. Love you!"

"Love you too Dad. Love you Mom."

Vicki leaned her body back down to continue to wrap wires. The car started in the driveway and pulled out. The familiar engine sound disappeared down the street into the setting sun.

Jim missed the ignition with the first stab of the key, as he did with the second. Two keys and two ignition locks pushed past his eyes into his brain. Using both hands, he slipped the key in on the third try. The truck bucked when he turned the key until he remembered to push in the clutch. The engine rumbled as the 250 horses strained for the freedom to run. He slammed the gearshift into first and mashed the gas pedal as he let his foot slip off the clutch.

The truck jerked forward and the rear tires spun throwing gravel at the other pickups in the parking lot. He kept the pedal to the floor as the truck fishtailed around curbs and light poles. The spinning of the tires only stopped as the truck gained the asphalt of the highway. The tires chirped with the shift to second. They chirped again as he shifted into third gear.

The land rose as Jim raced the truck down

the highway toward home and another fight with his wife. He topped the hill accelerating through eighty. The sun centered in the rearview mirror and lit his face with an orange glow. He lowered his eyes from the road as he reached his right hand down to search under the seat for the bottle hidden there. One more swallow was all he needed before the inevitable screaming with the standard threats of divorce. One more swallow.

Ahead, a line of cars turned left across the highway into the Little League baseball park.

The grandfather's clock in the front hall began to strike. Vicki lay on the floor in the living room, the driver's manual open in her hands. Buster, her new kitten, sat on her shoulder purring. Vicki looked up at the clock.

"Maybe they went out to get ice cream with the team for winning the game," Vicki said to Buster.

As the eleventh and last chime faded from the room, Buster's ears flicked upward toward the street before he settled back into peaceful purring. Vicki turned her ears toward street as the sound of a large powerful automobile stopped in front of the house. A second car, smaller, with a higher pitched engine, pulled into the driveway. Neither engine belonged to her parent's car.

The sound of car doors opening and shutting filtered through the front door frame. Vicki put Buster on the floor as she stood to go to the door. She rose up on her tiptoes and placed her eye at the peephole as the doorbell rang. The sheriff stood in the porch light outside the door. Vicki's aunt and uncle, Sylvia and Eb, were on the steps behind him. Vicki turned the deadbolt and opened the door.

Her uncle looked at her with misty eyes. "We need to talk."

Vicki backed into the living room never taking her stare from his eyes. She grabbed Buster from the floor and held him close to her chest. The sheriff took Vicki by the elbow, guided her to the couch, and sat her down. He sat next to her, but a slight distance away as though the slightest touch would be wrong. Sylvia and Eb moved into the chairs across the coffee table. The sheriff cleared his throat, hesitated, looked away, and then straight back at her.

"Honey, I hate to have to tell you this, but your parents and brother were killed tonight by a drunk driver as they turned into the baseball field."

Vicki sat in silence as she looked into the sheriff's eyes. She hoped she would see a glimmer of a joke in them, as morbid as a joke such as that would have been. Nothing but pity returned her stare. As she clutched Buster even tighter to her chest, tears began to flow freely from her eyes. Buster snuggled and purred as Vicki pressed him deeper into her chest as though he could mend her heart. For the next few moments all that existed in Vicki's world was Buster's light purr against her chest.

Sylvia broke the solitude. "Vicki, you need to go pack some of your things. You're going to have to move in with us for now."

As her tears fell on Buster's head, Vicki looked up. "Why? This is my home. I want to stay here."

Sylvia pointed her finger at Vicki. "Don't argue with me. You can't stay here by yourself."

Vicki jumped up and ran to her room. She slammed the door and pushed the locking button in. Moving to the old swivel chair at her desk, she placed Buster in his towel-lined basket as she sat. He curled up, shut his eyes, and purred softly.

She opened the center drawer of the desk and stared at the large envelope that sat on top of the pens, note pads, and paper clips. She lifted it and opened the clasp. Her hand slowly withdrew the two 8 X 10 photos that she had taken at the Fourth of July town picnic. She placed them reverently on the top of the desk.

The top one showed the four of them. Her parents were in their normal pose, her father's arms wrapped around her mother's waist with his chin on her shoulder. Vicki and Adam stood in front, their arms over each other's shoulders. Adam stood half a head taller despite Vicki being older by four years. Vicki's mind moved to that day with its three legged sack races, Frisbee contests, fried chicken, potato salad, ice cream, and then fireworks as the sky had grown dark.

Her hand moved the lower picture to the top. Her parents stood by themselves in familiar embrace. Both smiled at the camera, but her father's eyes looked more toward her mother. Adam's head poked in from the side with a mischievous grin across his face. Vicki had scolded him for trying to ruin the shot. However, when she saw the finished picture, she knew this photo exemplified the family she loved. The quiet of the moment left as first the doorknob rattled and then a fist banged into the door.

Sylvia shouted through the door. "Vicki, open the door. We've got to go."

"I'm not going," Vicki cried.

"Don't argue with me. You can't stay here by yourself."

More bangs hit the door.

"Go away. Leave me alone. I want to stay here."

The banging stopped. Muffled voices came from the hallway. A minute later, the front door opened. The engines of both cars started and then headed down the street. Vicki stayed at her desk, the picture of her parents with Adam in her hands.

A light tap sounded through the door. Eb spoke softly through the closed door. "Vicki, the sheriff and Sylvia have left. I'll be in the living room whenever you want to talk."

Vicki looked down at the photo again. The photo looked the same, but now it contained not her family, but three specters who smiled back at her. Vicki stared toward the door. She knew she had to open it and face the reality that had become hers now.

Vicki walked through the doors of the First Savings and Trust Bank of Casper with the letter from Mr. Gallagher of the Trust Department in her hand. It had come the week before to the service station and requested her to come by to discuss the Trust that her parents had set up for her.

Vicki knew very little about the Trust. She had attended a meeting about it with Mr. Gallagher, Aunt Sylvia, and Uncle Eb shortly after the funeral, but she remembered little from the meeting. Sylvia had told her to sit in the rear of the room quietly. Vicki did know that the Trust owned half the service station with the other half owned by her uncle. It also owned the still empty home that she had been forced to leave.

As Mr. Gallagher's secretary showed Vicki into his office, he rose from behind his desk, greeted her cordially, and offered her a seat. Vicki looked first at the green leather chair that Mr. Gallagher had indicated, then at the grease spots that covered her jeans. She sat down on the front edge of the chair, her arms held tight against her sides.

"Would you like anything to drink? We've got coffee, tea, or sodas."

"No, thanks."

As Mr. Gallagher moved to his seat behind the large dark desk, another man entered the office and shut the door behind him.

"This is Mr. Smith," Mr. Gallagher said. "He's an assistant Trustee here and was assigned by the court to help with the Trust set up for you."

Vicki rose to shake hands with the man. "Pleased to meet you, sir."

Mr. Smith took a seat on the couch against the wall so he faced Vicki.

"I want to thank you for coming in," Mr. Gallagher said. "We were a little concerned when we didn't get any response from the letter we sent to you at their house or the messages we left with your aunt."

"Huh? I never saw any letter and my aunt never said a word to me about any messages."

Mr. Smith pursed his lips. "That does explain a few things. But, that as it is, you're here now."

"The reason I asked for you to stop in," Mr. Gallagher continued, "is that now that you have reached your eighteenth birthday, which is the legal age of adulthood in this state, your aunt and uncle are no longer your guardians. You and I will be interfacing directly to work under the terms of the Trust set up for your benefit."

"You mean my aunt and uncle are out of the picture?"

"As of now, yes. However, I will tell you that your aunt did stop by to ask for our support in a motion to continue guardianship until at least your twenty-first birthday. I told her that in my opinion, your character was such that I would not support any such motion. So, since I have not received anything from the courts to the contrary, their guardianship ended last week on your birthday."

Vicki shook her head slightly. "She never said a word to me about any of this. So what does all this mean?"

"Well," Mr. Gallagher started. "What it means is that you will deal directly with me and Mr. Smith concerning the release of funds from the Trust until your twenty-sixth birthday. At that time, the Trust will be dissolved with any remaining funds turned over to you. Until then, we will work with you concerning payments to your aunt and uncle for your housing, food, and clothing while you still live there. You will have to prove need for any personal funds requested before any are released."

Vicki's heart quickened. "You said 'while I still live there'. Does that mean I can live somewhere else?"

Mr. Smith spoke this time. "Within reason. We have an obligation to the Court to be able to show that we are releasing funds in a manner that is in your best interest. The assets of the Trust are not unlimited, so if you wanted to purchase a house that would take, uh - let's say eighty percent of the assets, we would have trouble agreeing to that."

"I don't want to buy a house. I just want to move back to my home."

"I can support that," Mr. Gallagher said. "The Trust required that, if possible, the house remain as an asset until you reached your eighteenth birthday and had a chance to decide whether you wanted to live there or not."

"Something else I guess my aunt forgot to mention. I would like to live in the old house. In fact, I would like to move in as soon as I can."

"One last thing," Mr. Gallagher said. "It is your right to live where you want. I will have to warn you though, if we see that you are living in a manner that is not in your best interest, we will petition the Court ourselves for your aunt and uncle to be reinstated as your guardians until at least your twenty-first birthday. Having said that, I will also say that based on what I have seen of your character over the years that I have known you, I think you will act responsibly."

"Thank you for that, sir."

"Mr. Smith can make the arrangements for you to move in at your convenience."

Mr. Smith stood. "Let's go over to my office. We'll get the necessary paperwork filled out. Then we can go over to inspect the house, I'll give you a set of keys, and you can move in."

As Vicki carefully rose from the chair so that her pants touched as little as possible, Mr. Gallagher came from around his desk. He offered his right hand to Vicki.

"I hope that as you enter this next phase of your life, you will also feel that I am not only the Trustee in this case, but I am also a person that you can seek advice from. My door will always be open to you to talk about anything you need."

"Thank you, sir. I will not disappoint you or Mr. Smith."

Vicki followed Mr. Smith down to his office. She signed what seemed to be a ream of papers before they headed in their separate vehicles to the old home. Together, they walked through the house quickly for the inspection. They stopped at each of the rooms long enough to ensure that no damage was evident, but did not linger in any space.

Vicki had not been in the house since the week after her parents and brother died. The picture of Vicki's family lay covered in dust on her desk where Sylvia had made her leave it.

"Better not to have a lot of things reminding you of the past, you need to move on," her aunt had said.

Even Buster had been a problem. Sylvia and Eb had several loud arguments about Vicki keeping the cat. Sylvia wanted it gone and Eb wanted her to keep it. Eb had won, but Buster had lived his life since then stuck in

Vicki's room unless Vicki carried him out to her truck for a ride.

As they made their way back out on the front porch, Mr. Smith held out the set of keys to Vicki. "If you find anything needs fixing, please call me. I'll get someone right out."

Vicki watched from the porch as he got into his car and left. She turned to face the front door, remaining motionless for almost a minute. She had finally returned to the home that fate had ripped her from so violently two years before.

Vicki walked back into the house and slowly began to move toward the kitchen. Dust lay on top of every surface and the house seemed gloomy even with the ceiling lights on. The silence screamed the reality from that awful night.

The pantry was empty and the refrigerator dark with its door blocked open. She opened each cabinet in turn, carefully pulling down a dish here and a cup there as she remembered who always used which one. They were all hers now.

She turned and moved purposely out of the kitchen down the hall to her parent's bedroom. The neatly made bed sat unused with the spread tucked just so. The clothes in the closet hung in their orderly rows, segregated by sex and color. The dresser stood with its drawers full of folded items. Pictures of her parents, long before she knew them, sat on top like a shrine.

Her little brother's room was in the same condition that he had left it on his way to Little League. The bed had a quickly thrown together look. Half of the clothes in the closet hung on hangars and half lay on the floor. The drawers of his dresser, hanging half open, were stuffed haphazardly with socks and underwear quickly put away. Posters of his baseball heroes clung to the walls with a few corners hanging loose. The room was cold and still. Vicki's memories of the room put it full of rambunctious racket and laughter that would cause her mother to tell them to calm down.

A wave of horrible reality swept over Vicki. She backed out of the room, clicked the lock on, and shut the door. She ran down the hall to her parent's room to lock that door. As she fell against the wall of the hallway, her breath in an almost panicked tempo, the memories of her family flooded back into her mind.

Maybe it is wrong to move back in here. Maybe I should just stay with Aunt Sylvia and Uncle Eb. The image of Sylvia replaced that of her family and Vicki's breathing quickly paused. The ghosts of her family were much nicer than her living aunt.

Vicki flung open the drapes as she ran through all the other rooms in the house. Sun light flooded the dusty rooms and hallways. She lifted the window sashes to let fresh air blow into the musty spaces. A sense of life began to work its way back into the house.

Vicki stopped by her room, grabbed the curled photo of her parents and Adam, and returned to the kitchen where she mounted it on the refrigerator.

Sylvia and Eb were not home as she loaded her few possessions into the pickup. Buster's cage came first into the front seat. Boxes of books landed haphazardly into the bed of the pickup. Vicki stuffed her clothes into garbage bags. She threw the last of the bags in the truck as Sylvia arrived.

"You ungrateful child," Sylvia shrieked. "Were you just going to leave our house without a word of thanks for all we've given you?"

Vicki just looked at her aunt. "I'm going home." She got into the pickup and pulled away.

Vicki stopped by her uncle's gym on the way back to her home. "I'm sorry Uncle Eb. I just can't live there anymore. You know that Aunt Sylvia and I have never gotten along. I would have left anyway in June when I finished from high school."

"I know Vicki," Eb said. "It's been rough

on you since your parents died. I hope you're still going to finish school."

"O-yea, that's a given. I still want to work at the garage if you'll let me."

"Hell Vicki, I can't fire you. It's really half yours away. Maybe you should talk to Mr. Gallagher about you running the place after graduation instead of just being a mechanic. You almost run it by yourself now."

"You wouldn't mind?"

"No, I'd rather be here at the gym anyway. Are you going to keep working out here?"

"Yes, as long as it doesn't cause you any problems with Aunt Sylvia. I really enjoy the kick boxing instruction and working with the free weights."

"You let me worry about Sylvia. You head home now. You need to get settled in. You've got school tomorrow."

"Thanks Uncle Eb, for everything." She hugged him and headed home.

She unloaded her belongings into the living room then sat in her spot on the old sofa while

Buster lay on the arm. She stared at the pile of clothes, books, and knickknacks that represented her life for the last two years. They barely covered the throw rug. Some of it she would keep, some of it she would just throw away.

One thing that would definitely go was the collection of dresses that Sylvia had made her wear to the school dances. Vicki had no interest in the dances, but Sylvia said that Vicki needed to show all the young men that she was a budding young lady with style and taste.

Never mind the grease that was always under her rough-cut fingernails. Never mind that she never wore makeup. Never mind that she took shop rather than home economics.

She turned her face toward Buster. "Why can't people take me as I am like you do?"

Vicki grabbed up all the dresses, took them through the backyard to the alley, and threw them into the empty trashcans. She slammed the lids back on and started back toward the house. She halted as she got near the steps.

Her old bicycle sat under the porch with spider webs covering it like a shroud. Rust spotted it in blood red hues. Vicki walked over, pulled it out from its resting spot, and set it up on the kickstand. She sat down on the rough porch steps and stared at the old bike. Memories of her little brother flooded once again back into her mind. She missed him. She had never been able to give him the bike that he so looked forward to. As she had looked forward to the freedom of her truck, he had looked forward to the freedom of the bike. Freedom had escaped them both in different ways. Now Vicki looked forward to freedom at last. Freedom from her Aunt. Freedom to be herself. Freedom to grieve.

Her eyes filled with tears.

The lights of Casper reflected off the low clouds to the south. An early fall chill was in the air. Vicki rolled down the sleeves of her flannel and buttoned the cuffs, then pulled the partially open overhead doors fully down and slipped the locks into place. It had been another slow Friday night with only a few gas customers since the dinnertime rush. The other two mechanics had left at five to have dinner with their families.

As the sound of a distinctive engine came to her from the highway, Vicki quickly moved back into the showroom and locked the front door. She scampered to the electrical panel and flipped the cover open. Standing on her tiptoes, she shut off the top breakers. The lights in the work bays and the parking lot went dark. Only the light from the back office showed through the windows of the station. Vicki began to shut the door with thoughts of hiding. However, her truck, parked next to the building, was a dead giveaway to her presence. Watching out the front windows, she hoped the truck would pass by.

The distinctive sound grew louder as the truck sped by on the highway and then slid into a quick U-turn. The tires spun and smoked on the dry pavement as it sped back toward the parking lot. Gravel flew when it left the pavement, and the driver revved the engine in backfiring spurts as the truck rolled past the pumps. Then it stopped directly in front of the door. The driver stumbled out.

Vicki was standing behind the counter, the phone next to her hand.

The man in the passenger seat, Bud, swiveled his head toward Vicki. Silvery sunglasses hid his eyes. He turned his head toward the highway, looking one way, then the other. Raising a whiskey bottle to his lips, he drank a long swallow before returning it to its hiding place. Then he looked at Vicki again. The distorted reflection in the mirrored lenses disturbed her.

The driver made his way to the front door and pulled on the handle. "Locked," he said as he continued to hold it. Vicki could almost smell the whiskey through the door. He stared at the handle before he yanked on it again and then looked up at Vicki. "Open the door,

Vicki. I need to use the bathroom."

"I'm closed Eddie. Try the Shell station."

"Come on Vicki. I really gotta pee."

"I never knew you were so particular about when and where you pulled your pecker out."

Eddie smiled through the door. "You got me there. But you have to admit that we had some fun."

"You had some fun. All I got was a pregnancy scare and the sight of your taillights when I told you. Now get out of here before I call the sheriff."

"You want a drink? We could have a little fun again."

Vicki picked up the phone. "Leave!"

"Okay," Eddie said as he moved toward the truck. "See you later."

Gravel flew as the truck skidded back toward the highway. It sped away, tires chirping as the gears engaged.

Vicki turned off the rest of the lights and waited in the dark. The night grew still. Two cars passed by the station headed into town.

Her house was less than a mile away, but still she waited.

After ten minutes, she unlocked the door, then locked it behind her and hurried to the safety of her truck. She scampered in, pushed the door lock down, slipped the key quickly into the ignition, and turned it. When the engine roared to life, the low rumble calmed her nerves. She put the truck into gear to start home.

She rounded the corner onto her street. The lamppost in front of her home cast a warm glow on the empty street. The yellow porch light beside her front door beckoned toward the warmth of an evening fire, but her distrust of Eddie made her err on the side of caution. She pulled into the driveway, stopped, and killed the engine. The key remained in the ignition. Vicki rolled the window down an inch, then listened and watched.

Normal noises filtered through the neighborhood. A muted bark from the Johnson's dog betrayed its desire to come in from the cold. A branch scraped softly with the wind on Mr. Stanley's roof. The neighborhood exulted tranquility. Vicki shook her head as she pulled the keys free and opened the truck door. "This is ridiculous." She walked up the sidewalk and pulled the screen door. It creaked as she reached the house key toward the door lock. A hint of stale oak crept into the air just as someone grabbed her arms below the elbows and yanked her backwards. The keys dropped to the ground.

A man whispered behind her ear. "Evening Vicki."

She twisted her head toward the voice and her face reflected in mirrored sunglasses. Something moved in the periphery of the porch light that showed behind her in the lens. She turned her head toward the light.

Eddie placed the whiskey bottle on the ground and grinned. "Told you we'd see you later."

As he took a step toward her, the stink of

the whiskey overpowered the night air. He bent down and roughly kissed her on the lips. "Now, let's have some fun."

Vicki, a grimace set into her face, transferred her weight to the balls of her feet and tensed her calf muscles. She stared into Eddie's eyes as she waited for the mistake she knew would come.

Chapter 2

Rick backed his Harley to the curb in front of the Study Hall Bar. As he shut down the engine with one last loud roar, he surveyed the motorcycles already parked there. Familiar colors and trims told him that friends waited within. He pulled off his helmet and checked his hair in the rearview mirror before he dismounted. The bouncer waved him in as he headed for the bar door.

Rick nodded. "How's the party tonight?"

"A little slow with school out for the session."

Rick grinned. "I guess there's less chance my seat will be taken."

Rick moved into the low light of the room as laughter, TVs, and music filled his ears. A reserved sign sat on the bar by the corner stool facing the door. Rick smiled as sat down on the stool, pushed the sign to the side, and placed his helmet on the bar. The bartender ambled over with a draft beer that he positioned on a coaster in front of Rick. Then, he grabbed the helmet and placed it below the bar.

Rick nursed the beer while he slowly scanned the room. Only a few of the bar stools and half of the tables were occupied. Most of the tables only had one or two people as they drank, ate burgers, and watched the TVs. Most of the noise in the room originated from one table near the rear that had extra chairs pulled up. People also milled around the table. Most of those were women.

A gap opened in the milling crowd allowing Rick to view the people seated at the table. Randy, the owner of one of the motorcycles parked outside, sat in one of the seats. Randy's presence at the table was a good enough reason to get closer to check out the party. As Rick left his bar stool, he slid the reserved sign over so that it held both his seat and the one next to it.

When Rick approached the full table, Randy got up, beer in hand, and headed straight toward Rick until he was within earshot of him.

"Rick. Have I got a deal for you!"

Rick stared at Randy for a moment. "Only if I get to choose first."

Randy grinned as he dragged Rick over to an empty table. "Don't worry. I'm not trying to set you up this time." Randy swallowed a quick swig from his beer. "You're always up for fun. Want to try something really exciting?"

"I'm listening."

"A bunch of us are going to try skydiving tomorrow. One of the guys on the list got sick, or at least that's the message he left. His deposit is non-refundable. So all you would have to do is pay the remaining thirty bucks and you could go skydiving in his place."

"Skydiving? What do you mean?"

Randy stood and pulled Rick by the arm. "Come on over to the table. The instructor, Kevin, is here. He can answer any questions that you have."

Rick slid into the seat that Randy had left open next to Kevin. Kevin was tall, almost gaunt, with wispy blond hair that hung to his shoulders. A trimmed goatee framed his mouth and his eyes twinkled with an inner generated excitement.

Rick looked Kevin in the eyes. "So what's the story with this skydiving stuff?"

Kevin spoke fast. "Well, it's like this. Skydiving is jumping out of an airplane with a parachute. What these guys are going to do tomorrow is take the First Jump Course at the Florence airport in the morning and make their jump in the afternoon."

Rick looked around at the others seated and then up at the women that were standing close as they hung on every word Kevin said. Several of them looked intensely at the instructor with a familiar look. Sometimes women looked at Rick that way when he told them he rode a Harley. It was the look of excitement.

Rick reached into his wallet, pulled out three tens, and handed them to Kevin. "Deal. Count me in."

Randy slapped Rick on the back. "I knew you'd be up for it." He turned his head toward the bar. "Another round over here! We're going skydiving!"

Kevin handed out sheets of paper with directions on how to get to the airport, how to dress, and what time to arrive. Rick studied the sheet for a moment before stuffing it into his jeans' pocket. Kevin then left with a simple "See you tomorrow. Blue Skies."

The waitress delivered a tray of beers to the table. Randy grabbed two and placed one in front of Rick. The conversation turned to laughter as Randy and the rest of the group spoke with bravado about jumping the next day.

Rick sat silent as the unknown of the next

day crept into his mind. "That's what I get for trying to impress women," he said under his breath.

The sun was just above the horizon as Rick stepped onto his small balcony in northwest Tucson, his first cup of coffee in his hand. Classic Arizona morning rays crossed the sky like translucent orange contrails. His mouth opened into a long yawn betraying that sleep had escaped him most of the night. As hard as he had tried, he could not think of any way out of his obligation to go. *If only I hadn't said Deal.*

The words of his father had come back to him many times during the night, as they did every time he had second thoughts on something he had agreed to. *You give your word, you make a deal, you must follow through. It's what an honorable man does.*

Rick drained the coffee, put his cup down, and walked through the apartment to his front door. As he grabbed his keys from the front table, a cocktail napkin with a girl's phone number stared back at him. She had said to call when he got back from the airport. If he got back.

His leather jacket and helmet hung on a hook by the door. He grabbed them before he could change his mind. He took the outside stairs two at a time and jumped onto his motorcycle. Kicking the starter, he prayed the engine would falter. It roared to life. As he reached the street, he looked both ways and turned north toward Florence.

Rick met up with the group at Spanky's Café near Oracle Junction for breakfast. After a quick meal of chorizo and egg burritos, they motored up route 79 with Randy at the head of the pack. Rick rode in his normal wingman position, slightly behind and to the right. The Harley rumbled beneath Rick's legs as the wheels spun the miles away toward his fate.

Riding up front with Randy brought a sense of familiarity to the adventure, just another motorcycle run through the sparse desert. Mesquite trees, creosote plants, and cholla cactus stretched to the horizon on the left and right while the Superstition Mountains rose like a friend to the front. If Rick ignored the turn into the airport, the road ahead would take him to those wonderfully curved mountain tracks.

Randy signaled the turn as the group arrived at the airport road. He stopped just past the turnoff and made everyone get below the large faded Skydive Florence sign to take a picture. Rick was about to lose his breakfast, Randy wanted to take a picture. After several shots, the convoy motored up the airport road.

As they moved quickly up the road and around a long curve, the group approached a cluster of buildings. To their front, a large building covered with windows reflected the morning sun. A still two-sided light sat mounted high on the curved roof. An orange streamer on a pole in the corner danced in the light breeze. Smaller buildings stretched away to the east suggesting a once bustling community. Broken railings, missing windows, and faded paint betrayed quiet abandonment.

Randy signaled a right turn into the parking lot and stopped at the edge of the gravel. Rick pulled up next to Randy as he threw down his kickstand. A worn single-story building lay in front of them with peeling paint that hung from the fascia and plywood covering several windows. Platforms and an airplane carcass littered the surrounding grass. A sign hung on the side of the building. *First Jump Course Here.*

Rick turned his eyes toward Randy. Randy had a different look on his face than the one that had laughed in the bar the night before. The skin of his face was taut while his wide eyes stayed fixed on the sign.

Seconds later, Randy's face morphed back to normal with his big toothy smile. "Ye-Ha," he shouted. "Let's do this." He leapt off his Harley and walked toward the building as Rick trailed behind.

Kevin strolled out of the building dressed in shorts, a t-shirt, and flip-flops. He directed the people there for the class toward the door. "Those of you that are here to watch can hang out at that picnic table. You can see the experienced jumpers land from there. Don't go wandering around too much, there are airplanes moving around. Bathrooms are at the other end of this building. There's also a lunch counter on the side of the hangar. That's the large building with all the windows."

Inside the classroom, green paint peeled from the walls while broken tiles checker-boarded across the floor. The group made their way into old school desks set in rows in front of a blackboard. Rick selected a desk near the rear next to Randy. Multiple lines of graffiti craved into the desk welcomed him. With wide eyes, he read crude comments intermixed with some terms he had never seen before. Malfunction, funnel, free-fall, and bounce predominated as he looked on his desk and the ones on either side of him.

Kevin handed out pens and stacks of papers to the people seated in the front row. "Pass these back please. Everyone take a pen and a copy of the injury waiver. When everyone has one, I'll go over them so you can fill them out."

Rick whispered to Randy. "What does he mean by injury waiver?"

Randy grinned at him. "Dangerous shit, man!"

Rick grabbed his copy of the waiver and silently started to read down it. The first words after a place for him to put his name stopped him cold. *I understand that skydiving is a dangerous activity that can result in injury or death*. Rick stared at the words, his pen still.

Kevin spoke again from the front. "Please print your name on the upper line and then read each of the paragraphs. You will need to initial beside each paragraph and sign at the bottom. Before you start, let me draw your attention to the first sentence. Yes, this is a dangerous sport if not done correctly.

However, it is not as dangerous as you may think. The public's perception of parachuting is different from the facts. A lot of the training is done outside where you will be able to see jumpers open their canopies, land, and walk away smiling. We have to have you fill these out so the insurance company will insure the airplanes and the city will allow us to operate here. Anybody have any questions about this?"

Rick looked to his left. Randy's pen raced down the paper as he initialed the spaces with no apparent attempt to read the paragraphs. Rick read each paragraph and initialed them in turn, no matter what the words said. The words did not matter. A deal was a deal.

After all the students passed the waivers to the front, Kevin scanned them. He looked up and glanced around at the class "Mike? You forgot to sign at the bottom." Mike came forward and signed the waiver. "Okay," Kevin said. "Let's get right into it."

Kevin placed a parachute pack on a table at

the front and explained the different parts. Rick did not catch many of the terms, but his attention focused when Kevin spoke two words. "Emergency Parachute."

Kevin looked out into the class. "Can I get a volunteer to wear the gear for a minute?"

Rick raised his hand and was out of his seat before Kevin called on him. Kevin strapped the parachute pack on Rick quickly with a practiced familiarity. The pack weighted heavy on Rick's back while the harness cut into his shoulders. Kevin shifted Rick around in different directions and pointed out the parts of the parachute again. Rick focused his eyes solely on the emergency parachute. Kevin grasped Rick's left arm and placed it across the emergency parachute with Rick's left hand over the ripcord.

"Whenever you have these rigs on, you need to cover the emergency ripcord like this. It's also referred to as the reserve ripcord. The last thing you want to have happen is one of these coming open at the wrong moment. An open parachute in an airplane with an open door is a bad thing. Any questions?" No hands went up. "Okay. Let's take a 15-minute break and meet outside. We'll go through aircraft procedures and exits next. Bathrooms are at the end of the building."

Kevin unbuckled the parachute and lifted it off Rick's shoulders.

"Thanks for the help," Kevin said.

"No problem."

Rick headed to the bathroom. As he walked along the well-worn path, a couple from the class headed toward the parking lot. They both got into a car and drove away.

Kevin's voice came from behind him. "Not bad, only two Leavers. I expected more than that out of a class this size. Maybe my teaching skills are getting better."

Rick stopped and turned toward Kevin. "Do many people leave before jumping?"

Kevin walked past Rick and pushed the bathroom door open. "Some do. Most likely a couple more won't come back from lunch.

Like I said in class, most people's perception of the danger of this sport usually isn't anywhere near reality. Some folks think it's worse and some folks think it's less. The ones that start out thinking it's less dangerous are the ones who usually leave. The ones who think it's really dangerous and come out here anyway quickly learn that it's reasonably safe."

The class moved outside into the sunshine after the break. An occasional airplane taxied by and the distinct rippling crack of parachutes opening in the sky above distracted the attention of the class on a continuing basis. Students focused their eyes toward the landing area as skydivers floated their way toward the ground. Laughter from the jumpers filtered across the concrete as they walked toward the hangar with their open parachutes slung over their shoulders.

The class gathered around the carcass of an old airplane while Kevin explained aircraft procedures. He moved small groups around the inside the fuselage and demonstrated how to exit.

As the last of the students performed their practice exits, an airplane rolled past on the taxiway with a jumper kneeling in the doorway as he held the top-hinged door open. The jumper waved at two women stopped nearby in a golf cart. He closed the door as the airplane turned onto the runway. It roared away into the sky.

A flatbed truck pulled up in front of the class and the driver honked the horn. "Everyone on the truck," Kevin said. "A load of returning students had just taken off and we're going to go out to the student landing area to watch them land."

Rick climbed on to the truck and sat down on the carpeted bed. As they pulled away, a man from the class headed toward the parking lot. Rick's hand felt for his keys while the truck headed out across the airport. Rick held the keys inside his jeans pocket with his eyes focused on the man as he got into his car.

The truck followed the taxiway for a short time and then weaved down a desert track. It stopped at the edge of a large dirt area cleared of the desert brush, mesquite trees, and cactus. Craved out by a road grader, the circular field measured over a hundred yards in diameter. Next to the edge where the track entered, a ragged streamer swung in the breeze. The students followed Kevin out into the clearing.

Kevin stopped near the center of the open area. "This is the student landing area." He pointed toward the streamer. "That's the wind sock. I'll talk about it later in the class."

The truck driver climbed up on the bed of the truck and lay down. "Jump run," he yelled.

Kevin pointed skyward and everybody looked up. "Does everyone see the airplane? It's flying from the east and is almost overhead now."

The sound of an airplane engine filtered down from the sky. Rick could not tell where it came from and had no idea which way was east. His eyes panned left and right, then up and down. Nothing but open sky filled his vision. The sound of the airplane engine suddenly diminished.

"He's climbing out," Kevin said.

Rick saw nothing.

"And Go," Kevin said.

Rick scanned the sky to no avail.

A white and orange round shape blossomed high in the sky above him. The parachute drifted in the sky as Rick's mind raced. *What was the person hanging under it thinking? Was he terrified, excited, passed out? Would my reaction to the jump be fear or excitement? Would I have the nerve to go through with it?*

Rick kept his eyes focused on the jumper as he neared the ground. Kevin moved quickly toward the descending jumper and yelled, "Feet and knees together. Eyes on the horizon."

The jumper moved his legs together and held them there until he met the ground. He collapsed to his side and rolled onto his back. In a quick movement, the jumper regained his feet and ran toward the side of his still inflated parachute. The parachute collapsed to the ground as it lost its air.

"Good one," Kevin yelled.

Rick looked up toward the sky again. Another jumper hung lazily under a green parachute. A third jumper hung under something that looked like a colorful mattress. Stripes of green, blue, and gold raced across the sky toward the earth.

Rick walked up next to Kevin and pointed at it. "What's that?"

"That's the jumpmaster. He's jumping what's called a square canopy. That's what most of the experienced jumpers use."

The jumpmaster spun his canopy, almost getting vertical before he leveled out. As he approached the ground, he lowered his arms to his side and the canopy seemed to stop just as his feet touched the earth.

"That looks like fun," Rick said.

Kevin smiled. "Oh–it is. It is."

When the jumpers had all landed, everyone piled back on the truck for the ride to the hangar. Rick purposefully seated himself next to one of the just landed student jumpers. The jumper held his parachute close to his chest with his arms while he grasped his helmet and goggles in his left hand.

"Want some help?" Rick asked.

"If you could grab my helmet and goggles, that would be good," the jumper said.

Rick grabbed them from the jumper. "Name's Rick. Rick Jones"

The jumper smiled. "Bob Smith."

"How was your jump?"

"Great! That was my third jump. I'll go again as soon as they can get me on a load."

"That was your third jump? Wow. When did you start?"

"I attended the first jump course last Saturday. I made my second jump Sunday and would have jumped again but the winds came up. I hope to make my first free-fall jump tomorrow."

Rick did not respond as the truck accelerated and the noise made conversation hard. When the truck stopped at the hangar, the returning students hopped off. Rick handed the helmet and goggles to Bob. "Good luck on your next jump."

"Thanks. Have fun on yours."

The truck pulled off and accelerated toward the training area. The students clambered down off the back as it slowed to a stop.

"Take a ten minute break. We'll meet back in the classroom," Kevin said.

Rather than heading toward the bathroom, Rick walked over to the airplane carcass. He stood next to it for several minutes, his gaze fixed on the small metal step mounted above the wheel. The vision of the ground thousands of feet below him filled his mind. He imagined the noise of the wind. *What had those jumpers seen as they stood on the step for real? How hard will it be to hold on until I'm told to let go? What will it feel like when I let go? Will I have the nerve to do it?*

He moved away from the step as the rest of the class filtered past him. The visions of the void beneath the step lingered in his mind as he walked into the classroom.

The class spent the rest of the morning learning the emergency procedures to use if the main parachute did not open correctly. Rick paid close attention to this part of the class and took two turns in the practice harness.

Kevin called a lunch break when everyone had taken a turn in the harness. "There's a snack bar on the side of the hangar that sells burgers and sandwiches. Be back here in thirty minutes. We'll go over canopy control and landings next."

Rick bought a burger and soda. Several picnic tables sat in the shade on the north side of the hangar and his group had gathered at one. He grabbed a seat next to Randy and tapped him on the arm. "What did you think of that emergency junk?"

"It seemed pretty easy," Randy replied. "I'm just not worried about it. This stuff seems pretty foolproof." Randy slapped his knee with a laugh. "Which is good because we're all a bunch of fools."

The entire table erupted in laughter as Rick laughed along with them, though not as loud. Rick fell silent as he munched his burger.

Somebody near the door to the hangar yelled, "Jump Run." Rick looked skyward to see if he could spot the airplane against the blue sky.

Another voice called. "They're out."

The airplane remained hidden to Rick. A minute later, several cracks sounded as two jumpers appeared under colorful square canopies. Seconds passed and two other jumpers opened their canopies further away in the sky. The jumpers spiraled out of the sky as the reds, greens, and yellows of their canopies contrasted brightly against the clear blue sky. They touched down softly in the dirt across from the hangar.

Rick looked around at the other occupants of the table. They were still engrossed in Randy's jokes, the same old jokes he told at the bar. Rick left the table and threw his trash in the can. He walked toward the classroom.

"I'm going to go get another look at that emergency parachute."

Randy yelled at him. "Hey, don't worry about it. If you're number's up–it's up!"

The table erupted in laughter. Rick lifted his right hand above his head and raised his middle finger as he walked away. Laughter hit the air again as Rick shook his head. *I have to get smarter friends.*

Rick left the bright sunshine of the outside as he entered the classroom. Kevin sat at a desk, a half-eaten sandwich in his hands. Rick nodded to him and walked over to the parachute equipment that lay stacked on the table. He placed his hand on the reserve ripcord handle. The chromed steel drained the heat from his hand.

He looked over at Kevin, who stared back at him as he slowly chewed his sandwich. "This stuff works, right?"

Kevin swallowed a sip from his bottle of Coke. "What's your name man?"

"Rick"

"Well Rick, it works great and I think you'll do fine. You know why?"

"Why?

"Because you're scared enough to pay attention and take this stuff seriously, not like your friend."

Rick looked back at the reserve as he moved his hand away from the handle. His gaze remained fixed on it. "How long have you been doing this?"

"I've been jumping for fifteen years and teaching for ten."

"How many students have gotten hurt?"

"Nobody's died, but there have been a few broken legs and wrists. Listen closely to the class on landings. It'll teach you how you can keep that from happening."

"Deal. I'll do whatever you teach."

Kevin drained the last of his coke as the other students moved back into the room while Rick turned to get back to his seat.

"Hey Rick," Kevin said. "You might just find that you like this skydiving stuff."

Rick smiled at Kevin, still unsure of what the end of the day would bring.

The afternoon training consisted of canopy control in the classroom and landing practice on the platforms outside. Rick practiced the landing roll extra times as Kevin's comment about a few broken legs stayed in his mind. He brushed the desert sand from his jeans as Randy laughed through a botched roll.

When all the students were back in the classroom, Kevin reviewed all they had covered in the class before he handed out a twenty question multiple-choice test. Rick went down the questions and checked the answers without hesitation. As Kevin collected the tests to grade them, a man in a green jumpsuit and a woman in shorts and a tank top walked into the classroom.

The woman spoke to Kevin. "Are they about ready?"

Kevin looked up. "Almost, I'm grading the tests now."

"We'll wait outside."

They both moved outside the door and focused their eyes toward the sky.

After Kevin finished marking the tests, he sorted them into two piles. "Okay, if I call your name, go with those two jumpers. They'll get you geared up for your jump. If I don't call your name, stay here. We'll go over what you got wrong on the test until you understand everything enough to safely make your jump."

Rick heard his name called, along with most of the others, and left with the group. Randy was not among them.

The group walked across the road toward the large hangar doors. As they walked those few steps through the massive thirty-foot tall doors, they entered another world. Colorful parachutes in different stages of being packed covered the hangar floor forming a kaleidoscope of green, blue, red, yellow, brown, and orange. Men and women in bright jumpsuits bent at the waist as they twirled as if on a dance floor. Returning students dressed in white coveralls leaned against a large shelf mounted on the south wall while they waited for their next chance to jump. Rock music blared from speakers mounted above the windows. An amplified voice cut into the music and rattled instructions in a language known only to the educated.

"Beech load five. Tom L with six, Dusty with three, Jackie with three, Airplane's on its way down. Ten minutes. Meet the airplane."

"Cessna load ten. Jumpmaster George plus three. Airplane is fueling. Meet it at the pumps."

"First Jump load one. Airplane is on its way down. Meet it on the ramp ten minutes. Give me a manifest before you go out."

The two escorts shepherded their charges

to a large room in the back. Nails protruded a foot from the ceiling on three of the walls while the fourth wall had a long bench the length of it. Dirty white coveralls, patched with Duct tape on the knees and elbows, hung from the nails on two of the walls. Scratched helmets hung on the other wall.

The jumper in the green jumpsuit stepped up onto the bench. "Hi everybody. My name's Mike. I'm going to be one of the jumpmasters putting you out on your first jump."

"I thought Kevin would be doing that," one of the students said.

"He'll be doing some of you, but the class is so large that we will need several jumpmasters to be able to get you all jumped today." Mike indicated down to the woman in the tank top. "This is Judy. She'll help get you suited up and ready to go. Now, who wants to go on the first load of three?"

The students remained silent. No one moved for several seconds until Rick raised his hand. "I'll go."

Two other students raised their hands. "Me too." "Why not?"

"Good," Mike said. "Grab a set of coveralls off the wall. The sizes are on the collar. Then grab a helmet and come on out to the hangar floor. The rest of you can start picking out coveralls and helmets, but wait in here. If you need to use the bathroom, it's through the door in the back."

Rick picked out a set of coveralls with the least amount of Duct tape he could find. He tried on first one helmet and then another until he was satisfied with the fit. As he walked out the door to the hangar floor, a motorcycle engine roared from the parking lot. His heart raced until he realized that the engine was not his, but was Randy's. Squealing tires followed the engine roar and then it faded into the distance.

Judy waited just outside the door and herded Rick over to the shelf on the south side of the hangar. A pile of parachutes lay loosely stacked across it. Judy looked Rick over, glanced at the parachutes, and picked one up. "Slip this on like a coat." After her hands shifted the pack over his shoulders, she reached between his legs for dangling straps. In less than three minutes, Judy had the parachute straps buckled and tightened and the emergency reserve parachute strapped into place.

"Put your helmet on." She checked the helmet's fit, grabbed Rick's left arm, and placed it over the reserve ripcord. She then slapped Rick on the backpack. "You're good to go. Just lean against the ledge while we get the others ready." Judy turned to suit up the next student.

Rick leaned lightly against the ledge as though any pressure on the parachute would end in disaster. His left arm remained pressed against the reserve and his hand caressed the handle.

A voice came from his left. "You ready for this?"

Rick turned his head to face the voice. Bob,

suited up identically to Rick, stood there with a helmet in his right hand. His left covered the reserve handle.

"I guess so. Are you going up again?"

"Yup. Next load. I'll probably still be at the landing area when you land."

A jumper in a red jumpsuit with a small parachute backpack over his shoulder walked up to Bob. "Okay Bob. To the airplane."

"See you out there," Bob said to Rick.

"Yea. Later."

Kevin walked up to Rick as Bob headed toward the hangar door. Kevin had changed into a blue jumpsuit with yellow stripes. He had a small parachute backpack draped over his shoulder. "I figured you'd be one of the first."

"I wanted to get it over with before I changed my mind."

"Your friend changed his mind and left. He told me I didn't know what I was talking about and he wasn't going to take any more of my bull. You'll probably get a different story when you see him later." Kevin looked over to Judy. "This load ready?"

"Yes, just got to give manifest the list of names."

"I'll take this load up. Tell Mike to take the next load."

Kevin looked at Rick and the other two students geared up and waiting. "Come on. Let's go skydive."

Kevin led the trio out of the hangar and into the sunlight. Rick followed behind him hunched like a condemned prisoner on his way to the gallows.

The airplane halted in front of them and the propeller chugged to a stop. Rick stared in at what would carry him skyward. The passenger seats and interior fabric were gone. The bare metal of the framework lay exposed. Metal ribs jutted from the inside of the smooth aluminum skin with occasional pieces of duct tape covering sharp edges.

The pilot did not lend an air of credibility to the operation either. Dressed in shorts, t-shirt, sandals, and a baseball cap, he stretched in his seat as he turned his head toward his approaching passengers. Only mirrored sunglasses and a wristwatch lent an air of professionalism to the situation.

Kevin loaded Rick in last and seated him next to the door with his back to the instrument panel. The tail of the airplane was visible out of the rear window along with a little bit of the ground. The student that sat in the back of the Cessna craned his neck while he shifted his eyes quickly side to side as if he was searching for a way out.

The pilot called out "Clear" and the engine roared to life. The airplane rolled and in less than a minute, it turned onto the runway. The noise level decreased as Kevin latched the door.

He looked around the cabin. "Everybody ready?"

Not a head moved.

"Good! Let's go skydiving."

The pilot throttled the engine up and the

airplane thundered down the runway. The ground moved faster and faster past Rick's rearward view. The airplane vibrated, slowly at first, then more violently as it picked up speed until it lifted off the ground. The vibrations changed to a gentle sway. The rumble from the wheels of the airplane grew quiet as they spun down from the takeoff roll and the sound of the engine changed to a gentle roar as the pilot fiddled with different controls.

The seconds changed to minutes as the airplane reached higher into the sky. Kevin reached behind Rick's parachute pack, removed the static line from the rubber band keepers, and hooked it to a ring on the floor.

Rick tried to lift himself up to catch a glimpse of the ground, but his parachute was too heavy and the cramped space allowed little movement. The parachute dug into his back, yet he dared not shift his body for fear something would catch and tear. All he could see out outside was the tail of the airplane and the horizon as it moved further away.

He shifted his eyes back inside. He first gazed at the ceiling toward the control cables while they moved back and forth with the sway of the airplane until the motion began to sicken him. He then stared toward the student seated in the rear. Rick could not tell if that student was as scared as he was or just relaxed. Rick looked up to the kneeling Kevin. The pilot said something into Kevin's ear and Kevin burst out laughing as he stuck a thumb up near the pilot's face. Rick wondered how Kevin could be so relaxed, given what they were about to do.

Everything had moved too fast. Rick pushed his mind to concentrate on the days' worth of training to block out the engine noise and wind. Women were not worth this. He promised himself that if he survived, he would never do this again. He gaze focused again at Kevin as he knelt in front of him. A gentle smile that betrayed an underlying calmness answered his stare.

The engine sound reduced as the airplane turned left and leveled out. Kevin looked around the cabin and turned the latch. "Door," he yelled.

The door swung up on its top mounted hinges while the wind sound in the cabin violently increased. Bits of paper and cloth flew around Rick's head. When the fusillade of debris ended, Kevin looked around the cabin again, caught Rick's eye, winked, and leaned his head out into the wind stream. He looked down at the ground.

Kevin brought his head back into the airplane and bent down until his mouth was close to Rick's ear. "You ready?"

"Who? Me? Yea, I guess so."

"You'll love it." Kevin looked over to the pilot. "Cut!" He stared back at Rick. "Climb out."

Rick hesitantly reached his left arm toward the strut as he twisted his body so that his left foot headed toward the step. Kevin grabbed Rick's backpack and pushed him forward as the full force of the wind hit Rick in his chest. Rick's left arm shook in the windblast as he struggled to grab the strut. His left hand latched onto the metal, then his right caught as he pulled himself upright. His left foot pressed against the step while his right dangled over the abyss. Rick heaved a deep breath and then looked back into the airplane.

Kevin looked down at the ground and then back at Rick. "Go!"

Rick turned his head forward and another deep breath filled his lungs as he jumped off the step. His eyes failed him as a blur of green filled his lower vision and a mist of blue filled the upper. A pull from above lifted his shoulders and swung his feet forward. His vision returned as the olive green parachute blossomed above him. The shape of the parachute was perfectly round.

His ears resumed their job as the wind noise ceased and the sound of the airplane engine faded into the distance. Only the rustle from the thin nylon above him hit his ears, all else was still. Rick's eyes focused on the parachute directly above him as the lower edge of the fabric pulsated like a jellyfish moving through the sea. Thin lines radiated from the lower edge to his shoulder straps like tentacles. The lines looked fragile, like string on a kite.

Rick's mind raced. Panic began to set in with thoughts of the lines breaking. He envisioned his body tumbling out of the sky toward the ground. He reached up and grabbed the steering toggles to have something to hold onto if the lines broke. Adrenalin and endorphins pumped through his veins. The lines held. Excitement began to replace fear as his vision returned to normal once more.

Rick looked around for the first time under canopy. The ground was three thousand feet below him. Square cotton fields, laid out in orderly patterns, stretched far to the west while the open desert pushed east until it touched the Superstition Mountains. The sky and ground filled Rick's eyes with a new sense of space and time. The distances presented were surreal. Only the rustle above him and the sway of the harness existed. Nothing else moved.

Rick's grip on the steering toggles relaxed. His gaze moved from the horizon to the round parachute above him. The solid appearing yet flexible shape continued to pulsate ever so slightly like a breathing, living thing. Rick breathed in time to his new partner. Excitement filled his soul.

He then turned his eyes from the round parachute above him to the ground. He searched for the landing area and pulled down on the left toggle until his nose pointed toward it. The horizon line moved up in his vision as movement toward the ground became apparent. In another minute, the ground floated quickly up. Rick pulled the right toggle to turn his nose the same direction the windsock was pointing.

"Feet and knees together," a voice yelled.

"Eyes on the horizon."

Rick responded automatically. The ground met his feet. He tumbled to his side. He stayed on the ground as his body twitched slightly from the adrenalin that still pulsated through his veins. His vision stayed fixed on the blue sky above him and a smile crept over his face. The shoulder straps tugged as the breeze kept his parachute inflated behind him while the sun shined warmly on his face.

A figure moved between him and the sun. Rick's gaze turned toward the figure. Bob stood there, his parachute in his arms. "You okay?"

Rick smiled up at him as a laugh filled his throat. "Yea. I've got to do that again."

Chapter 3

As the sun began to set over the mountains west of Prescott, Vicki turned her truck into the empty student parking lot and parked close to the doors of the building. After she turned off the engine, her head came to rest on the steering column for a long minute. She raised her head and looked toward the ominous double glass doors. With a sigh, she stepped out of the truck, locked it, and took a deep breath before moving.

She looked up again at the doors. "Here goes nothing."

Vicki moved up the footpath, pulled open the glass door, and turned right toward the offices. Most of the rooms were dark as she walked down the center of long hallway and glanced left and right at the closed doors. One office door sat open near the end and the lights in it were on. The baritone voice of Mr.

West, her advisor, resonated down the hall as he talked, undoubtedly on the telephone. Vicki stopped outside of the door before she knocked lightly on the wooden frame. Her left hand unconsciously twisted the pigtail on that side.

Mr. West looked up with the telephone held to his ear and motioned her in. She crept thru the doorway and made her way to the long wall of the office. Photos from a bygone era covered the wall. The images flew once again into Vicki's eyes. Pilots with their caps set at rakish angles, Fire Bombers low as they dumped red slurry, and large piston-engine airplanes parked on dirt airstrips in remote corners of the planet. Many showed a much younger and thinner Mr. West. They all seemed to be adventures he had experienced in the days before he came to the school.

Mr. West finished his call and placed the receiver in its cradle while Vicki moved to a seat across the desk. He picked up his unlit cigar from the unused ashtray. "So how did the interview with Desert Airlines go?"

Vicki fidgeted in her seat as she twisted her pigtail again. She opened her mouth, looked back at the pictures on the wall again, and paused a few seconds before answering. "Well, I guess the interview went fine. They offered me a job at their Phoenix base in their avionics shop." She paused again, then turned her head toward Mr. West until she looked him in the eye. "But, I didn't take it."

Mr. West leaned back in his chair and looked at the ceiling for a moment before his gaze dropped toward her. "Why not? They're a solid company with good benefits. They're growing and I'm sure that you would have opportunities to grow with them."

Vicki glanced up at the pictures on the wall again. "Well, to tell you the truth, I just couldn't see myself being cooped up in that shop day after day adjusting equipment for somebody else to install." She pursed her lips. "Don't get me wrong, I like working on avionics. I like all parts of aircraft maintenance. Getting my Aircraft & Powerplant certificate is probably the best thing I've ever done. I just don't want to sit at a bench day in and day out."

Mr. West cocked his head and started to open his mouth. Before he could speak, Vicki spoke again. "Also, I just couldn't see myself living in Phoenix. There are too many cars and people for me. Putting my RV into one of those crowded trailer parks down there just wouldn't work. My cat would never get to go out. We'd end up spending our lives inside and we'd both go crazy in a couple of months."

Vicki fell silent and sat tensed as she continued to twist her pigtail. She shifted her eyes away from his stare.

Mr. West let out a short chuckle. "You know something, I totally understand."

Vicki looked straight at Mr. West, released her pigtail, and slumped in her seat as the tension drained away. Relief replaced nausea.

Mr. West pointed with his cigar at a picture

on the wall. "You see that picture of those two young pilots standing next to the B-24 slurry bomber. That's Harry Sparks and me many years ago. We flew together and worked around each other for I can't remember how many years. That was him on the phone just now. I think you might be interested in what he had to say."

Vicki sat up as she looked at the picture of the two men.

"Harry runs the Florence Airport between Phoenix and Tucson. He has a couple of DC-6 Slurry bombers and a few skydiving planes. He just added a DC-4 cargo plane to his collection. He's going to send it to Alaska to haul fish. He's looking for another A&P to work on the skydiving planes and provide help on the DCs. Interested?"

Vicki sat quiet. The right words did not come to her. She finally answered. "Is there anything special about working on skydiving airplanes compared to what I've learned here?"

Mr. West waved the cigar through the air. "Not really. There's a Beech D-18 and two Cessna 182s. They aren't fancy. They strip skydiving airplanes out to reduce weight. Each one has maybe one working radio. They're flown hard and put away wet. The working conditions are rudimentary and dusty. A lot of the work is done outside on ladders or platforms." He put the unlit cigar in his mouth.

Vicki did not wait a second to speak this time. "How can I get a hold of Mr. Sparks to talk to him? Can I set up an interview?"

Mr. West smiled with the cigar clinched in his teeth. "I already set up an interview for you. I figured that Desert Airlines wouldn't be your cup of tea so I called Harry. He's expecting you tomorrow sometime in the morning. Can you do that?"

"No Problem! I don't know how to thank you Mr. West. You've been such a help to me these last two years."

"Don't thank me yet. Take a look around

down there and talk to Harry. Then decide if I'm doing you a favor or trying to hang an Albatross around your neck. Now get out of here so I can finish up and go home."

Vicki got up from the chair and headed to the door. "I'll come by Monday and let you know what happened."

Mr. West pulled the cigar out of his mouth. "Don't bother. Harry will call me five minutes after you leave to either thank me or curse me." He paused for a second and smiled again. "Vicki, think you can find the airport or do you need directions?"

Vicki smiled, turned, and hurried down the hall.

The next morning, Vicki woke before the dawn. She brewed herself a cup of tea while the sky outside the window lightened. She stroked Buster as the cat purred. "Don't worry, buddy. I'll get us to a place to live we both will like."

The teacup empty and a bowl of cereal

later, she grabbed her keys and camera. She listened to the sounds of the wakening trailer park as she opened the door and glanced around. Locking the door behind her, she waved to Buster as he pushed his nose against the kitchen window screen. The truck started effortlessly and she headed out on the long drive through Phoenix toward Florence. An hour later, she was in heavy city traffic.

The traffic broke on the south side of Phoenix. The big box stores and endless residential subdivisions moved to the rear view mirror as the open desert unfolded before her. Vicki's shoulders relaxed as her grip on the steering wheel became loose and one-handed. The exit to Florence came into view with an exit ramp that merged into a two-lane road that twisted through a short mountain pass. Monstrous saguaros, with the holes of the homes of Cactus Wrens in their sides, lined the steep hillsides. Cholla and Ocotillo cacti thrived on the lower slopes. A coyote stared at the truck from a rock on the hillside.

The pass fell behind her as the landscape flattened into large farm fields with this year's crop of cotton and onions. She drove by a small Quonset hut hangar at a dirt airstrip with two crop duster airplanes parked beside it. The pictures on Mr. West's wall came alive in her mind.

As she merged onto Highway 287, Vicki looked for signs of the Florence airport. A large hangar became visible in the distance long before she found the Airport Road sign. As she slowed to make the turn, a sign for the skydiving center became visible. She headed down the Airport Road and the large hangar drew closer as multiple old one and two-story buildings came into view. Some of the buildings had windows broken out while others had a look of aged completeness.

Vicki pulled into the large gravel lot and parked in a space next to the hangar. As she stepped out of the truck, she took in the serene surroundings. The desert stretched endlessly toward the sun that hung low in the sky. A light wind ruffled the leaves of the few trees growing near the hangar. A hint of laughter filtered through the air from some place unseen. Vicki smiled.

Cars parked in haphazard rows throughout the lot. Another group of cars and a couple of motorcycles sat parked near one of the smaller buildings. A group of men and women gathered around an aircraft fuselage and another group sat at a picnic table. As Vicki moved purposely around the side of the hangar, she passed into the world of Mr. West's wall.

Three monstrous four-engine airplanes sat parked side-by-side across the concrete. A fuel truck idled in front of one as a man on the wing grasped the filler hose. Platforms and ladders lay scattered around the beasts. As Vicki reached the concrete, a worn Cessna came into view parked at the fuel pumps. A longhaired young man in shorts, t-shirt, sandals, and a baseball cap held a dipstick in his hand. He gazed intently at the end.

Vicki approached the man. "Hi. I'm looking for Mr. Sparks."

The man slid the dipstick into the engine, closed the inspection cover, and motioned toward the hangar. "Check in manifest." He turned and yelled toward the hangar, "Cessna load one, let's go!"

The man swung the top-hinged passenger door of the Cessna up, climbed into the pilot's seat as he pulled on a pair of mirrored sunglasses, and then strapped on the parachute that sat on the seat. Vicki backed away from the airplane and headed toward the hangar.

Four men in colorful one-piece jumpsuits with parachute packs on their backs came out of the hangar toward the Cessna. Vicki varied her path to avoid them but turned her head to follow their progress as they passed by her. The men paid no attention to her as they focused only on the airplane and each other. They bantered between themselves. Vicki tried to understand what they said as they passed, but she only picked up a few words such as star, track, and dump between laughs and shouts of "Skydive." The Cessna propeller began to turn and the engine caught.

A slight grey-haired man leaned against the edge of the large hangar door with his vision focused on the Cessna as it started to move. His eyes followed the airplane while it taxied by and shifted only for a moment to Vicki as she approached. The airplane passed and the engine roar subsided enough for conversation.

Vicki smiled at the man. "Hi. Are you Mr. Sparks?"

He looked at her solemnly. "I'm sorry, he passed away."

Vicki froze, stunned as the blood drained from her face. Nausea came over her. She would have to call Mr. West and let him know his friend was gone.

The man then smiled broadly, looked her in the eye, and stuck out his hand. "Got-ya!

Mr. Sparks was my father. My name's Harry. You must be Vicki."

She met Harry's eye contact with her own. The handshake was firm but not overbearing. His eyes sparkled a bright blue that matched the sky. The wrinkles of crows' feet and graying hair betrayed his age, but his eyes provided him a youthful appearance.

"Yes sir," she replied as she released his hand. "I'm Vicki."

Harry continued smiling. "I said my name's Harry, not sir."

"Okay, Harry."

Harry motioned toward the runway. "Let's go watch the Cessna take off. I just finished the annual on it last night and I'd like to see if it works."

Vicki walked with Harry out on the concrete to a spot that they could see the runway clearly.

"Did you have any trouble finding the airport?"

"No. It was pretty simple."

The airplane engine roared and the Cessna began its takeoff roll. It lifted off, turned quickly to the east, and began to climb into the rising sun.

Harry smiled. “Great, no more paper work. Why don’t we walk down and take a look at the DCs.”

They walked quickly down the flight line past another Cessna and a Beech D-18. Oil shimmered in coffee cans placed beneath the Beech’s two engines. The DC-6s and DC-4 sat on the other end of the concrete, their size made the skydiving airplanes look like toys.

“Have you ever worked on any 4’s or 6’s?”

“No,” Vicki said as they walked. “My only experience has been with the Cessnas and Pipers that the A&P School has in Prescott. I’ve never been near anything that big.”

Harry climbed up the entry ladder for the first of the DC-6 slurry bombers. Vicki followed without hesitation. “How about working on round engines? Did you do anything with them up there?”

Vicki wished she had different answers for this interview. "Not an operating one. The school had a WASP R-985. I helped take it apart and put back it together a couple of times, but it didn't run. It was only for training purposes."

Harry crawled over the large slurry tanks and stopped at the over-wing window. He unlatched it and climbed out. Vicki followed but was careful to swing the window back down slowly so that it would not bang against the frame. Harry walked down the wing to the outboard engine until he stared down at the upper left part of the cowling. Vicki followed, being careful to stay on the rivet line, and moved up next to him.

"It looks like they fixed the oil leak. These engines have a problem with the upper oil return line. It vibrates a little loose every 50 hours or so and starts putting oil over the wing. It's hard to reach the fitting without taking the cowlings completely off. We normally just wait until we see it start leaking.

Truth is you could let it leak for a couple of weeks without losing much oil. It always looks worse than it is."

With that, Harry moved back down the wing toward the fuselage and slipped through the window hatch. After Vicki followed through the hatch, she stopped to latch it while Harry crawled back over the slurry tanks. He was waiting at the bottom of the ladder by the time Vicki reached the door. As soon as Vicki's feet hit the ground, Harry headed around the landing gear and between the immense engines. Vicki moved behind him staying between the arc swing of the propellers.

Harry glanced back. "Let's go over to the DC-4. Dean is just finishing up replacing a cylinder on the left inboard and still has the cowlings off." They hurried across the aircraft ramp. "Dean has been the mechanic on the jump planes for the last two years. He's going to go up to Alaska with the DC-4 as flight engineer and mechanic. That's why we're looking for a replacement A&P."

The two moved around the front of the DC-4. The exposed left inboard engine had a work stand around it. Harry scampered up the side of the stand. "How's it going?"

Vicki climbed up the side of the stand until she stood next to Harry. As he tightened the bottom left cylinder nut, Dean smiled at Harry and nodded toward Vicki. "Just about ready to cowl it up. You want to take a look?"

Harry smiled. He moved his eyes a mile a minute taking in every nut and bolt. "No, it would probably just scare me. If you need any help cowling it up, I'll be in the hangar."

Dean nodded. "Buzz and Willie are inside the cockpit installing the radios. I'll get them to help. If there are any problems, I'll come get you."

Harry nodded, swung himself over the railing, and climbed down the side of the stand. Vicki climbed over the rail and followed as Harry waited at the bottom.

"Let's go back to the office and talk."

He turned toward the hangar. Vicki followed behind as she softly spoke under her breath. “I hope he asks me something I can answer yes to.”

As she followed him into the hangar, Vicki passed into another world. Men and women walked around dressed in colorful jumpsuits that seemed to be the uniform for skydiving. Multi-colored parachutes, both packed and unpacked, lay scattered across the hangar floor. Some jumpers worked on or packed parachutes while others in small groups bent over at the waist engaged in some sort of dance. The mood of the hangar was cheerful with a sense of charged electricity to it. Music played from speakers on the wall.

Harry led her past a line of jumpers that waited at a counter with a sign over it that said Manifest. He walked by it and opened a door further down. Gold lettering on the door announced Airport Office.

“Come on in.” Harry walked over to a table, grabbed a cup, and poured coffee into it.

He motioned toward the coffee pot. "Grab yourself a cup and let's talk a little."

He sat down in a swivel chair behind a desk that overflowed with papers, manuals, and old aircraft radios piled up in one corner. Invoices overflowed from an inbox. The outbox sat empty. Vicki poured herself a cup of coffee adding a generous portion of dry creamer and sugar to kill the taste. As she sat down in the chair across from the desk, a woman walked in from an inner doorway.

"Hi. You must be Vicki. I'm Sally, Harry's wife."

Vicki stood and extended her hand. "Pleased to meet you ma-am."

Sally smiled. "Oh, please drop the ma-am stuff. It's Sally."

Vicki smiled in return. "Okay...Sally."

Sally sat down on the leather couch that was to the side of the desk and settled in. This was a team interview and Vicki would have to meet Sally's approval also. Vicki sat back down.

Sally was the first one to speak. "So tell us a little about yourself. How did you get into the aircraft maintenance field?"

"Well, when I was growing up in Casper, Wyoming, my parents owned a garage. I started pumping gas there when I was ten. Over the years, my father taught me how to work on cars and trucks. I found I was good at it and liked it. The only thing I didn't like was all the grease and grime."

"Do they still own it?"

"My parents and little brother got killed in a car accident a little over five years ago." The all too familiar look of sadness came over Harry and Sally's faces. Vicki quickly continued so as not to dwell on that point in time. "I lived with my aunt and uncle until I was eighteen. I kept working at the garage part time until I graduated from high school and then went full time. A couple of years ago I had some trouble and —"

Harry sat forward in his chair. "What kind of trouble?"

Vicki hesitated. She didn't want to go there. She wanted those demons left buried. "I – uh – I was involved in an assault."

"Were you arrested?"

She felt her face drain. The peacefulness she had felt when she stepped out of the truck was gone. Her mind raced as to what she and Buster would do next. "I – uh – yes."

"Why?"

Vicki slumped in the chair as she twisted her left pigtail. "It was my fault. I hit a cop. I got probation for a year, but that's over now."

Harry stared straight at her, almost through her. His eyes were a blank page. Vicki could not tell what was to come next. His gaze slowly moved toward Sally. Harry nodded slightly at Sally, who smiled softly and nodded back.

Sally sat forward on the couch. "So how did you end up at the A&P School?"

Vick sat straight in her chair and turned toward Sally to avoid Harry's stare. "Well, I decided I needed to make some changes in my life and needed to move elsewhere. I bought an RV, loaded up my tools and cat, and started heading south. I was passing through Prescott one day and saw the sign for the school. I checked it out and decided to enroll. I always tell people that I really enrolled because when I took a tour of the shop, nothing had grease on it. I felt I had died and gone to heaven."

"Do you like the work?" Harry said.

Vick turned back. His face was softer than a minute ago. "Well, I've always liked fixing mechanical things. I've found that aircraft maintenance is more exacting than car and truck work. That works very well with how I like to do things. I especially like the lack of grease and grime."

Sally laughed. "It's not all clean like it is in that school. You don't know how many clothes Harry has ruined when an oil line broke and he had to fix it in the field.

Harry continued. "When did you meet Sam West?"

"I met Mr. West the first day of classes when he was assigned to be my advisor."

"Is he still smoking those cigars," Sally asked.

Vicki smiled. "O-yea. I was always thankful that he couldn't light it up in class or his office."

The conversation died as Harry and Sally silently stared at each other. Unspoken words raced across the void. Sally then turned her head toward Vicki.

"I know that it required a lot of courage to tell us about the trouble you had. One of the things we value most in people that are around us is honesty and taking responsibility for their actions. Sam told us you had been in some trouble years back, but not what it was. For you to admit it gives me a good feeling about your character."

Harry spoke as Sally finished. "Sam already told me about your classes and grades. I watched you as you moved around the DCs out there. You moved deliberately and yet cautiously. You were also careful to treat the airplanes with respect. I can and will teach you how to work on airplanes, but I don't want to have to teach you to have respect for them. Not respecting airplanes can get you or somebody else killed." Harry set down his coffee and turned his eyes toward Sally. "You want to do the honors?"

"Sure."

Sally turned toward Vicki. "We'd like you to come work for us. We start mechanics at $10.00 an hour with no added premium for overtime. You would work on the skydiving airplanes mainly but would help on the DCs as needed. You would also take care of pumping fuel for any transit aircraft that stop by. Your workdays would be Monday through Friday with weekends off. But, if you're on the field and we need help, we expect you to pitch in."

Sally paused. Vicki realized that she had stopped for Vicki to answer. "That sounds good. I think I would like to work here."

"Wonderful! From what Sam told Harry about you, we hoped it would work out."

"One last thing," Harry said. "We won't say anything about your past to anyone. What you want to tell people about where you came from and why is your business. Also, we won't bring it up again. But, I don't want to ever hear about you hitting anyone."

"Okay. Thanks."

"When do you think you could start?" Harry said.

Vicki thought for a moment before answering. "Well, I can drive back up today and get the RV ready to go tomorrow. I can't get my tools from the school until it opens Monday morning, so I could be here in the afternoon on Monday. I'll need to find an RV park nearby to set up in. The only issue after that would be getting back to Prescott for my truck."

"You wouldn't need to pay anyone for a place to live," Harry said. "There are plenty of old building pads around here you can park on. There's water, power, and a sewage tap at most of them. That would work better for us anyway. There would be more chance for you to be available to work off hours if we need you. As far as your truck, we could fly you back up to Prescott Tuesday so you could pick it up." He turned toward Sally. "What do you say? Do you want to go up to have lunch with Sam and Jean next week? You could continue on your quest to try to get him to stop smoking those cigars."

"I think that would be great. Does that sound okay to you, Vicki?"

"That sounds fine. But I have to tell you I've never been up in an airplane before."

Sally laughed. "What? You learned to work on airplanes and never got a ride in one? Now I have something else to be mad at Sam about."

"Please don't be hard on him. He offered, but I always told him I needed to study. Actually though, I was afraid that I would get airsick."

Harry chuckled. "No problem. Sally can do the flying. She will be very gentle with you. I'll sit in the back on the way up. We'll be sure to carry a few barf bags just in case."

Sally stood and shook Vicki's hand. "Then it's settled. You can start work on Thursday. That should give you a chance to get your RV set up and get yourself settled in. I'll take you on a tour of the airport. We can look at the old building pads to see which one you'd like to set up home on."

"That would really be nice," Vicki said.

Harry stood and shook Vicki's hand. He grabbed a worn set of headphones from a peg on the wall. "I'll leave you two to sort that out. I need to go preflight the Beech. There's probably a load ready for it. If I'm up flying when you leave, it was really nice meeting you. I look forward to working with you."

Sally led Vicki through a rear door unto the parking lot. A dusty golf cart sat parked with its cord plugged into an outlet on the wall. "Let's use this for our tour. We would wear ourselves out walking all around to see everything."

Vicki swung herself down into the passenger seat. "That sounds good to me,"

Sally drove toward the smaller buildings off to the side of the hangar. "Let me show you the showers and the laundry room first. They get pretty crowded during the weekends with all of the skydivers, but during the week they're usually empty." She drove the golf cart past a group of people gathered around a stripped fuselage of a Cessna. "That's the first jump course for today. If you ever decide that you would like to try skydiving, we give discounts to employees."

Vicki glanced toward the class. "Thanks but no thanks. I'll just work on the airplanes for now."

"Okay, but if you ever change your mind, just let Harry or me know."

They pulled up to the front of the building. The individual showers were basic and relatively clean. The women's restroom looked in good repair and the paint was fresh. A double door led from the hallway into the center of the building.

"This is what we call the Rec. Hall. The skydivers use it on weekends for parties and to watch TV, but during the week it's usually empty." They left the building and walked toward the golf cart. Sally pointed to the far side of the building. "That's the classroom for the First Jump Course, but it's almost never used during the week."

As they reached the golf cart, Sally motioned toward a pile of scrap wood. "The skydivers like to have a bonfire on Saturday nights over there. Some drinking and loud partying, but it's all in good fun. Harry and I will come over here to have a beer with them occasionally, but we normally leave them to their own devices. You would most certainly be welcome if you decided to go over there during a fire."

Vicki just nodded and smiled at Sally. They sat back down in the golf cart.

"Let's go look for a place for your RV."

"That would be good. Then I should get on the road back to Prescott."

As they started to turn around, a Cessna taxied toward them so Sally pulled the golf cart off to the side into the dirt. The Cessna rolled by as the jumper in the door waved. Sally smiled and waved back as she turned the golf cart toward the old building pads.

Vicki and Sally walked around the several of the pads before Vicki settled on a spot. It was away from the other RVs and trailers and had hookups in a good position. Scattered cacti grew nearby. A small mesquite tree sat across the pad from where her bedroom window would be and would block the morning sun. The desert stretched to the east, broken only by flat concrete pads, with nothing nearby that could hide a person.

Vicki stood where her RV door would open and looked around. "I think this will do great for Buster and me."

Sally then guided the golf cart over to

Vicki's truck. "You have a good drive back. Please say hello to Sam for me. I'm sure that Harry will call him before you get there so he'll already know about your job. We'll see you Monday afternoon."

"Thanks for everything."

Sally nodded and drove the golf cart toward the rear of the hangar. Vicki drove over to the pad she had just selected.

"Home Sweet Home," she said before she turned the truck and headed out the airport road.

Vicki pulled up to her RV as the sun hit the mountain to the west. Buster sat in the kitchen window and let out a loud meow before he disappeared from view. As Vicki came through the door, Buster meowed in varying tones while he jumped back and forth from his dish to the food container.

Vicki scooped Buster up, hugging him tightly. "We've got a new home and I think it's going to be great.

She put Buster back at his bowl and filled it to the brim. Moving to the sofa while Buster crunched his food, she surveyed her little home. The well lived-in RV stared back at her. Books lay stacked on every counter. Clothes hung from a jerry-rigged line. Photos of Jerome and the red rocks of Sedona hung pinned high on the walls. "Where to start? Where to start?"

The next day Vicki cleaned the RV. All of the books, clothes, and knickknacks collected over the last two years went into the many storage spaces. The pictures pinned to the walls went into a drawer. Lastly, she muscled the storage trailer onto the hitch and checked the lights.

On Monday, she fed Buster and had her own breakfast before driving her truck to leave it parked next to the RV manager's spot. She disconnected the power cable, water lines, and sewer connection on the RV, stowing them neatly. The slide came in and the leveling jacks came up. Vicki climbed into the driver's seat and pulled out toward the road as Buster jumped into the passenger seat.

"Here we go buddy. The next adventure in our lives."

She reached the road and turned toward the school.

Mr. West unlocked the student tool room and helped Vicki roll her toolboxes to the door next to where Vicki had parked. They emptied the bottom sections of the toolboxes to carry them to the trailer but together they were able to lift the smaller upper sections still loaded. After the toolboxes were strapped into place and the trailer locked, Mr. West lit the cigar he had clenched in his teeth. Blowing out the match, he tossed it into the parking lot.

"Harry called Saturday. They are planning on flying you up here tomorrow to get your truck."

"I have to warn you about something. Sally sounded like she is going to harass you because you never took me on an airplane ride."

"Well good. Maybe that will keep her from harassing me about these cigars."

"I don't think so, she mentioned them too."

"That woman's been trying to get me to stop smoking cigars for almost forty years. You'd think by now she would have given up."

"I guess you've known them a long time."

"Known them long? Hell, I introduced them. Jean and Sally were roommates in the Wasps in WWII. Harry and I were training together nearby. I started dating Jean, but Sally kept coming along on our dates. So one night I brought Harry along to try to get some time alone with Jean. Danged if they didn't up and get married three weeks later. Not to be outdone, Jean and I got married the next week. We've been trying to one-up each other since then."

"I think that's wonderful. But I do have to tell you now that grades are final and my tools are loaded, I also think you should stop smoking."

Mr. West pointed at the road with his cigar. "Get in that RV and get out of here before I go change your grades. And just for that, you're buying lunch on Tuesday. Moreover, don't you dare take Sally's side at lunch. We've been having this battle for forty years and she doesn't need any help."

Vicki walked up to Mr. West and hugged him. "Thanks for everything, Mr. West."

"No problem, kid. And would you please drop the Mr. West stuff. I'm no longer your teacher, I'm your friend. It's Sam."

"Okay, Sam," Vicki said. A tear caught in her eye as she climbed into the RV. As she pulled away from the curb, she waved. Another tear dropped down her cheek.

Vicki drove the long way around Phoenix to the west of the city. She missed most of the noonday traffic with only a few backups delaying her as she went through the industrial areas along 51st Ave. After she crossed the bone-dry Salt River, she was soon into the open desert of the Gila River Indian Reservation. She steered the RV down the two-lane desert road and then through the town of Florence as Buster slept in the passenger seat basking in warm sunshine. The hangar, now the welcome beacon of home, materialized in the distance as she cleared the town.

Harry helped her unload her toolboxes and get them stored in the tool room. He handed her a key to the tool room and showed her where the light switches were.

"Sally wanted me to invite you over for dinner tonight so you wouldn't have to worry about cooking until you get fully settled in. Just come on over to the house around six,"

"That would be great. I'll be there."

Dean, the mechanic she had seen Saturday at the DC4, walked up to Vicki as she turned to move the RV. "If you need anything for your RV hookups, let me know. We've got a bunch of extra stuff stored in the back of the parts room."

"Thanks, but I'm sure I'll be fine." She quickly hurried back to her RV and drove it to her chosen pad. Unhooking her trailer, she dragged it around so it could act as a small storage shed. Before long the hookups were connected, the jacks were down, and the RV leveled. Vicki cranked the slide out and extended her awning. Buster sat in the front window the whole time and his head twisted back and forth toward birds as they fluttered from tree to tree. Vicki opened the trailer and pulled out the lounge chairs. As she moved them to the concrete pad in front of the RV, she spotted a figure standing next to the hangar.

Dean! He stood there just staring at her.

Chapter 4

The sun broke over the horizon bringing the first signs of the day's coming intense heat. The air weighed heavy from the previous night's rain. Though the storms had cooled the air, the moisture promised more thunderstorms in the afternoon. The Cactus Wrens fluttered back and forth through the trees, calling with their harsh chars as they danced through the air. The heat would soon silence them and force them into the shade of their protective homes.

The rays of the sun angled their way through the zipper crack of the tent until they shined into Rick's eyes. Rick flipped open the flap and crawled outside. Lighting the camp stove, he loaded the dented coffee pot and placed it above the blue flame. He poured a cup when it finished its dutiful perk and lifted the steaming black liquid until the strong aroma entered his nose. Settling in his camp chair, he looked toward the Superstitions and the building clouds, slowly sipping his coffee.

The summer monsoon season had quickly grown old as the afternoon storms stopped jumping early. When motorcycle riding every weekend had been his sport, Rick would go into the mountains north of Tucson or East of Phoenix to escape the heat and storms. Only a jump into the irrigation canals in the surrounding cotton fields allowed escape from the heat at the airport.

Rick got up and banged on the door of the van parked next to his tent. "Wake up sleeping beauty. It's time to have some fun. There's skydives to make."

Bob slid open the van side door. The smell of the fresh coffee brought him a little closer to actually being awake as he filled his cup and hoisted it to his lips. He plopped down in his own camp chair. "Seen any signs of life from the hangar yet?"

Rick already had his jumpsuit and helmet

out of the tent. "Nothing yet, but I'll bet the pilot's already there."

"Think the storms will come back in early today?"

"Yea. That's why I want to get going so I can get both jumps in before they have to shut down. I'd hate to have you party alone tonight."

"No chance of that. We'll both make it."

Rick picked up his gear bag, jumpsuit, and helmet before grabbing his cup of coffee. He headed toward the bathrooms at Rec. Hall. "See you over there. I'm going to get on the first load possible. Maybe I can even get my graduation jump in before yours. That would be a hoot."

"Won't happen. I'll be on the manifest before you get there."

"Put me on if you get there first,"

"No problem."

Rick sipped his coffee as he walked along. No breeze disturbed the desert air. Birds fluttered around the mesquite trees.

Movement to Rick's left caught his attention. A large orange cat walked out of the bushes and moved toward him. Rick knelt down and put his cup on the ground. "Now what are you doing out here?" The cat came over to Rick's outstretched arm and rubbed against it. He carefully lifted the cat into his arms. It struggled for a moment and then settled down as Rick walked back to the campsite.

"Look what I found. I wonder whose it is."

"It probably belongs to that girl mechanic, Vicki. I've overheard her say something about a cat to Sally. It must have wandered away from her RV."

"You're probably right. I'll take it over there."

Rick headed toward Vicki's RV. He crossed a couple of empty building pads and mounted the one with Vicki's RV. The area under the awning contained empty lounge chairs. After placing his gear on one of the chairs, Rick knocked on the door.

"Hello. I've got your cat."

No answer came. Rick moved toward an open window and called again. "Hello."

A voice came from his right. "What are you doing to my cat?"

Rick turned toward the voice. Vicki set her camera on the picnic table and moved purposely toward Rick. She grabbed the cat from his arm and backed away as fast as she had approached. She held the cat up to inspect him and then dropped him through the gate into the covered pen. The cat ran quickly into the basement hatch disappearing into the bottom of the RV. Vicki turned toward Rick with her fists clinched as he backed away.

She started advancing toward him with a grimace on her face. "What were you doing with my cat?"

"I found him walking in the desert. I was just bringing him back."

Vicki kept advancing. "The door is locked and the gate was shut. How would he have gotten out?"

"Maybe through that window he just jumped out of."

Vicki stopped. She quickly turned her head toward the RV. Buster sat on the picnic table, licking his paw and rubbing it over his head. The screen for the bedroom window sat on the ground. Vicki picked up the cat and held it close on her chest.

"I'm sorry. Buster's been with me his whole life. I guess I'm a little over protective at times"

"No problem. He must have gotten excited by all the birds singing and pushed out the screen."

"I guess. I never noticed the birds."

"By the way, my name's Rick."

"Mine's Vicki. Thanks for bringing him back. I own you one."

Rick looked at the camera on the picnic table. "Nice camera. Do you take a lot of pictures?"

"Yes. It's kind of a hobby of mine."

"I'm making my student graduation jump

today. Could I talk you into coming to the student landing area and taking a picture of my landing? I'll buy the prints."

"I'll take the pictures and give you the prints. It's the least I can do for you bringing Buster back. The only problem is the DC-4. We installed a replacement engine on it this week and they're testing it this morning. If there're any problems, I'll have to help fix it."

"I saw it was back. I thought it was going to be in Alaska all summer."

"It was. They were hauling a load of fish to Seattle and had a problem with number 2 engine. Rather than fix it in Seattle, Harry had them bring it down here. It'll go back as soon as the engine checks out. But, it should be ok so I should be able to catch you."

"Great. I'm going up now for a last training jump. I'll probably do my graduation jump in a couple of hours or so."

"I'll come over to the manifest to see what load you're on. If the timing works out, I'll catch the truck to the student landing area."

"Thanks. See you then."

"Okay. Thanks again for bringing Buster home."

Dan, the Cessna pilot, headed out toward the airplane with his parachute and headset as Rick walked into the hangar. Bob stood at the manifest window in his jumpsuit. He was immersed in a conversation with Sally as Kevin carried student parachutes out of the equipment room.

"Where have you been?" Kevin said. "Did you get lost? Pick out a rig and give it a safety check."

"Sorry," Rick said. "I had to see a lady about a cat."

Kevin just stared at him, and then shook his head. Rick went over to the rigs stacked on the packing ledge and sorted through them as he searched for pack fourteen. Ever since he had been able to pick out his own equipment as an advanced student, he had always tried to get free-fall rig number fourteen. It fit his body well and seemed to open smoother than the other rigs. He soon found it and put it off to the side. He did not have a favorite reserve since he had never had to use one so he just grabbed the top one.

Rick inspected the pack from front to back. Satisfied with the main parachute rig, he turned his attention to the reserve. The checks for the reserve were the same for the main.

As he finished up, he glanced toward the manifest window. Kevin stared at him. Nothing escaped Kevin's ever-moving eyes. One time when Rick headed to the airplane all suited up, Kevin had stopped him and untwisted a leg strap. It would not have affected the opening, but it would have been uncomfortable on the ride down. Rick had not seen Kevin anywhere near the student dressing area.

"Go ahead and get suited up," Kevin said.

Rick zipped into the brown and orange jumpsuit that he had purchased the weekend before. The nylon felt comforting as it snuggled tight against his chest like a cocoon. He fastened the Velcro wrist cuffs closed, stretched his arms up, and seated the wing cords. He swung the main parachute pack to his back until it settled on his shoulders. The chest strap hooked with a solid snap. He bent over, grabbed the two leg straps, hooked them in place, snugged them up, and stowed the loose ends in their rubber band keepers. His practiced hands clipped the reserve parachute on the front rings next and he cinched the side straps tight. Practicing a pull, his hand met the main parachute ripcord handle with a known familiarity. After grabbing his helmet and goggles from the ledge, Rick walked over to where Kevin was finishing the adjustments of his own gear. Bob waited suited up next to him.

Kevin then performed a safety inspection on both students' equipment. He knowingly ran his hands up and down the rigs, pulled on straps, checked that all the Velcro mated properly, and adjusted the harness where necessary.

He smiled at the two. “Pretty good. You might get this right yet. Let’s go.”

The three of them walked toward the airplane while Kevin quizzed each of them about their jumps. The other two other jumpers on the load, Tom and Amy, waited at the airplane. They would jump out after Bob, Rick, and Kevin. Tom and Amy got in the airplane first and sat in the back. Rick got in next and sat down backwards with his pack up against the back of the pilot’s seat. Kevin entered next and sat facing backwards with his parachute rig against the instrument panel. Bob entered last and knelt facing forward next to the pilot. Bob pulled the door shut and secured it.

The engine chugged to life and the airplane moved down the taxiway. Dan turned onto the runway. “Everybody ready?” Dan yelled. With multiple affirmative yells from the jumpers and a thumb up from Kevin, Dan advanced the throttle and the airplane picked up speed.

Rick kept his eyes fixed on the tail as it lowered when Dan pulled back on the yoke. The ground fell away as the airplane gently swayed in its element. Tom closed his eyes and looked asleep. How some jumpers could sleep on the ride to attitude eluded Rick. His own heart beat abnormally as adrenalin coursed through his veins on every jump.

Soon, Rick's altimeter read 3500 feet. He reached over, punched Bob in the side, and showed a thumb up. Bob smiled down at him and then turned his head back to look out the side window. The engine suddenly quieted.

"I've lost oil pressure," Dan yelled. "Everyone's going to have to get out. Open the door, Bob! Get Out. Get Out."

A shot of adrenalin pumped into Rick. His hands shook as he started to work his feet free from the entanglement of Tom's legs. As the door came open, Tom grabbed Rick by the arm with one hand while he motioned with his other for Rick to sit back down. He smiled and winked. Amy did not move but had a grin on her face. Bob leapt from the airplane and Dan throttled the engine back up. He turned the airplane slightly and the door settled down to where Kevin could latch it.

"That was fun," Tom yelled. "I saw Bob's face as Dan yelled for him to get out. He really had Bob scared."

Amy stared at Rick's face with a smile. "What's the matter Rick? You look like you almost died." Tom and Amy both burst out laughing.

By the time the airplane reached 10,500 feet, Rick had shifted from his sitting position to his knees and moved next to the door. Kevin pulled Rick close to him so he could speak into his ear. "It's all yours. When you're ready to go, give me a headshake and then do your exit. I'll catch up."

Rick nodded to Kevin and presented him a thumb up.

Dan turned the airplane left as he called out, "Jump Run!"

Rick kept his eyes fixed on the pilot. Dan throttled the engine slightly back, looked over at Rick, and nodded. Rick checked back with Tom and Amy. They were both on their knees and gave quick nods

"Door," Rick called out.

He turned the latch and the door swung up. Rick stuck his head out into the windblast and looked down at the hangar and buildings. They resembled a toy set placed on a patchwork quilt of tan and green. The view of the ground two miles below made his heart race as a new shot of adrenalin coursed into his veins. He gestured the hand signal to the pilot for a 10-degree turn to the right and waited another 15 seconds before he signaled the pilot to cut the engine back to idle. As the engine noise diminished, Rick nodded a headshake to Kevin and dove out the door.

As his body hit the air stream, he arched with a practiced familiarity while the wind flowed onto his face. Rick turned his body so that he could look back up at the airplane. By the time he found it in the air above him, it had flown 200 feet away. Kevin still knelt in the door with his eyes focused on Rick. Rick resisted the urge to wave at him as he stuck to the plans of the dive.

He turned his body to face the west and began his series of maneuvers for his final student jump. As he finished the last back loop, Kevin dropped down in front of him from above and settled into a position about 10 feet away. Rick checked his altimeter. 7,000 feet. He focused his gaze back on Kevin as Rick stuck his legs out to move forward. The movement was jerky and sloppy like a sailboat without a keel blown around in rough seas. Rick slowly closed the distance between them. As he made headway, he checked his altimeter again. 6,000 feet. Rick stuck his legs out a little straighter until the distance to Kevin reduced more rapidly. Kevin put his arms out as Rick approached and caught him by upper shoulder grips. When he released his grip, Rick floated backwards before he straightened his legs a little and stopped the movement. Rick looked at Kevin's chest mounted altimeter and saw they were just above 4,000 feet, his mandatory break off altitude. Rick waved the break off signal to Kevin and turned 180-degrees. He straightened his legs and brought his arms to his sides as he moved away from Kevin in a halting porpoise-like track.

He held this position for a few seconds before returning to his normal arch. He then waved his arms before he looked over his shoulder to ensure that the air above him was clear. His gaze turned to the approaching earth before he reached for his ripcord. He hesitated as he stared at the ground. The trees rushed toward him and grew larger with every millisecond. He reached for his ripcord with his right hand as his left arm automatically went above his head to balance him in the airflow. The ripcord tightened until the pins pulled from their keepers and the pack against his back loosened. Rick looked over his shoulder at the pilot chute as it moved skyward with the deployment bag in its wake before he turned his face forward to prepare for the opening shock.

His body was jerked vertical as the parachute fully caught air. The sound of the rushing wind ceased and all was quiet around him. Rick looked up at the parachute that blossomed fully open with the lines running straight. A quick glance at his altimeter showed he had opened at 3,000 feet.

"Everything right on the money."

Rick lifted his legs slightly to settle himself in his harness as he relaxed for the remainder of the now familiar canopy ride. The view of the desert vastness with the little farming towns in the distance never grew old. Familiar, but not old.

The ground approached and Rick setup for his landing as he turned his parachute into the wind. His feet and knees came together without thought for the landing. He hit the ground, rolled to his right to absorb the impact before he regained his feet and ran around his canopy to spill the air. With a smile on his face, Rick gathered his canopy into his arms and walked toward the waiting truck. Bob lay on his back on the carpeted bed.

"You okay, Bob?"

Bob stayed on his back and continued to grin. "Yup. You're just looking at a real skydiver enjoying the sky. It's great not being a student anymore."

He sat up with his hand raised above him. Rick raised his in turn and they high fived.

"So that fake emergency exit was pretty funny from where I was sitting. You looked pretty scared."

"I can't believe they did that to me."

"When did you figure it out?"

"As soon as I heard the engine rev back up. I really felt stupid."

"Don't worry. I'm sure you'll have lots more things to feel stupid about in the future."

"Just sit down and shut up, you stupid student."

Kevin debriefed Rick back at the hangar and signed Rick's logbook to clear him for his graduation jump. Rick headed straight over to manifest to sign up for the next open load with a jumpmaster aboard. He grabbed rig number 14 to pack it so he could use it for his next jump. While he packed, Bob walked up with his logbook open in his hand.

Bob had a laugh in his voice. "Read it and weep! Read it and weep! I'm not a student anymore."

"Did Kevin talk to you about the beer rule yet?"

"Beer Rule?"

"Yea. It seems there a tradition amongst the skydivers that anytime you do something memorable in the sport for the first time, like getting off student status, you own a case of beer. We're supposed to bring it to the party at the fire tonight."

"Are you sure that he's not just pulling your leg."

"I asked Sally about it. She said that it's true and I believe her."

"You believe her? Hell, she'd pretend to flirt with you to get a free beer."

"Really, I think it's true."

"I guess we'll have to go buy some beer after dinner."

Rick finished packing the student rig and laid it on the packing ledge with his jumpsuit on top to hold it. He walked outside, turned his eyes skyward to watch for the Cessna to come on jump run.

As he gazed into the clear blue above him, Vicki walked up. "Are you going up soon?"

Rick maintained his vigilant watch for the Cessna. "Next load."

"Okay. I'll be available to catch your landing."

Rick stopped his search of the sky and looked at Vicki. "Thanks. It'll really be great to have a picture of that."

Someone yelled, "Jump run."

Rick immediately looked skyward again

and located the airplane high in the vast blue sky above him. Rick's practiced vision caught the four experienced jumpers as they left the airplane as a group and stayed close as they fell. The jumpers danced the flying dance of skydivers, relative work. They flew their bodies together in constantly changing geometric patterns that they had practiced earlier bent over in the hangar. Rick's own chance to do that dance would come soon enough. With student status gone, he could jump with other jumpers that would help him learn that flying dance. He would learn to dance with the best of them.

The jumpers hit their break off altitude, tracked away from each other, and opened their canopies almost simultaneously in different quadrants of the sky. The manifest speaker came to life as the jumpers flew their canopies toward the landing area, the flights punctuated with turns and spirals.

"Cessna load 8. Get it on. Huey, Jill, George, Ed, and Rick for his graduation jump.

Airplane's on its way down."

The announcement of Rick's graduation jump brought applause and catcalls from the hangar floor. A smile stayed on his face as he did his safety check before donning the gear. George, the jumpmaster for the load did a quick safety check on Rick and then the five jumpers walked out together toward the airplane as it taxied toward the hangar. The pilot stopped the airplane on the apron with the engine running. The jumpers climbed in with Rick getting in last, and the airplane taxied to the runway before heading skyward.

Dan had just turned onto jump run as Rick looked toward him for the signal to open the door. Rick's body tensed; half from the anticipation of the jump and half from the concern that the others in the airplane would pull a stunt on him as they had on Bob. Dan throttled the engine down and nodded a quick headshake. Rick looked around the cabin to make sure that everyone was ready and yelled "Door!" while he simultaneously twisted the latch. The door swung up out of the way and Rick stuck his head out the door to pick his exit point.

Suddenly, he felt hands push against him. Initially, he resisted. Then, he relaxed as the hands did their deed and he fell from the door. As soon as he was clear of the airplane, he arched his body and found stability. His eyes looked over his shoulder as he pulled his ripcord and the pilot chute left his back. It moved away slower than normal, an inch at a time. Rick's heart quickened, but held his arch as he continued his count. The deployment bag lifted off his back as if in slow motion with the lines flopping out behind it. By the time Rick reached eight in his count, the parachute over his head began slowly filling with air. Just as he finished nine, the parachute was open full.

Bob and Vicki ran toward him as Rick approached the ground near the center of the landing area. He hit, rolled, jumped to his feet, and ran around to the side of his parachute. It collapsed to the ground as the wind spilled out of it. Rick started gathering it up.

"So did they push you out of the airplane?" Bob said.

Rick bunched the last of the canopy to his chest. "You knew about that?"

"Yup. Kevin told me that's what they were planning on doing to you. He said they like to do something different to put students off balance and see how they react. Since they did the fake emergency on me, they decided to give you the old heave ho."

"It was kind of fun actually. The only weird thing was my chute opened weird, almost like things were in slow motion."

"Kevin told me about that during my debrief. It's called a sub-terminal opening. Kevin said that since you had just exited the airplane you were going slower than you do at terminal velocity, so the chute opens slower. It's another thing they don't tell you so they can see how you handle it."

Rick finished gathering his chute, "I

wonder now that we're off student status if they'll still do junk like that to us."

"Probably."

Vicki walked up. "Stand next to each other. I've got one more shot to finish the roll."

Rick and Bob moved next to each other.

"Smile."

Bob threw his arm over Rick's shoulder. "How could we not?"

Chapter 5

Vicki stared at the thunderstorms of the monsoon as they built to the north while the student truck slowly made its way out of the desert. "How long do you think it will be before those storms hit us?"

"I don't think it will be too long, maybe an hour or two," Rick said. "While I was under canopy, I saw a gust front heading toward us."

"I guess I better go put my lounge chairs away before I head out."

Vicki jumped off the truck when it stopped at the hangar. Harry stood outside with his headset around his neck as he looked at the load manifest.

"Do you need me for anything? I'd like to go into town to take care of a few errands."

"Sure, go ahead. The engine on the DC-4 checked out fine. Dean and Buzz are cowling it up."

"Thanks. I'll be back in a few hours."

Vicki walked around the hangar and headed toward her RV. The folding chairs went under the chassis and she rolled the awning in. After chasing Buster inside, she shut the cabinet door that contained the hole to the outside caged area. She removed the roll of exposed film from her camera and loaded a fresh roll.

"I'll be back soon," she said to Buster.

Locking the door behind her, she headed toward her truck. As she started to open the door, a shadow crossed her. She dropped her keys, turned, assumed a fighting stance, and scanned the area around her for danger. No one was near. Canopy shadows raced across the parking lot as several jumpers turned toward the landing area. One of the canopies had crossed in front of the sun and caused the shadow. Vicki relaxed her stance, picked up her keys, opened the door, and sank into the driver's seat. She hesitated a moment with her head on the steering wheel to calm her heart before she started the engine. Without thinking, she locked the driver's door even though the window was down. She slowly pulled away from her RV to begin the five-mile drive into town.

The first stop was the PhotoStop, the only one-hour photo place in Florence. Vicki wanted to get the pictures of Bob and Rick to them in case they left early when the storms rolled in. She dropped the exposed roll into the attendant's outstretched hand.

"Only one roll this week?"

"Yes, we had to change an engine and I worked until dark every night. Do you think you can put these on the top of the pile so I can get back to the airport soon? There's a storm coming in."

"No problem. You ought to learn to enjoy these storms. Once they end there won't be any rain for months. By next year you'll probably be out dancing in the rain when they come."

"We'll see. I'll be back in a little. I've got a few errands to run."

Shoppers in town for Saturday crowded the sidewalk. Vicki walked along with the flow of people as they window-shopped and made their purchases. Across the street was the Auto Parts Warehouse though the name was a bit of a misnomer since the store was not more than 20 feet wide. Traffic was light on the street so Vicki crossed from where she was and entered the store.

Nobody noticed Vicki as the two clerks busied themselves with the farmers and weekend mechanics lined up three deep in front of the counter. As Vicki walked the aisles, she scanned the shelves and drank in the smells of grease and rubber. Her mind drifted back to the time before her parents died, back before her life turned upside down, back when she had a family and a home.

Her mind came back to the present as one of the clerks shouted, "Next!" A tear appeared on Vicki's cheek. She wiped it away as she headed out the door without any of the items she wanted.

She walked several blocks south and pushed through the doors of Joyce's Gym. The smell of sweat permeated the air while the harsh bang of clanking weights mixed with the constant rumble of the treadmills. Music played in the aerobic room as middle-aged women followed the lead of a slender instructor. Vicki waited in the line at the front desk. Two large prison guards waited in front of her. One of them noticed her after he signed in.

He moved his eyes up and down. "Need any help with your exercises little lady?"

"No thanks." Vicki turned to the clerk at the desk. "Is Joyce here?"

"Yes. I'll get her."

The clerk walked to an open door behind the desk as the guards headed toward the locker room. Joyce walked out of office with a clipboard in her hands, smiled at Vicki, held a finger up into the air as she stopped and turned around. She popped back into the office emerging a moment later with a stack of papers. She motioned Vicki down to the end of the counter.

"Your check cleared on Wednesday so I placed the order."

"Great. When will the stuff be in?"

Joyce shuffled through the stack and pulled out a stapled clump of papers. She studied the top one for a moment. "Let's see. The free weights and workout bench will be here late next week. The Standing Punching Bag will take another week or so."

"That's great. I have the old barracks that Harry said I could use as a workout room all cleaned out and almost ready. I've just got to paint the window panes opaque."

"You're welcome to use the equipment here for free until your stuff comes in. Having an experienced kick boxer working out here would be good for business."

The two prison guards came out of the locker room dressed in spandex shorts and loose muscle shirts. The one that had talked to Vicki smiled at her and flexed his bicep.

"No thanks. I'll just lift heavy wrenches until everything comes in."

The gust front of the monsoon storms hit as Vicki walked out of the gym. She pushed into the swilling mess. The sidewalks emptied as the wind whipped the dust horizontally at the windows. Vicki moved briskly down the street with her hand above her eyes. She focused toward the grocery store up the block. The store entrance was crowded with about twenty people standing near the door with no grocery bags. They held bags from other stores as the wind beat dust against the front glass.

Vicki moved through the aisles to gather the supplies she would need for the next week. Into the basket went cat food to keep Buster fat & happy, cereal, milk, tea, honey, apples, bananas, canned ravioli, and a six-pack of beer. She rolled her cart toward the cash registers.

The crowd still surrounded the door as Vicki finished at the checkout and she weaved her way through them. The rain had started. She left the grocery store in a dead run through the downpour with the two bags in her arms. The empty sidewalks allowed Vicki to sprint in a straight line to her truck. She threw in the bags, rolled up the windows, locked the doors, and raced back toward the PhotoStop.

The wind howled and pushed the rain sideways down the street. Water flowed, first at a trickle, then in a gush as it quickly filled the pavement from sidewalk to sidewalk. Vicki pushed through the doors just as another sheet of rain hit the glass. She stopped to wipe the water from her arms and face before making her way to the counter through the shoppers that stared out the windows. The clerk looked up from his machine as she moved to the counter. He grabbed a package of pictures from the ready rack and handed them to her.

As the clerk went back to the photo machine, Vicki thumbed through the stack. She shuffled past the ones of Buster and cacti until she came to the ones of Rick's landing. She had set the camera to burst mode and the six shots showed the landing roll in sequence. As she studied the shots, she pushed pictures away one by one. Finally only two remained. Vicki stared intently at each before she picked one up. She also grabbed the shot she had taken of Bob and Rick standing together.

"Could you make an eight by ten of each of these?"

The clerk came back to the counter, looked at the shots, and then at the strips of the negatives. He pointed to the landing shot. "Can you tell me which number this one is? In the burst they all sorta look alike."

Vicki picked up the negatives by their edges and looked through them. "It's number thirty three. The other shot is number thirty six."

The clerk filled out the order form and

placed the negatives in an envelope. "Wednesday ok for you?"

"That's fine. I won't pick them up until next Saturday, so take your time."

The clerk ripped the claim number off the top and handed it to Vicki. "See you then."

The rain ended as Vicki turned onto the airport road. When she rolled down her window, fresh damp air flooded in. She parked her truck next the RV, unloaded the groceries, and headed toward the hangar to see if Rick was there so she could give him the pictures.

When Vicki entered the hangar, it was almost empty. Jumping had stopped for the day due to the weather so most of the jumpers had vanished. Several of the remaining jumpers sipped beers as they talked amongst themselves while watching a group playing hacky-sack by the packing ledge. Vicki steered a route around the game to where Rick knelt in the center of the hangar floor as he worked the folds of a square canopy. Bob, Harry, and

Robert, the drop zone rigger, closely watched.

Robert moved forward as he pointed at the canopy. "Clear the side panels before you Z-fold it. If you don't clear them, you'll end up with little holes from line burn."

Rick grimaced "Dang. Forgot that again."

Rick cleared the side panels then folded the parachute into the deployment bag. He stowed the lines in their keepers, placed the assembly into the bottom of the container, and threaded his pull up cord through the side panel grommets.

Robert stopped him. "That's far enough. Pull it back out to let Bob have a go."

Rick pulled the canopy clear of the bag and shook the folds out. He threw the whole thing into the air. It landed in a wrinkled mess.

"Have fun," Rick said.

Bob grabbed pilot chute bridle and followed it to the top of the canopy. His hands grabbed the tabs at the top and he started to sort them.

Vicki walked up to Rick. "Come on over to

the packing ledge. I've got the pictures of your landing."

"Cool."

Rick and Vicki walked to the ledge. Harry followed. Vicki pulled the envelope with the pictures out and flipped through them.

"Here you go. This is a burst shot of your landing. I picked out that one to have an eight by ten made of it. They are also making an eight by ten of the one of you and Bob."

"Great. How much do I owe you?"

"I told you. Nothing. Thanks for bringing Buster back."

Harry stared over Rick's shoulder. "I didn't know you liked to take pictures."

"It's been a hobby of mine for years."

"What kind of camera do you have?"

"It's a Pentax A3000."

"Does it have the electric shutter release?"

"Yes."

"Come back to the parts room a minute. I've got something you might be interested in."

Harry led Vicki into the parts room and turned on the lights. He reached onto a shelf marked Miscellaneous Parts and pulled out a metal box. One side of the box had clamps while the other had a hole. He handed it to Vicki.

She twisted it around, looking at it from all sides. "What is it?"

"It's a camera mount made to go on the strut of a Cessna. There used to be a jumper here that sold pictures of exits. He did it for several years. We sold a lot of them to first jump students. He even sold a few to experienced jumpers. He gave up the sport last year and just left it here. No one else here takes pictures, so I just removed it and put it on the shelf."

"How does it work?"

"The clamps go around the strut and the camera mounts inside the box. You loosen that bolt to aim it. The wires for the shutter release are still installed on one of the Cessnas. I've got them stowed above the strut inspection plate. The trigger switch is mounted to the pilot's yoke so he could take the shot as the people exited."

"I wondered what that extra button and those loose wires were for."

"If you would like, I'll mount it again. We charged people twenty dollars for each 8 by 10 picture. Manifest collects the money and Sally mails the photos out. You provide the camera, film, and get the photos made. I'll pay you twelve dollars for each photo. We pay pilot a buck for each shot."

"What size lens did he use?"

"28mm."

"I've got one of those. Did the camera ever fall off?"

"No. The camera screws onto the mount and then the box cover closes over it. Only the lens sticks out."

"Okay. I'll try it. I'll take the mount back with me to see how my camera fits."

Vicki grabbed the mount and headed out the back door of the parts room toward her

RV.

Sally's voice came from behind her. "Hey Vicki, wait up."

Vicki slowed until Sally caught up. "Have you got any plans for dinner?"

"Not really. I was just going to heat up some canned ravioli."

"Harry and I are going to the Manuel's Cantina in Florence for dinner. We'd like you to come along as our guest. Most of the jumpers go there for dinner. With Rick and Bob's graduation, it should be a hoot to watch the festivities. They even have a live band."

"I don't know. I'm really worn out from work this week. I wanted to get to bed early."

"Oh, we never stay late. I promise we'll have you back by nine."

"Okay. Thanks."

"We'll pick you up at 5:30."

"See you then."

Harry led the threesome through the doors of the restaurant as lively music filtered into the evening air. As they followed the hostess around the crowded tables, strange smells attacked Vicki's nose. They stopped at a table next to the dance floor that had a reserved sign on it.

"I called ahead for this table," Harry said. "It's far enough from the bar that we don't get sprayed by the drinking games and close enough to the restrooms that I don't have to run."

He laughed and then with a wave of his hand caught the attention of a waitress. She came right over. "Good Evening, Senòr Sparks. What can I get for you?"

Harry turned to Vicki. "Would you like a beer?"

"Sure, I'll have one. But that's my limit."

Harry turned back toward the waitress and spoke in Spanish. The server scribbled on her pad then hurried off as Vicki settled down in her chair.

The Mexican band played a festive song as several couples danced. The bar across the room had skydivers standing three deep as they laughed and bantered loudly to each other. Bob and Rick stood at the edge of the crowd at the bar with Bob holding a beer in his hand. Rick held three. They were in a laugh-filled conversation with Kevin, who held two beers, one in each hand.

Vicki looked at her watch. *If it is this rowdy this early, what will it be like in a few hours?*

The waitress returned with their beers and placed silverware, napkins, chips, two small bowls of sauce, water, and menus down on the table. "I'll be right back to take your order," she said as she hurried off.

Vicki opened the menu. The choices were unrecognizable. She turned toward Sally. "Would you help me? I have absolutely no idea what to order."

"Do you like spicy food?"

"Yes. But not too hot."

"Try a chip with the chucky red sauce and tell me what you think."

Vicki grabbed a chip and dipped it in the

sauce. She placed it in her mouth. It mildly spiced her tongue and left a pleasant taste. "That's nice."

"Now try the smooth red sauce. I'll warn you, it's hotter."

Vicki dipped the chip and placed it in her mouth. The reaction was instantaneous as she threw the rest of the chip down and reached for her beer. She emptied a large swig into her mouth and swished it around. After she swallowed, she laughed as tears came down her cheeks. "I think the first one will do fine."

Sally laughed. "Sorry. I didn't think it would do that to you. I guess I've been down here so long I've gotten used to it. How about I order you something that's pretty mild?"

Vicki wiped her eyes with her napkin. "Okay."

The waitress returned and Harry ordered in Spanish. She then looked at Sally. Sally also spoke in Spanish.

Vicki heard her name as Sally ordered. When the waitress left, Vicki turned toward

Sally. "What did you order for me?"

"A Chicken Burrito plate smothered in Green sauce. It's pretty mild. I'm sure you'll like it."

Rick walked up to their table with his three beers. "Mind if I sit down?"

Harry motioned toward the empty seat next to Vicki and Rick sat in it. He placed the beers on the table near Harry. "I lost the coin toss with Bob for designated driver tonight so I thought I'd bring the beers I can't drink over to you."

Vicki started to tell Rick that one was her limit, but before she could open her mouth, Harry grabbed the beers and placed them in front of his plate. "Thanks Rick. I'm sure we'll put them to good use."

Vicki's face flushed as the thought of a ride home with a drunk crossed her mind. She silently wished she had stayed back at her RV.

Rick turned toward Vicki. "Thanks for taking those pictures of Bob and me today. They're really neat."

Vicki's gaze remained fixed on the three beers. "No problem."

"I better get back to keep Bob out of trouble."

He stood to walk away but stopped and turned back toward Vicki. "Will you be at the party at the fire tonight? It should be fun."

"No. I'm going to turn in as soon as we get back."

"Okay. I'll look for you if you change your mind. Thanks again for the pictures." Rick headed toward the bar.

"So how are you enjoying living at the airport?" Sally asked.

Vicki turned her eyes from the beers and toward Sally. "I'm really enjoying it a lot. After the DCs left, I started walking around a lot at night. The solitude of the desert at night is very relaxing. I occasionally hear a coyote howling, but besides that the only sound out there at night during the week is the rotating beacon."

"Some of the places Harry has had us

staying at over the years didn't even have that noise. I remember one airport in Alaska that the silence was total. I was glad to leave that one. Certain familiar noises relax me at night, be it a rotating beacon, an airplane flying overhead, or Harry snoring."

"That's true for me too I guess. Having Buster purring on my chest at night helps me sleep. Without him I think I'd be lost."

Sally laughed. "I wish Harry purred instead of snoring."

Harry broke up laughing and kissed his wife. Vicki giggled as she sipped her beer.

The waitress soon brought their food. After gingerly taking a first bite, Vicki dove into the plate. "You're right. This is really good."

Harry picked up one of the beers that Rick had deposited on their table and handed it to a skydiver that was walking by. "Here George. Free beer."

George grabbed the beer. "Thanks," he said as he continued walking.

Vicki looked at Harry inquisitively as he

picked up the other two beers in turn to hand them to other passing skydivers. He noticed her stare. "I always consider it bad form to not accept drinks from somebody celebrating something. However, once they're mine, I feel I can give them away in turn. That way everybody's happy." Vicki smiled at Harry's little lesson in skydiver bar etiquette. She relaxed a little more and dug back into her plate of food.

After they had all finished their dinners, Harry got up and walked over to the bandstand. He talked into the singer's ear before heading back toward the table. As the band began a slow number, Harry walked over to Sally's chair. "May I have this dance?"

"Why of course."

She stood up as Harry pulled her chair out. He led Sally to the dance floor and they assumed a classic dance pose. As they slowly moved to the music, they both stared into each other's eyes. Other couples joined them on the floor, moving to the slow tender tune with their arms wrapped around waists and necks. Some had their eyes open and some had them closed. A soft yearning beat into Vicki's heart as the image of her parents slowly dancing in the moonlight on the back porch filled her mind. As the song finished, Harry and Sally walked back hand in hand to the table.

Harry looked at Vicki while he still held his wife's hand. "You ready to go?"

"Yes. I just need to pay my bill."

"Don't worry about it. You're our guest tonight. The restaurant will just tab us. Sally will stop by next week to settle up."

"Okay." The three walked through the high-spirited crowd toward the door as numerous skydivers called thanks to Harry for flying the Beech. When they got out on the sidewalk, Harry led the way as Sally and Vicki walked next to each other.

Vicki pulled close to Sally. "I hope you don't mind me saying so, but I thought it was so sweet of Harry to ask you to dance."

Sally laughed. "He's been doing that every

time there's a band since we got married. He says he wants everybody to know that he's taking home the prettiest girl in the bar."

The drive back to the airport went quickly as Harry talked about the DC4 flying out Monday and what cargo contracts he had acquired. Vicki was glad to see it go, because with it Dean would leave. Dean watched her while they worked and the constant staring caused the hair on the back of her neck to stand up.

They dropped Vicki off at her RV and drove away toward their house. Vicki unlocked the RV and stepped inside as Buster greeted her with a loud meow. "Poor baby." She poured food into his bowl and Buster attacked it vigorously as Vicki sat down on the dining area bench seat to watch him. Her little world of Buster and the RV was comforting.

When Buster finished eating, Vicki went out into the night and sat on her lounge chair with Buster in her lap. The monsoon clouds had cleared out and the stars of Milky Way massed above her. The rotating beacon on top of the hangar cast its alternating green and white light across the desert like a slow motion strobe. The desert stillness brought a sense of peace to Vicki after the rowdiness of the bar.

Vicki's quiet solitude ended as the party started at the fire pit. Loud talking came across the night air from the direction of the Rec. Hall and then music began to drift through the night. The bonfire sent light across the parking lot as the scrap wood in the pit began to blaze high into the night sky. Down the airport road, the headlights of cars from the restaurant materialized. While most of the headlights continued to the parking lot, several turned toward the old building pads. One of the sets of headlights stopped at Bob and Rick's campsite. The headlights died and a flashlight beam came on. The beam of the flashlight moved toward the fire while it swung wildly around. Vicki put Buster in the RV, locked the door, and headed toward the noise to see what kind games skydivers played at graduation parties.

She moved slowly toward the fire as she stayed in the shadows away from the light of the rotating beacon. Her path angled to a large mesquite tree that rose like a sentinel in the fire light. The trunk hid her presence less than fifty feet from the light of the bonfire. Skydivers bantered back and forth about everything and nothing. With only her left eye peering around the trunk, the party, in all its glory, unfolded in front of her. The skydivers were all there, beers in hand and voices raised. Dean and Buzz stood off to the side drinking from a Tequila bottle.

Kevin walked out of the classroom with a chair in one hand and a beer in the other. When he got next to the fire, he put the chair down and climbed on top of it.

"Quiet you scurvy dogs. Quiet I say. There's honor to bestow tonight. Rick and Bob, come forward."

The crowd quieted as Rick and Bob made

their way toward Kevin. They soon stood before his dais.

"Today you left the title of Stupid Students behind you. But, you are still scurvy dogs not yet fit to float in the presence of the sky gods assembled here before you."

Cries of "dogs, dogs, dogs" laughingly filled the air from the crowd.

"Quiet I say or I take the beer and leave," Kevin yelled. The crowd quieted again. "Since you now do not have student rules to guide you, I give you the three rules of experienced skydivers." He drained his beer and threw the empty can into the fire. "Another beer, I can't talk without beer."

Several coolers sat on the dirt near the fire. George went to the coolers and grabbed Kevin a can. Kevin put the can to his mouth for a long swallow. He then looked solemnly down at Rick and Bob. "You must follow these rules or death will find you."

"Death, death, death," came from the crowd.

"Quiet or the beer's all mine."

The chant died out.

"Rule number one—Don't do anything in the sky that will hurt me."

The crowd clapped and hooted.

"Rule number two—Don't do anything in the sky that is going to hurt anyone else."

Howling came forth from the crowd.

Kevin raised his hand for silence. "And, last but not least, rule number three. Always have fun."

The crowd burst into applause.

Kevin swallowed another long swig from his beer and then raised his can high into the air. "Fellow masters of the sky. I give you Rick and Bob, the newest and wettest skydivers at the drop zone."

Ice water out of a cooler behind Rick and Bob crashed down over their heads. Two skydivers had walked up unseen behind the two for what was undoubtedly a solemn duty. Rick stood there dripping wet smiling. Bob shook his body like dog spraying water over the people near him. Vicki blurted out a laugh out as the skydivers ran to get away from the spray.

Dean jerked his head her way. Vicki's laughter stopped short. Dean lifted the Tequila bottle, took a long swallow before wiping his mouth with his sleeve, and then grabbed Buzz by the arm. They moved away from the fire toward her.

Vicki retreated into the shadows of the hangar as the safety of her RV beckoned. She ran crouched, weaving through the cars. Her heart raced as she got to the end of the parked cars and looked back toward the two men while they staggered in a halting gait. Their path headed straight for her RV. Vicki moved across the open part of the parking lot. She stopped and knelt every time the rotating beacon sent a flash of light that lit up the desert night around her.

As she got close to the RV, she broke into a full run for the door. The men staggered toward her only fifty feet away as she reached for her key. Buster shrieked a meow.

Buster! What would these two do to her cat if they got inside her RV?

She had to protect Buster. She ducked around the back of the RV and stopped. Her stomach tightened and her skin became wet with a cold sweat as her breathing quickened. She bounced on her toes and did several practice kicks into the air. She fisted her hands.

The men walked up to the door of her RV and stopped. Dean reached for the handle and twisted it. The lock held. He stared at it and tried again.

Buzz moved his head side to side as looked at the RV. "Hey man, this isn't your trailer."

Dean belched. "Whoops. I know it's around here somewhere. Maybe it's over that way."

Together they stumbled past Vicki's hiding place as she crouched slightly, ready to spring. They continued their way into the darkness, illuminated only by the flashes of the green and white beacon.

Vicki leaned against the back of her RV shuddering as relief came over her in waves. She watched the two men long enough to ensure they were not coming back then raced back to the door and unlocked it. She slammed it shut behind her and pushed the bolt securely into place. Grabbing Buster, she ran into the back bedroom and crawled to the back of the bed. She lay there shuddering until an exhausted sleep overtook her.

Chapter 6

Rick backed the bucket truck into its spot under the canopy and set the air brake. He flipped his hard hat off and it landed on the seat beside him with a thud. Pulling his hairbrush out, he checked his hair in rearview mirror and made quick work of his helmet hair. He grabbed a plastic bag from the floor to gather the empty soda cans, chip bags, and sandwich packs scattered around the cab. As he stepped down from the truck, he slung his tool belt over his shoulder and headed toward his foreman's pickup. The heavy lineman's hammer slapped his thigh as he walked. When he reached the pickup, he dropped the tool belt on the ground, opened the passenger door, and plopped down on the bench seat.

"What's the time code for the last job you had me do, Mr. Ryan? I don't have that location on my work orders."

Mr. Ryan searched through the stack of plans on the seat. "By the way Rick, I've got some overtime work this weekend if you're interested. It would be time and a half Saturday with double time Sunday."

Rick spoke without a second's hesitation. "No thanks, I've got things planned for all weekend."

"Are you still doing that parachuting stuff?"

"Yes sir, and loving every minute of it."

"You know you're crazy, don't you?"

Rick smiled. "Yes sir, and loving every minute of it."

Mr. Ryan laughed loudly then recited the time code. "Well, stay safe."

"You have a good weekend, Mr. Ryan,"

Rick got out, picked up his tool belt, and headed toward the office building. Once inside the building, he threw the plastic bag of his lunch trash into the can by the door. He moved into the central hallway to head to the payroll office. A long line stretched from the paymaster's window. Rick tossed his timesheet into the Lineman's bin then stepped to the rear of the line. It slowly advanced as the paymaster retrieved envelopes and counted the contents out. As Rick talked with a cable splicer in line in front of him, a woman called his name.

"Hey, Rick. Could you stop by and talk to me for a minute before you leave?" Rick looked over to where the voice had come from. It was Carrie, one of the newest timekeepers.

"Sure. No problem."

Rick's turn at the window came with the ritual counting out of the bills and change completed efficiently. With his envelope in hand, he headed over to Carrie's desk. He sat down in the chair beside it and dropped his tool belt on the floor as Carrie put down the timesheet in her hand.

"Have you ever been up the Roosevelt Lake? My cousin is here for the weekend with my parents and hers. We want some place to drive while the parents do their shopping. I would like to drive her up through the mountain roads to the lakes, but I'm not sure which ones are the prettiest."

"Sure. I know a good route." He detailed the roads he used to take through the mountains on his motorcycle as Carrie scribbled notes. She repeated the directions back word for word.

Rick stood to leave. "On your way back, you will be passing by the airport just south of Florence where I skydive. If you have time, why don't you stop by just to look?"

"Maybe we will. We want to stay out of town until time for dinner with the folks. The last thing either of us wants to do is give our mothers an opportunity to pick out clothes for us."

"If you do make it, I'll be in the hangar or in the air. Just ask anybody for me, we all know each other. If I'm in the air, I'll be back on the ground within a half an hour. Hope you can make it."

"Okay. Bye."

Carrie shifted her attention back to the timesheet. Rick walked down the hallway and out the parking lot door to his car. He dumped his tool belt into the back seat, quickly forgetting that Carrie might show up. His mind went to the airport and skydiving.

Rick pulled into the parking lot of the apartment complex. Bob's van waited in front of his building. He pulled up next the driver's window as he revved his engine. Bob casually lifted his cowboy hat off his forehead and opened one eye.

"As soon as you're finished trying to impress the girls, we're ready to go. I already got your skydiving and camping gear loaded in the van. Grab your tooth brush so we can get out of town." Bob replaced the hat over his eyes.

Rick hurried into his apartment and was back out to the van in two minutes. He slid the cargo door open and threw his overnight bag into the collection of parachutes, jumpsuits, helmets, a tent, assorted other camping gear, and a cooler. "You want me to drive us down so you can get some beauty sleep?"

Bob slid his hat to the back of his head as he started the van's engine. "No. I'll take it. This is your 100th jump weekend. You need to be good and rested so you don't screw up."

Rick slid the door closed and hopped into the passenger seat. With the radio blaring, Bob backed out of the parking spot and turned out of the lot toward the west.

Rick turned down the radio. "Stop at the Quick Mart so I can buy my beer."

Bob pulled the van into the lot and parked by the door. "How about buying a good brand this time? I'm tired of drinking that light beer you like."

"You need to get gas?"

"Already got it. You owe me a couple of jump tickets. You need any help picking out the beer?"

"No thanks. I'll get it."

Bob nodded, picked up a paperback from the engine cover, and opened it while Rick jumped out of the van and headed into the store. He picked two cases of light beer out of the cooler, placed them on the counter, and motioned toward the coffee condiments.

"You mind if I take some coffee creamers?

The attendant looked at the beer and then up at Rick. He spoke with a smile. "Sure. No problem. I like my beer with lime, but to each his own."

Rick grabbed the creamers and put them into his jacket pocket, then pulled a twenty out of his wallet. "I like mine with lime too. These are for a cat."

The attendant handed Rick his change. "I guess that's better than having a drunken cat."

Rick laughed, stuck the change in his pocket, and grabbed the beer. Hurrying outside, he slid open the side door of the van and climbed in. The beer went on the floor and the creamers in the cooler. He climbed over the piles in the back into the passenger seat as Bob put his book down, started the van, turned the radio back on, and headed toward the west again.

The heavy late afternoon traffic slowed their progress. Oracle Road finally came up. Bob turned the van north and they soon left the stores and houses behind them. The open desert stretched across the front windshield. Bob turned the radio up over the wind noise as Rick rolled down his window. Rick stuck his hand out into the wind and let it fly up and down to the beat of the music. The afternoon smells of the creosote plants and mesquite filled the van.

When they reached Florence, they pulled into the half-empty parking lot of Manuel's Cantina. Carlos, the bartender, placed their To-Go orders and the two men waited at the bar sipping waters with lime. The restaurant was different on Fridays compared to the Saturday nights they spent there. The smells were the same, but the texture of the sounds was different. Fridays nights had families with giggling children and crying babies as the jukebox played softly in the background. On Saturday nights, it overflowed with skydivers while the room reverberated with loud laughter and rambunctious shouts as the local Mexican band played lively music.

When their food came, they headed the van on its way to the drop zone. The sun had just touched the horizon as they turned off the airport road into the gravel lot. The empty parking lot revealed a quiet scene that would be broken in the morning. Bob pulled the van around to the front of the hangar stopping just short of the large open doors. As Rick and Bob got out, Vicki and Harry passed by pulling a Cessna by a tow bar. Rick and Bob ran to help and pushed on the struts. When they got the Cessna away from the hangar, Harry unhooked the tow bar from the front and handed it to Vicki. Vicki hoisted it over her shoulder as she turned back to the hangar.

Harry looked at Rick and Bob. "Either of you want to go for an airplane ride? We just finished the annual so I need to take it up for a return to service flight."

"I'll go," Bob said.

"You go ahead," Rick said.

Rick headed back toward the van as the Cessna taxied away. He opened the side door and reached into the cooler to retrieve one of the coffee creamers. Stepping out of the van, Rick watched as the Cessna reached the runway. The engine roared and the airplane thundered down the runway before lifting off. As it faded into the evening sky, Rick headed into the hangar.

Vicki worked by her toolbox, a rag in her hands as she wiped her tools off and put them away in their proper drawers. Buster lay on the packing ledge half-asleep, one eye barely open.

Rick held the creamer out. "Buster. Want some creamer?"

Buster's head jerked up and he meowed loudly. The cat jumped off the ledge and hurried over toward Rick. Rick popped the top off the creamer and placed the container on the dusty concrete floor. Buster dropped his tongue into the contents with gusto.

Vicki smiled. "It's really nice of you to get those for Buster. You're nicer to that cat then a lot of people here."

Rick knelt and stroked the cat's back. "No problem. I think he's a cool cat."

Vicki closed the last tool drawer and began to drag her toolbox toward the tool room. She stopped and turned to Rick. "What was it like on your first jump? Were you scared?"

Rick looked up from the cat. "Yea. I was scared out of my mind. I wasn't sure I could do it. Why?"

"I'm going to take the first jump course next week. I decided to take Harry and Sally up on their offer of a discount."

"That's great. You'll do fine. It's a rush."

"That's what everybody keeps telling me. When did you stop being scared?"

"I don't know. When I got down from my first jump, the fear had already turned to excitement. It was during my first long free-fall that I decided to stay in the sport. I had time to look around at the desert and the mountains in the distance. The view just hooked me. I ordered my advanced rig as soon as I got down."

"Thanks. At least I know I'm not alone." Vicki pulled the toolbox the rest of the way to the tool room. She locked the door as the Cessna taxied up to the tie downs in front of the hangar. Harry and Bob hopped out and walked into the hangar.

"It flew great," Harry said as he headed toward the office.

Bob remained in the opening between the hangar doors, his stare fixed on the setting sun. The familiar evening rays cast alternating glows through the hangar windows as Vicki grabbed the tow bar and headed out toward the Cessna.

Buster had finished the creamer and Rick lifted him into his arms. "Hey Bob. Vicki's going to jump next week."

Bob continued to gaze at the sunset. "I know. Harry told me. Another Whatfo bites the dust."

Vicki stopped and looked at Bob. "What do you mean? What's a Whatfo?"

"That's someone who doesn't jump and asks 'What for you jump out of perfectly good airplanes?' That's a Whatfo."

"I'm not a Whatfo. I know exactly why you jump. You're crazy."

Rick called out as Vicki turned back toward the Cessna. "That's true, so true. But it's a fun kind of crazy."

After Vicki finished tying down the Cessna, she brought the tow bar back into the hangar and hung it on the back wall. Taking Buster from Rick, she hugged the cat to her chest. "You guys have a good night."

"We've got a bunch of Mexican from Manuel's we're going to heat up in the Rec. Hall if you'd like some," Rick said.

"No thanks. I have some stuff in the fridge in the RV to eat up. See you guys tomorrow."

She waved as she headed out the hangar doors.

After eating, Rick and Bob drove over to their favorite building pad to set up camp. The campsite sat far enough away from the fire pit to avoid the noise of the rowdiest parties while the surrounding mesquite trees near the pad blocked the rotating beacon's alternating green and white lights. "A great second home," Rick told everybody.

The moonless night sky opened the Milky Way to their view. Rick set up his tent while Bob started a small fire in a stone ring on the pad. A light breeze moved the smoke to the east. Bob settled down into his well-worn camp chair and opened a beer. He opened a second one and handed it to Rick as he settled into his own camp chair. Their eyes reflected the dancing firelight while the crackle of the mesquite wood broke the silence of the night.

Bob stirred the wood until the fire picked up. "Why do we do this?"

"Like Vicki said, we're crazy. However, it's a good kind of crazy. I think it's safer than riding my Harley."

"Definitely. I've seen you ride your Harley."

Both laughed as their eyes stared deep into the crackling flames.

The next morning Rick woke before the dawn and fired up the camp stove with the coffee pot ready. The red sky flowed with the golden rays that formed just before the sun broke the horizon line. A chill in the air confirmed that summer had ended and the fall season had begun. The leaves in the trees rustled in the light breeze as occasional birds fluttered about from tree to tree while they sang their morning songs. A rabbit hopping along stopped to munch on the few tuffs of grass that grew. The coffee came to a boil and Rick poured himself a cup.

The side door to the van slid open and Bob stuck his tussled head out into the morning.

He stumbled sleepily across the concrete pad before he plopped down in his camp chair, a poncho liner wrapped around him. Another five minutes passed before Bob reached down and poured himself a cup of coffee. Cars flowed down the road as the sun rose above the horizon into the sky.

Bob finally spoke. “Any idea what Kevin decided on for your 100th?”

“He told me last week that he was thinking of a twelve way using the Beech and a Cessna.”

“That would be cool. Hopefully the first jump course won’t be so big that it will take the Cessna from you.”

“Yea, hopefully.” Rick drained his coffee cup and rinsed it with clean water. “Well. I’m heading over. I still have to make three more jumps before my 100th. You gonna hang out here?”

“Yup. I’m going to wait for it to warm up a little bit more. When’s this babe you’re expecting supposed to get here?”

"Not until this afternoon if at all. I think she was just being nice when she said they might stop by."

Rick knelt on the hangar floor as he packed a student parachute. A pair tennis shoes stepped up next to him. He looked up and Carrie stood there with another young woman.

"Hi Rick," Carrie said.

Rick got to his feet. "Hi. I'm glad you showed up."

"Rick, this is my cousin Joan. Joan, this is Rick, the guy who works out of the same building that I work at."

Joan stepped forward and, with a slightly seductive smile, offered her hand. "Pleased to meet you."

Rick shook her hand. "Nice to meet you." He turned to Carrie. "How was the drive?"

"Really great. The directions you gave worked wonderful. We got to see Roosevelt Lake along with all the little lakes. We had some time left so we thought we'd stop by to see what you do down here on the weekends."

"That's great. Listen, I need to finish packing this parachute for a student load that's going to go up soon."

Rick looked around until he saw Bob leaning against the packing ledge talking with some other jumpers. "Hey, Bob. Got a minute?"

Bob headed over. "Sure."

"Bob, this is Carrie from work and her cousin Joan. Mind entertaining them for a few minutes while I finish this rig up?"

"Sure, no problem, I'll go show them the Beech."

"Okay. I'll meet you out there in a few minutes."

"Ladies. If you'll follow me, I'll start the fifty-cent tour."

Carrie and Joan followed Bob out the hangar door while Rick continued to pack the student parachute. He finished it in five minutes then swiftly carried it into the student gear room. Kevin walked in as Rick marked the log to show he had packed the rig.

"Hey Rick. Do you have time to pack another rig? I'm still one short"

"Sorry, I got some friends here visiting so I want to show them around."

"That the two babes out at the Beech with Bob?"

Rick started for the open doorway. "Yea. A woman from work and her cousin."

"You'd better hurry on out there. I saw a couple of jumpers walking that way with flirting in their eyes."

"Thanks." Rick quickened his pace as he hurried across the hangar. He rounded the opening in the hangar door almost at a run. Bob and the two women stood in front the Beech looking up at the engines. There were no other jumpers nearby. Kevin had pulled his chain again. Rick slowed his walk to a normal pace. As he walked up to the airplane, the women climbed through the doorway into the cabin.

Rick stuck his head through the doorway. "How's it going?"

"This is neat," Carrie said. "I've never been near airplanes this small. I've only flown once before and that was a big jet to Miami for a cruise with our family. Bob was just telling us that you're going up soon in this one."

"Yea. The load for my 100th jump is going up in about 30 minutes. I hope you can hang around for it."

Carrie looked at Joan. Joan smiled as she nodded a slight yes headshake.

"Okay, we can do that." Carrie said. "We will have to leave early enough so we can get back to town before it gets dark. I don't know these roads very well and the folks are expecting us for dinner."

Rick continued the tour of the drop zone as he tried to explain everything that was going on. The lack of questions combined with the women's puzzled looks revealed failure on his part. Relief crossed Rick's face when the manifest called out over the PA that the Cessna had turned on jump run. "There's a group of jumpers getting ready to jump."

Bob scanned the sky for the Cessna. "Got it." He pointed to the location of the approaching airplane. Rick found it, walked over to the women, and pointed toward dot in the sky.

"I don't see anything," Joan said.

Rick pointed toward the north and kept his eyes focused on the jumpers in free fall. "The jumpers are out of the airplane. In about a minute, you'll see their parachutes open. Keep looking up that way." The jumpers approached opening altitude. "Any second now." The jumper's parachutes blossomed open with a distinctive crack.

"Neat," Carrie said. "Do you see them Joan?"

"Yes. This is so cool."

The manifest PA sprang to life. "First jump course load three. Cessna's on its way down. Meet it on the ramp. Rick's one hundredth jump. Kevin, Rick, George, Tom L, Judy, Tom K, Jackie, Dusty, Jeff, Brian, Scott, and Amy. Jumpsuits on and dirt dive in front of the hangar in five minutes."

The women kept their gaze on the descending parachutes while Rick turned to Bob. "I've got to get ready for my jump. Mind keeping them company while I do this?"

"No problem. Go have fun. I'll take them out to the landing area when you're under canopy so they can see you crash and burn."

"Thanks a lot."

"No problem."

Kevin positioned the jumpers for a practice exit. Four jumpers, who would ride to altitude in the Cessna, waited several feet from the others. Kevin finished the lineup for the Beech. The group jostled with each other as they waited.

"Quiet down," Kevin said to the rollicking group. "This is going to be a simple round twelve-way star for Rick's hundredth jump."

Several jumpers clapped while others whistled. Kevin raised his hand for silence. "Rick, this isn't about you learning anything or testing your flying skills. This is about you having a memorable 100th jump and having to buy beer for the fire party tonight." The other jumpers burst into applause. Kevin paused for a moment for the noise to abate. "Dusty is front float, spotter, and will work the door. Rick is center float and will do the count. Front and rear floaters and first in the door will take Rick off in a four-way star as the base for the formation. Nobody enters the star next to Rick except Judy or me. Break off will be at 4500 feet. Everybody except Rick track away. Rick, you'll move to the center for opening. Any questions?" Nobody had any. "Good. Let's go through a couple of practice counts and run outs. We'll do a few more with gear before boarding the airplanes."

The jumpers ran through their practices with the ease and familiarity known to experience. They retrieved the rest of their gear from the hangar before they moved toward the airplanes. Bob, Carrie, and Joan stood next to the hangar door watching.

Rick stopped by the small group. "Wish me luck."

"Have fun, man," Bob said.

"Good luck," chorused the two women.

Carrie turned to Bob as Rick and the other jumpers practiced the dive again. "Why aren't you jumping with Rick?"

"Rick and I have about the same number of jumps. I'll probably do my 100th next weekend. Kevin didn't want to put two inexperienced jumpers on a big load like this. We jump together on smaller loads all the time."

"You mean having a hundred jumps is considered inexperienced," Joan asked.

"Yup. Many of those jumpers have over five hundred jumps. A couple have over a thousand."

"Wow," Carrie said. "Do you come out here every weekend like Rick does?"

"Yup. We drive down together to stay the whole weekend."

"Doesn't your girlfriend mind you being here so much?"

"Don't have a girlfriend, just a parachute."

The jump run call came back from Harry to the rear of the Beech as it leveled out at 12,000 feet. He had flown the formation load past the normal 10,500 feet exit altitude.

Dusty reached for the latch on the door and yelled. "Door."

The airplane filled with a cold rushing wind as Dusty removed the door, stowed it in rear of the cabin, and stuck his head into the wind. He kept his gaze toward the ground for a few seconds before he pulled his head back in. "Five right." He waited a few seconds before he stuck his head out again for a moment before he turned and looked at Rick.

"You ready to Skydive?"

Rick nodded enthusiastically.

Dusty yelled into the airplane, "Cut—

Climb Out."

The noise of left engine of the Beech reduced as Harry brought the throttle back. Three of the jumpers, Rick included, reached for handles on the outside of the airplane and pulled themselves into their exit positions. Rick started the exit count with a cadence taught to him and practiced to perfection. "Ready—Set—Go." He moved his body with the expected rhythm in time to the count.

Rick released his grips from the handrail on "Go." The four jumpers came off the airplane as a single flying clump. Dave dropped his grips on Rick's harness as Dusty and Bill's free hands gripped Dave's arms. The next two jumpers in the lineup were in position to enter the formation within seconds. The formation sprang open into a six way. Wave after wave of additional jumpers added to the formation. Judy entered to the left of Rick as Kevin prepared to enter as the last man. Kevin grasped Rick's right arm and shook the existing grips. The formation opened up. Rick was in his first twelve-way as another milestone in his skydiving career had completed.

Rick glanced at his altimeter. The formation had just passed 7,000 feet. He looked down to imprint the appearance of the ground. The technique helped keep track of his altitude with a glance. Kevin stressed this to every jumper on the field.

"Never forget that the ground is always coming at you fast," he would say. "If you do, it will kill you. You can't win against Mother Earth, you can only hope to break even."

Rick always listened seriously to those little sayings that Kevin spouted. One day some little word of wisdom might save his life.

Rick glanced around at the other jumpers in the formation. Smiles propagated from the group as a few jumpers stuck out their tongues and shook them like rattlesnakes in the desert sun. This moment of levity in the air with eleven friends heightened the excitement. Rick smiled at each of them as he gained eye contact across the sky. The altitude came for the formation to end.

Kevin left first with an exaggerated wave of his arms and a quick 180-degree turn. He moved his arms to his sides as he stuck his long legs straight out. His body moved like lightening away from the formation as the other jumpers turned and assumed the same basic body position. None could match Kevin's speed away from the formation. Maybe the proportions of Kevin's body allowed it or maybe just the years of experience, but nobody moved away from a formation as fast as Kevin did. He could separate himself from the others at over twice the speed of anyone else.

Rick waved his arms a final time and glanced over his shoulder. The space above him was clear, so he reached back with his right hand to the rear of his parachute container. Suddenly, something grabbed his foot and spun him to the left. Judy caught him as he came around and pulled him close before she planted her lips on his. She held this kiss for a long second, and then released him as she turned to track. While she pulled away and looked back between her legs, a little wave motioned from her right hand. Rick watched her leave for a second before reality kicked back in. Canopies opened all around him as he checked his altimeter. It read 2900 feet, 100 feet below his expected opening altitude. He reached behind his pack and grabbed the familiar soft ripcord. Rick pulled it from the keeper and the air snatched the pilot chute from his hand into the airstream. The container went slack as the deployment bag lifted off his back. The canopy rapidly slowed his speed as it quickly blossomed over his head.

Judy continued her free-fall as she turned onto her back to wave again at Rick. She then turned over on her belly before finally deploying her own parachute.

Rick let out a happy excited scream as he grabbed the steering toggles to release the brake lines. He pulled on each steering toggle in turn to put himself into a series of fast turns and spirals. The stabilizers on the sides of the canopy snapped as his speed increased toward the earth.

Rick spotted Bob with Carrie and Joan just off the landing area as he approached the ground and pulled his steering toggles to his chest to slow his approach. He timed their release so that he landed in front of the trio. The women clapped while Bob called out, "Show off!" Rick gathered his canopy into his arms and walked over to the trio.

"That was neat, Rick," Joan said. "Weren't you scared?"

"No. I trust my parachute."

"Sorry to say this," Carrie said. "But, we need to get on the road."

"Okay," Rick said. "Too bad you can't hang around. We're going to eat Mexican in Florence soon."

"Maybe next time."

Joan moved closer to Rick. "It was really

nice to meet you. Maybe we can get together next time I come to visit Carrie."

"Sounds good."

"Talk to you later Bob," Carrie said. The two women walked toward the parking lot.

Rick and Bob watched the two walk away. "Isn't Carrie just about the cutest thing you've ever seen," Rick said.

"She sure is." Bob hesitated a moment and then turned to face Rick. "Hey. Do you have any claim on her?"

"No. I asked her out a couple of times, but she wouldn't go."

Bob dropped his gaze to the ground. "Listen, I need to tell you something. Carrie gave me her phone number and asked me to call her sometime." Bob looked back up. "If that's a problem, I'll throw the number away."

Rick looked at his friend. The flush of worry covered Bob's face. Rick smiled. "No problem. I don't know what she sees in you, but I'm sure she'll come to her senses soon and run away straight into my arms."

"If it's any consolation, her cousin thought you were cute."

Rick used his free arm to grab Bob around the shoulders. "Let's get to the hangar so I can pack. It's time to head to Manuel's. Maybe one of the women in the first jump course would like to have a little fun tonight."

"No problem. I'll even buy you some beers."

You can buy me dinner tonight for stealing my date."

Judy sat down at the table with Rick and Bob. "So, Rick. Did you like the kiss pass?"

He smiled at her. "Yea. It was quite a surprise."

Judy moved closer, smiled seductively, and flipped her hair. She leaned over and put her arms around his neck. Her lips were inches from his face. "I just figured that you deserved one for a hundred jumps. So did I get virgin lips? Have you ever had a kiss pass before?"

Rick felt his face flush. "No. You were my

first."

Judy laughed as she stood up. "That, my dear, will be a case of beer." She headed back to the bar.

Chapter 7

"Let's break for lunch," Kevin told the class of three. "Be back here in 45 minutes. Everyone passed the test so you should be in the air by one. There's a snack bar on the side of the hangar that sells burgers and sandwiches."

Vicki and the twins, Nancy and Frank, walked out of the classroom into the bright sunshine. Parachutes filled the air. The twins headed to the picnic table where their parents waited while Vicki turned toward her RV.

"You want to join us for lunch?" Nancy said. "My mother fixed a big picnic and there's more there than we'll ever eat."

"No thanks," Vicki said. "I need to check on my cat."

"Okay, but if you change your mind, just come on over."

Vicki headed across the crowded parking lot toward the RV. Buster sat on a box in his covered caged area and let out a loud meow as she approached before he disappeared into the basement hatch. As Vicki turned the key in the lock, the distinctive crack of opening parachutes sounded behind her and she turned east toward the sound. Four open canopies hung in the distance, all pointed toward the drop zone. The jumpers, too far away and too low to make it back to the landing area, would land in the open desert. A long walk back awaited them on the ground. Rick and Bob's distinctive canopy colors hung in the group. The color patterns on the other two canopies also looked familiar, though neither a name nor a face came to Vicki's mind.

Vicki opened the door to feed the noisy Buster. She filled his food dish then grabbed herself a small bowl of cold ravioli, a banana, and a glass of milk. As she went outside to enjoy the midday sun, she locked the door behind her. The food went on the little table as Vicki sat down on one of the lounge chairs.

In the distance, four figures, parachutes bunched in their arms, trudged along around the cacti and mesquite trees. Vicki ate her lunch as the figures drew closer. Buster came through his basement hatch into the covered cage and cleaned himself in the warm sun.

"Bad Spot?" Vicki yelled as Rick, Bob, Michelle, and John moved within earshot.

"John wanted to practice his spotting," Bob said. "We've decided on the walk in that he needs more practice."

John pointed back toward the East. "I mistook that big barn to the east for the hangar."

"Doesn't matter what the reason was," Michelle said. "You blew the spot and you're buying the first round tonight."

"Okay."

"Rick," Vicki said. "Could I talk to you for a second?"

"Sure." Rick climbed on the concrete pad and sat on the empty lounge chair with his canopy bunched in his lap. The other jumpers continued their trek toward the hangar. Vicki waited until they walked out of earshot before she spoke.

"I'm going up on my jump after lunch and I'd like to ask a favor from you."

"Sure, whatcha need?"

"I'd like to ask you to look after Buster if anything happens to me."

"That's crazy talk. Everything's going to be fine."

"You say that and so does everyone else, but something could happen. Sally has said she'd take care of him, but she's never even petted him. You like Buster." She paused and looked at Buster licking his chest inside the cage. "I mean, I don't expect you to keep him or anything like that, just make sure that he finds a good home."

"I still think that's crazy talk. But, if it will make you feel better, I'd be glad to do it for you. However, I'm not going to have to do anything, you'll be fine."

Vicki lightly touched Rick on the arm.

"Thanks. That's a relief to me."

"No Problem. Enjoy your jump."

Vicki looked at her watch. "I better get back to class or Kevin will think I'm a Leaver"

Rick picked up his parachute and started for the hangar. "Later."

Vicki reached inside the cat area and picked up Buster. She hugged him tightly and dropped him back in. "I'll be back later buddy. Hopefully."

Vicki lay on the ground outside the classroom as canopies floated through the air when Nancy and Frank walked up.

"What are you doing?" Nancy asked.

"Just watching canopies," Vicki said. "If you lay on the ground, your neck doesn't get stiff."

"How'd you learn to do that?"

Vicki stood up and brushed the sand from the back of her jeans. "Just hanging around watching jumpers a lot."

"Does your boyfriend jump?"

“I don’t have a boyfriend. I work here as a mechanic.”

“A girl mechanic,” Nancy said. “That’s neat. How come you haven’t jumped before this?”

“I’ve only been working here a few months. I was just settling in and wanted to get the job under control first.”

Kevin walked out of the classroom. “Is everyone ready to go?” A trio of nods answered him. “Okay, let’s head to the hangar. I’ve got us manifested on a Cessna load going up in a half hour.” He turned and headed toward the hangar. The trio of students followed him with Nancy almost skipping in the front while Vicki trudged behind. Nancy and Frank’s parents brought up the rear of the small group.

Kevin suited each of the group up while the jumpmaster for the load, George, did the final equipment checks. Vicki tensed as Kevin tightened the straps on her legs, but relaxed slightly as Sally and Harry came up to watch.

They were all ready to go when the manifest speaker called their load.

Vicki was following George and the two other students out toward the airplane when an arm fell across her shoulder. Vicki tensed for a moment and began to pull away until Sally spoke. "You ready for this?"

"I think so. This is a lot different from anything I've ever done before and I am a little scared. Are you going to go out to the student landing area and watch me land?"

"I sure am. Harry will be there too."

"He won't fire me if I mess up, will he?"

"I don't think so. One day I'll tell you the story about my first jump. I messed up so bad I was surprised that Harry didn't divorce me."

"I didn't know that you jumped."

"I did for a while when we were younger, but I quit when I got pregnant the first time and never started back up. I've thought about it. I did like the excitement and the freedom that I felt up there. I'm what you call a Useto."

"A Useto?"

"Yes. As in I used to do that."

Vicki laughed. "Better than being a Leaver. I thought about doing that."

"You'll do fine. Pardon the pun, but this skydiving stuff is as easy as falling off of a log."

"If you say so."

As the two reached the Cessna, Sally left Vicki's side and walked up to talk to the pilot. Nancy, Frank, and George moved to the other side of the airplane to allow the parents to take a couple of pictures. Vicki waited under the wing while the bantering laughter of the family drifted around the airplane. Her eyes looked up at her camera mounted on the strut. The twins had both purchased exit pictures. Dan would snap her picture also.

"Where's Vicki?" Nancy said. "We should get her in some of these."

"She's standing over by the door," someone answered.

"Vicki, come on over here and get in the picture," George called. "You only do this once for the first time."

Sally looked at Vicki. "Go on, get in the picture. You'll be sorry if you don't."

"Okay," Vicki said as she headed for the other side of the airplane. The parents snapped several more shots and then Sally directed the parents toward the student pickup vehicle. George brought the students over to the door to load.

"Vicki. I want you in first. Climb in on your knees and then sit down behind the pilot's seat facing backwards. You're next Nancy. Climb in and sit on the floor in the back of the airplane."

Dan stopped his prefight checklist and looked at Nancy. "Welcome aboard. Is this your first jump?"

"Yes," Nancy said as she climbed in.

"That's nice. This is my first time flying."

Nancy stopped moving for a second, and then smiled. "You guys are so funny. You had me there for a second." She turned around and sat down. George placed Frank next to the pilot by the open door.

"Will Nancy jump after me?" Frank asked George. "She had wanted to go first since she's the oldest by two minutes."

"Nope. Big guys go first and little girls go last. It works better that way. It'll be you, Nancy, and then Vicki. We like to get the guys out of the way so we can have our way with the women before throwing them to the wind." Everyone in the airplane laughed at the joke except Vicki. Her internal defenses came up as her arms involuntarily tightened and prepared to strike.

George continued. "You and Nancy will be in the air at the same time. But you may be on the ground by the time we throw Vicki out."

Nancy called out from the rear of the airplane. "This is going to be so neat!"

Dan called "Clear" and cranked the engine until it caught. The airplane rolled forward when he released the brakes. When George pulled the door closed and latched it, the space around Vicki tightened even more than she thought possible. She tried to concentrate on the engine noise or the antics of Nancy rather than her upcoming jump. Nancy looked around George to make faces at her brother. A sense of dread passed through Vicki's mind as her stiffened face contrasted with Nancy's happy excited smile. Dan turned the airplane onto the runway and powered the engine up. Whatever might happen, Vicki was trapped until the time came for her to jump. As the airplane rolled toward takeoff, George looked around and yelled, "Skydive!"

The wheels of the airplane left the ground. Vicki knew her fate was sealed.

A blast of wind hit Vicki as George opened the door on jump run. The sweat on her forehead chilled and sent a shiver down her spine. Nancy smiled and stuck her right thumb up as their eyes made contact. Vicki provided a half-hearted thumb up in return. The cut command came from George and he ordered Frank out the door. George held the static line high as

Frank moved his hands along the strut and placed his left foot on the step above the wheel. After a few moments, Frank turned his gaze back to the inside of the airplane.

"Go," commanded George.

Frank faced forward again before he disappeared from view. The airplane rocked and a banging sound came from the side before George pulled the deployment bag in and shut the door. He rose up into a crouch and slide over in front of Vicki, his face only inches away from Vicki's head. His breath added more moisture to her skin. Vicki's left hand went into a fist.

"Turn around and scoot up to the front," George yelled to Nancy. George grabbed Nancy's harness as she moved.

"It's okay," George said. "I'm just helping you to turn around."

Vicki relaxed slightly as Nancy slid toward the instrument panel and George moved toward the front.

George lowered his mouth to Nancy's ear.

"I'm going to reach over you now to get your static line so I can hook it up." He pulled her upper body forward as he bent over her.

Vicki hands went into fists again. She needed to get out of the airplane soon or she would freak out and punch George.

George hooked Nancy's static line to the ring on the floor. "Are you ready to skydive?"

Nancy responded with an enthusiastic yes headshake as a big smile crossed her face. The airplane leveled out and Dan nodded to George.

"Door," George yelled. He twisted the latch. The door flew open and he immediately stuck his head out. He brought his head back in and looked at Nancy.

"Cut!—Climb out." A few seconds later, George yelled, "Go." The airplane rocked and the banging returned.

After he retrieved the deployment bag, George shut the door and slid into the rear of the cabin.

"Your turn little lady. Move on over here."

Vicki kept her hands balled into fists as George reached for her. He grabbed Vicki's parachute harness and pushed her toward the front of the airplane. Vicki's shoulders tensed.

"It's ok," George said. "Everything will be fine."

Vicki scooted to the front of the airplane cabin, her fists tight and ready to strike.

George looked down at Vicki. "I'm going to hook up your static line now."

He pulled her upper body forward to reach behind her pack to grab the static line. Vicki's arms were pinned to her sides. When George moved back and her upper body was upright again, Vicki could only stare at the door. The adrenalin in her body caused her arms to shake while her fists tightened and prepared to strike out. The plane leveled and Dan nodded again at George.

George called out, "Door."

The swirling wind invaded the cabin a third time as the door popped open. Vicki's hands stayed balled tight.

George winked at her. “Relax, don’t struggle. You’re going to enjoy this.”

Dan turned his face toward Vicki. His mirrored sunglasses silhouetted her distorted reflection against the sky outside. Vicki grabbed the doorframe with her left hand to force herself out of the airplane.

Before she could act, George yelled, “Cut—Climb Out.”

Vicki did not hesitate.

The wind blew stronger than she had imagined as it pushed her back into the airplane. She hauled herself out again and struggled as her left hand grasped onto the strut. She pulled herself out with her one grip and fought the wind for several more seconds to get her right hand into position. As her right hand grabbed the strut, George’s grip on her container released so Vicki was free from the men. She looked back inside at George as he smiled out at her. Dan’s head remained turned toward her as the reflected sky showed in his sunglasses. Vicki remained tense while her gaze stayed firmly fixed into the airplane.

"Go."

Vicki leapt off the step in an arch as she tensed her arms in anticipation of the need to hit someone. She swiveled her head left and right as she scanned the open void close to her for danger before a force pulled her shoulders upward. With her fists clinched, she turned her eyes skyward as the parachute blossomed open above her. She looked all around her until she convinced herself she was alone in the sky. The airplane flew away from her as the deployment bag disappeared into it. A few seconds later, George jumped from the airplane and fell below Vicki's level until his canopy opened far below her.

The air grew peaceful as the airplane retreated in a descending left turn, the rustle of the parachute fabric above her providing the only sound. Vicki relaxed her arms as she enjoyed the sky above and the ground far below. No danger existed here. A wave of peacefulness flowed through her body as

Vicki relaxed more than she had anywhere on the ground for the last three years. She twisted in her harness and turned her head to take in the vast landscape of desert, mountains, and farmland laid out in front of her like a three dimensional map. There was nothing to worry her, nothing to frighten her, nothing to harm her. She closed her eyes as she lifted her head to the sun as it shone down and brought warmth upon her face. Finally, she had found the place that allowed her the tranquility she had searched for so long. She would gladly jump again for the solitude of the parachute ride.

The ground with the dangers inherent to it came at her sooner than she desired. The student landing area waited beneath her as she turned her canopy into the wind. Her landing roll ended before she even had time to think about it and she jumped up to run around the parachute to collapse it. She had the entire parachute in her arms as the student pickup vehicle pulled up next to her.

Sally got out of the passenger side of the cab. "Good landing."

"That was the best feeling I've had for a long time.

"I told you that you would have a good time. Come on, let me help you up into the back and let's get back to the classroom for your debrief."

"Sally, when can I do this again?"

"You'll have to talk to Kevin, but you can probably go again today if you want."

Vicki climbed onto the back of the truck and sat on the bed next to Nancy and Frank.

"When can we go again?" Nancy said.

Kevin looked at the three students as they sat in the desks before him. "Do you all want to go again?" All three shook their heads yes. "Wow, I've never had an entire first jump class all want to make a second jump on the same day before."

George yelled from the back of the room. "Case of beer!"

Kevin looked at George and smiled. "Well, it's taken you four years, but you finally caught me. I guess we all slip up eventually."

George headed back to the hangar to manifest the group. Kevin prepared them for their second jump. On the second jump, each of them would go through the motion of pulling a ripcord as a preparation for their first free-fall jump. Kevin demonstrated to the three how to bring their hands and arms in to pull the ripcord. Soon the three students moved their hands and arms like synchronized swimmers while they yelled "Arch, Look, Reach, Pull," in time to the motions. Kevin, soon satisfied with his charges, led them to the hangar.

"Is there any way I could go out first this time?" Vicki said as George performed the safety checks on her parachute. "I'm sure that I'll do better if I go out first."

George looked up from his checks. "Sure, no problem. You did seem a little tense up there. Some people are like that. Watching the other people jump makes them nervous."

"Thanks."

Ten minutes later, the trio of students and their jumpmaster were in the air again. Vicki did her practice ripcord pull with ease before she settled down into her harness for the peaceful tranquility of the parachute ride. The sun warmed her face again as she closed her eyes and lifted her head skyward.

Nancy landed next to a mesquite tree and her parachute draped over it. The three of them and the pickup driver worked a half-hour to free the parachute. The driver directed the students as they pulled and slid the parachute from the branches so no damage would occur. Nancy and Frank's parents snapped pictures. The parachute finally came loose from the tree.

The driver helped Nancy gather the canopy up. "You own a case of beer," he said.

"Why does she owe beer?" Vicki asked.

"For the first time she put a canopy in a tree. It's tradition."

"Sounds more like a drinking game."

"It's okay," Nancy said. "I'll do it. I've decided that I'm going to do this again. I'll play by whatever rules there are."

The truck slowly made its way across the desert road and then onto the concrete apron. Vicki settled her head onto the pile of parachutes just in time to see a large formation of skydivers as they broke their aerial formation and separated for deployment. She pointed to the sky and yelled, "Look!" As they all gazed skyward, the jumpers pulled their ripcords. The air filled with the crack of opening parachutes. Within seconds, colorful canopies raced across the sky. The jumpers above hooted and hollered indicating that a good skydive had taken place.

"Oh, neat," Nancy said as the jumpers flew their canopies across the sky. "Do they do that many all the time?"

"Sometimes. I bet they'll be partying hard at the restaurant tonight."

"Do all of you go to a restaurant after this?"

Nancy asked.

"Yes, most of the jumpers do. It's a little place in Florence called Manuel's Cantina. They have Mexican food, a bar, live music Saturday nights. I usually ride over there with Sally and Harry, the airport owners."

"Do you think anyone would mind if we went?" Frank asked.

"Of course not," Vicki said. "Everyone is welcome."

"What do you say, Nancy? Shall we send the parents packing so we go to the party?"

"You bet! After all, it is our 21st birthday. Only, you get to be the designated driver so I can party."

"No problem big sister. No problem at all."

By the time they got back to the hangar, the sun lay too close to the horizon to allow another jump that day. The three decided that they would all jump together again the following day. Vicki grabbed her first jump certificate and ran to her RV. She opened the door to a loudly meowing cat that immediately jumped up to his food bowl.

"I see you're not interested in how my day went,"

Vicki dumped food into the bowl and then sat down on the sofa as she studied her first jump certificate. The Calligraphy Typeset along with Sally's eloquent script lent a sense of formality to the document. As Vicki traced her name with her fingers, the sense of peace and freedom left over from the canopy ride flowed through her mind. She looked around the RV for a place to post the certificate where Buster could not use it as a scratching post. Buster jumped down from his food bowl and hopped onto Vicki's lap.

She held the certificate if front of his face. "See this? This is freedom for me. I have finally found freedom."

Buster rubbed his chin on the paper before biting into it.

"Oh, no you don't. You don't get this one."

She stood up, removed a thumbtack from a picture high on the RV's wall, and put the certificate in its place. She settled back down on the sofa while looking up at the certificate. She petted Buster until she heard the car pull up.

"See you later kiddo," she said to Buster as she went out the door.

Vicki, Sally, and Harry walked through the door of Manuel's into the dining room packed with skydivers like students in a Cessna. The three of them had to weave through the crowd for over a minute before they reached the table with a reserved sign on it. As they sat down, skydivers started placing bottles beer on the table in front of Vicki in a continuous stream.

Vicki looked at Sally. "What are they doing?"

Sally laughed. "I guess that they are just congratulating you for your first jump. It happens sometimes when one of the staff starts jumping."

Rick placed a beer in front of Vicki. "Congratulations. I told you everything would be fine. I hope you'll think about jumping with me after you get off of student status."

Vicki closed her hand around the beer. "Thanks."

Vicki looked at the collection of different brands of beers on the table in front of her, which numbered now more than thirty and grew by the minute. "What should I do? I'm not going to drink more than one of these."

Harry smiled at her. "First, grab six of them and take them up to the band."

Vicki did as Harry said. As she sat back down, Nancy and Frank approached the table.

"Mind if we join you?" Nancy asked.

"Sure," Harry said. "Grab a seat and take a beer."

"Thanks." Nancy she sat down next to Vicki and grabbed one of the beers on the table. Frank sat down with a soda in his hands next to Sally.

Frank looked at the collection of beers in front of Vicki. "Why did you order so many beers?"

"I didn't. People have just been dropping them on the table." Vicki turned to Harry. "Now what do I do?"

"Stand up on the chair and yell 'Skydivers—Free Beer!' Then, sit down as fast as you can with a strong hold on to your own beer." He looked over at Nancy. "I'd suggest you hold on tight to yours too." Vicki looked at Harry with a questioned look on her face and then looked at Sally.

Sally moved her beer into her lap as she smiled. "Just do it."

Vicki grabbed the beer Rick had left and slowly mounted her chair. Then, as loud as she could, she yelled out, "Hey Skydivers, Free Beer Here!" She quickly sat and protected her beer as a wave of people rushed up and grabbed the beers off the table.

"Thanks Vicki," "Thanks," "Mochas Gracias," "Way to go Vicki," came the voices. The beers disappeared from the table in less than thirty seconds.

Chapter 8

The jumpers broke their grips at 3,500 feet. Rick turned 180 degrees, brought his arms quickly to his sides, and stuck his feet straight out. He shot away from the others like a bullet. He looked back at Vicki in her track as she moved at a snail's pace away from the center of the group. Rick noted her body position and would talk to her later about it. That is, if Judy had not noticed her also and talked to her first.

With close to 900 skydives, Judy retained the title of senior jumper on the load. This far surpassed Rick's 200 jumps and Bob's 175. Vicki's 65 jumps made her the baby of the group. Judy planned the dive, assigned the exit order, and would debrief the dive.

As Rick's internal clock chimed, he glanced

at the ground to guess his altitude. *3000 feet.* A quick check of his altimeter showed that his guess erred by 200 feet, the needle pointed to 2800. Rick waved his arms in preparation of opening as he glanced over his shoulder at the clear air above him. He pulled his deployment handle and released the pilot chute to the wind. The bag lifted off his back while he began to sit up in his harness to prepare for opening shock as the canopy cracked open.

The violent opening shock contrasted with any that he had experienced before as Rick's left shoulder suddenly rose and he swung off center. He reached for his steering toggles but, before his hands could grasp them, the canopy spun him to the left. Rick's body became heavy as the spin increased. He grabbed the steering toggles and yanked down on them to release the brake settings. The right toggle returned pressure while the left did not. Rick pushed his gaze past the toggles. The left steering lines had tangled in the rear suspension lines. The deployment slider flopped above the tangle and held the canopy partially closed. Rick pulled the right steering toggle down until it lay even with the useless left one. The spin stopped, but the canopy rocked as it grabbed air one second and then spilled it out the front the next.

Rick scanned the air around him and saw Judy's canopy off to his left. His canopy was falling toward the ground much faster than Judy's whereas normally, the speeds would be equal. Trying to land the canopy at this speed would break bones. Rick glanced down at his shiny and unused reserve ripcord.

With another glance toward his quivering canopy, Rick released his steering toggles. The canopy began its spin again as he looked at the handles on his chest. His right hand went around the soft orange cutaway handle while his left moved to the reserve ripcord. He inserted his thumb into the ripcord as he wrapped his fingers tightly around the cold metal. As he prepared himself for what was coming, he prayed that Robert had known what he was doing when he had repacked the reserve. He peeled the Velcro of the cutaway handle until it came free. He pushed his right arm out. Before the handle got a foot from his chest, the main parachute risers released sending Rick back into free-fall.

His body arched automatically as he picked up speed toward the ground. He pulled the reserve ripcord handle out of its elastic keeper and pushed his left arm outward. The handle, with its attached cable, came to a stop. His eyes grew wide as he looked at the handle in his hand with it stuck six inches from his chest and the cable taut. A twinge of panic filled Rick's veins with adrenalin as his speed toward the earth increased with each passing moment.

His training kicked in as he dropped his cutaway handle and moved his right hand over to his left. Both arms pushed outward with a fear driven strength until the tension in the cable disappeared when the pins cleared the closing loops. The cable came out of the guide tube as the harness loosened around Rick's shoulders. The reserve pilot chute flew from his back with the small deployment bag trailing. Rick instinctively went back into his arch. Over his shoulder, the white nylon fabric of the reserve parachute appeared from the bag. The parachute opened with a sharp crack as it filled with air. Rick's feet swung forward of his body until his toes were almost even with his head before they swung back to vertical. Rick breathed a sigh of relief as he stuck the reserve handle down the front of his jumpsuit. The bright white round parachute breathed softly as it rippled in slow wind. Rick drew breaths faster than the canopy.

Rick landed just outside of the student landing area. His main canopy, which had twisted itself into a tight mass of nylon and lines as it descended, landed in the open desert not far from him. As Rick carefully gathered his reserve parachute into his arms, the snapping of stabilizers on a square canopy in flight approached from behind him.

"Heads up," Judy yelled as she expertly landed three feet to his right. She spun around gathering her own canopy into her arms before it touched the ground. "I do believe that's a case of beer."

"Gladly. The way I'm shaking right now I could drink the whole thing myself."

Judy laughed. "First reserve rides will do that to you. What happened?"

"My left steering lines were tangled below the slider and it put me in a spin. When I pulled the right one down and stopped the spin, the canopy just rocked back and forth."

"Did you yank down hard on the left one a few times?"

"No. Would that have cleared it?"

"Probably not, but it's always worth a try if you've got the time."

"How do I know if I've got the time?"

"If you don't know, then you don't have the time. In addition, if you don't know, then you've broken the golden rule of skydiving.

"I know. Always know where you are

above the earth."

"Good guess. Let's go get your main. I saw the truck heading out this way before I landed."

"I dropped my cutaway handle. I had to use two hands to pull the reserve handle."

"It probably landed between here and where your main parachute hit. Let's spread out to look. If you don't find it now, you never will."

The two separated themselves by several yards as they walked toward twisted pile of nylon that lay dead on the desert floor. They moved their eyes back and forth across the sparse ground.

Rick saw it first. "There it is."

"That saved you a case of beer. Now there's no proof that you dropped it."

Rick picked up the cutaway handle, continued to the clump of the main parachute and picked it up. "This will take forever to untangle."

"Robert will have it straight in five

minutes. It's really simple the way he does it."

Carrie pulled up in the truck. "Need a ride?"

Judy and Rick got into the back of the truck and Carrie drove them toward the hangar.

"Say Rick," Judy shouted over the noise of the truck and the wind. "I wanted to ask you if you've ever considered getting your jumpmaster rating."

"I hadn't really ever thought about it."

"I think you should. Your flying skills and safety awareness are good. You seem to enjoy working with less experienced jumpers. I think you would be good at it."

"What would I have to do get it?"

"You would have to sit through a first jump course, teach a couple of parts of another first jump course under supervision, and pass a test given by the National Association. Also, you have to act as jumpmaster for five jumps with an experienced jumper acting as a pretend student."

"Do you really think I could do it?"

"Most of it will be easy for you with your skills. The hard part will probably be finding an experienced jumper that will let you strap a static line rig on them. Many jumpers don't like putting one of those back on. I'd ask some of the less experienced jumpers like Vicki, Nancy, or Frank. They're still close enough to student training that it probably wouldn't bother them."

The truck slowed to a stop as it reached the hangar doors.

"I'll think about it," Rick said.

"You should talk to Kevin," Judy said as they scooted off the truck bed. "He would actually run your training. He's the Designated Examiner."

The jumpers burst into applause with assorted catcalls as Rick walked into the hangar. He bowed to the crowd as he dropped the tangled mass of nylon and lines that used to be his main parachute. Robert walked up with a large trash bag and whipped it open.

Rick stared at the trash bag. "You're not

going to throw my main away are you?"

Robert laughed "No. This is for your reserve so you don't get any more dirt on it than you already have. Just dump the reserve and your container in here. I'll get it repacked as soon as I can."

Rick dropped the reserve parachute into the bag. He then loosened his straps and stepped out of his harness. He began to lift it into the bag when Robert stopped him. "Take your altimeter and the two hook-knifes off first. The fewer sharp things that could snag the fabric in there, the better."

Rick stripped the accessory items off before he placed the harness in the bag. Robert tied the top of the garbage bag shut and headed for the packing ledge. "Get your jumpsuit off and I'll show you how to straighten out your main. We'll need another pair of hands to do it, so grab someone else to help."

Rick unzipped the long front zipper of his jumpsuit and peeled the fabric off his shoulders like a snake shedding its skin. He sat on the floor, pulled his tennis shoes off, and slid his legs one by one out of the jumpsuit. As he slipped his shoes back on, he glanced around the hangar. Vicki stood over her laid out main canopy as she slipped out of the coveralls she used as a jumpsuit. He headed over to her.

"Hey Vicki. Do you have a couple of minutes to give Robert and me a hand?"

Vicki sat on the floor finishing putting her shoes back on. "What do you need?"

"Robert's going to show me how to untangle my main. He says need a third person."

"Sure, I'll help. How was your reserve ride anyway?"

"It was exciting. I had a tangle in my steering lines."

"Well, better you than me. I'm not looking forward to my first one."

"I'm sure not looking forward to my next one."

Robert had started on Rick's canopy as

they walked up. He gathered the packing tabs attached to the top of the canopy panels in his hands then shook the fabric forcefully to flatten the panels before passing the tabs over to Rick. "Hold on tight to these." Robert moved down to the knotted mass of lines attached to the two risers. He grabbed the risers and held them out to Vicki. "Hold these by the bottom rings." He then backed up slightly as he looked at the tangled mess. After a few moments, he grabbed the steering lines at the canopy end and worked them down toward the risers.

"Will you have to disconnect the lines from the risers to straighten it out?" Vicki asked.

"No. The lines were straight before Rick messed them up so they'll straighten out okay." Robert pulled on the steering lines gently as he looked at the tangled mess of lines. He held one steering line up above his head while holding the rest of the lines toward the ground. "Rick, step through here with the canopy." Rick walked through the lines and returned to his original spot. Robert dropped the steering lines and grabbed several suspension lines. He held them up slightly above the others. "Vicki, pass the riser in your left hand through here." This exercise went on for several minutes as Robert grabbed different lines to separate them while Rick and Vicki passed the canopy or the risers back and forth when Robert directed. Finally, Robert grabbed the steering lines one last time at the canopy attachment point and walked them clear down to the risers. "Just lay it down as it is. It's clear. I'll check it again after you hook it back up to your harness. I've got a jump to do now, but I'll start repacking your reserve as soon as I get down."

"Thanks," Rick said.

Robert hurried off toward the hangar door. He scooped his jumpsuit and parachute off the floor.

Rick turned to Vicki. "Now that was amazing."

Vicki headed toward her open parachute.

"I'll agree with that."

Rick moved over to the packing ledge and leaned against it. Judy's comments about a jumpmaster rating returned to his mind. Not able to jump again until Robert repacked his reserve, Rick decided to wander over to the student training area to look around and maybe talk to Kevin.

Bob pulled the van to a stop at the campsite. Carrie hopped out of the passenger door and opened the sliding side door. Rick pulled himself off the bed in the back as he grabbed the case of beer that he had bought in town after dinner. He slid the door closed and handed the beer to Bob.

"Do you mind taking this over to the fire for me? I've got something I want to do before heading over there."

"Okay," Bob said. "I'll tell everyone it's your first reserve ride payoff so they don't harass you when you get there."

"Thanks. I won't be long."

Bob and Carrie headed hand-in-hand toward the already blazing fire at the pit while Rick turned to head toward Vicki's RV. The alternating green and white flashes from the rotating beacon provided him occasional glimpses of the path. As he got closer, he could make out Vicki's RV in the flashes and the small light that glowed in the front part of the RV. Rick, hoping that Vicki had not turned in yet, walked up to the door and knocked on it.

"Vicki, it's Rick. Do you have a minute? I've got something to ask you."

Rick stepped back about three feet from the door as the exterior light came on. Vicki peeked around the shade that covered the door window. A moment later, the curtains that blocked the front window shifted as a shadow crossed in front of the light. The shadow moved back to the door window.

Vicki called from inside the RV. "What do you want?"

"I want to ask your help on something,"

Rick said. Then, as a quick afterthought, he continued. "It involves free jumps for you."

The RV door cracked open and Vicki stepped out onto the concrete pad. She glanced left and right as she closed the door behind her. Her stance was tense. Rick moved back a few more feet toward the lounge chairs around the small table. "Mind if I sit down?"

Vicki remained by the RV door. "Sure."

Rick sat on the lounge chair furthest from the RV. "I've decided to get my jumpmaster rating and I would like to ask if you would help me."

Vicki visibly relaxed. She made her way to the other chair and pulled it slightly away from Rick. She sat down with her back to the light from the RV.

"What do you want me to do?"

"I need someone to act as a student for five jumps, three static lines and two free falls. I'll pay for the lift tickets and the repacks. All you have to do is be willing to jump with the student rigs."

"Wait here a minute," Vicki said.

Vicki went into the RV and came out a minute later with a helmet in each hand. A metal bracket stuck out from the top of each one. She placed the helmets on the table near Rick. She then scooted her chair up to the table and sat.

"I'll do it if you'll do something for me. I've decided to start jumping with cameras. This helmet is almost finished to use with one of my still cameras. I'm working on this one to fit a new mini video camera I've ordered. I'll do your student jumps if you'll do some jumps with me so I can practice using these. I need to do some structured jumps for distance separation and fall rate practice. I'll pay for the jumps and I'll even give you some copies of any shots that turn out. Though who knows what they'll look like at first."

Rick picked up one of the helmets to look it over. "That's real good machine work on that bracket."

"Thanks. Harry taught me how to use the

lathe and the mill. Actually though, that is the fourth attempt to get it right. The others didn't fit either the helmet or the camera right. So what do you think? Want to trade off."

Rick stood and stuck out his hand to shake. "Deal."

Vicki stood up too and shook it firmly.

Rick left her at the RV and headed toward the fire pit with the party in full swing. Laugher filtered through the night air as jumpers tried to outdo each other in their jump stories. As he moved through the edge of the rabble, jumpers ribbed him about his reserve ride. Offers of packing instruction were frequent. Several jumpers also offered to pack for him in exchange for jump tickets. Rick good heartedly let the comments pass as he searched for Kevin. Reaching the line of coolers, he grabbed a beer before he continued his search. He found Kevin sitting at the outermost picnic table with George and Judy. They all acknowledged him as he sat down and joked with him about the reserve ride.

When Rick had worked in sufficient comebacks, he turned to Kevin. "I've decided to go for my jumpmaster rating."

Kevin raised his beer in a salute. "Good decision. Have you thought about who you are going to get to do the practice jumps with you?"

"I talked to Vicki. She said she'll do it."

"Good choice. We can get together tomorrow to go over a schedule and the rules for the training jumps."

"How long do you think it will take me?"

"It'll take you about a month or two to do the training and the practice jumps. We'll have to contact the Conference Director to come out to administer the test when you're ready. I've got a copy of the training manual you can borrow to study but you should order your own from the Association."

"I'll do that Monday."

The fire had died to embers. The cooler, empty and turned over on its side, spoke silently of another successful party. The number of jumpers at the pit had shrunk as the adrenaline of the day worn off and the alcohol took its toll. A few diehards huddled next to the fire to absorb one last touch of warmth. They cradled cans of beer with a swallow or two left in them as though the act of draining them would cause the night to end.

The Milky Way, stretching majestically across the night sky, cast a faint light that reflected off the trees, cacti and the desert sand. The huge cluster of stars resembled a massive fireworks display on the Fourth of July frozen in time. Only the alternating green and white flashes of the rotating beacon broke the stillness of the night.

Rick used a stick to stir the embers into one last flame as he prepared to abandon the scene and head for the shelter of his tent. The fire flared again as he pulled himself upright using the stick like a crutch. The last swallow in his can waited to move down his throat. He watched the small flames dance above the burning wood for a few more moments before he turned to say his good nights to the remaining jumpers. Before he could speak, a voice filtered through the darkness.

"Car coming in."

Far down the long airport road, headlights shown dimly in the distance. The few jumpers that remained lifted their eyes toward this intrusion into the solitude at the end of their evening. The headlights grew as the car raced toward the turn around the end of the runway and slowed quickly as it reached it. As the car followed the curve, the streetlights showed the shape and color.

Kevin spoke from the darkness across the pit. "It's Nancy and Frank. I wondered where they were today. They missed last weekend too."

The car moved knowingly through the parking lot and pulled to a stop at the edge of the grass. The engine died and car doors slammed as two figures moved through the splash of the green and white lights of the beacon. Nancy ran up to Kevin while Frank followed close behind. Rick ambled over toward them.

Nancy talked fast with excitement. "Kevin. Have you got any experience with Two-Way Freestyle jumping?"

"I've read about it in the Association magazine, but I've never seen it in person."

"We were out in California at the Chino Valley Drop Zone to make a couple of jumps last weekend. We saw some videos of people doing it. It's the most beautiful thing I've ever seen in my life. It's like two people dancing while suspended weightless above the earth."

Nancy, almost at a state of hyperventilation, paused to catch her breath.

Frank picked up the explanation in a calmer voice. "We hired coaches to make some training jumps to learn the basics. When we go back to California next month, we're going get some more training. They're going to have the first competition of it at Easter next year and we want to enter. We may not win or even place this time, but with our dance experience we think we can put together a good routine."

"What dance experience?" Rick asked.

"We've both been dancing since we were kids," Frank said. "Nancy dances now with the Phoenix ballet and I teach modern dance at a studio in Phoenix. Before we began skydiving, we would spend every weekend night at the dance clubs. We used to win most of the competitions."

Kevin threw his empty beer can into the fire. "I can't help you with any of that type of jumping. I really don't know anybody here that's done it. I know Judy goes to the California Drop zones for women's record attempts so she may know something about it. Other than her, you're probably on your own here. I would be interested to follow you out a few times to see what you're doing. What's it like?"

Rick's ears left the conversation as Nancy bubbled on about the new style of jumping they had discovered. He gazed into space as he realized that not only had he not known about Frank and Nancy dancing, he did not know what any of the other people at the drop zone, aside from Bob and Carrie of course, did away from the airport. He had never really thought about Kevin or any of the other jumpers having jobs or lives outside of the drop zone. For all he knew, some could be plumbers, carpenters, mechanics, or even doctors or lawyers. No one talked about anything here except jumping.

He shifted his eyes across to the jumpers that remained as they listened to Nancy. Rick wondered what kind of lives they had led before the sky beckoned them. *Had they played sports? Did anyone else ride a motorcycle? Did they go to movies? What did Kevin do away from the drop zone?*

Rick looked toward the darkened RV that sat by itself across the parking lot. *What had Vicki done before she ended up at this desert airport?*

He turned back toward the fire pit and the glow of the dying embers. This place and this sport defined his existence now, the center of his universe squarely on this spot. Nothing really remained of the biker life that had existed before that first jump, only the Harley that sat parked most of the time in the little fenced patio of his apartment. Rick had no contact with any of his old riding friends, save a headshake or a wave as he passed one riding down the street. Even his old constant search for women to party with had morphed into a search of the hangar floor as he looked for the next skydive to get on.

The outside world did not exist for Rick except as a place to earn money for more jumps. As he looked toward the tents set up on the grass, he wondered how many others here worked solely for that same goal.

He lifted his head and gazed again at the Milky Way. The power of the sky had taken hold of his life. It left him with only the single desire to focus on the next skydive. An addiction that gripped his very soul.

A shooting star crossed his vision as it hurdled down toward the earth. Rick felt a strange kinship with that rock like a fellow journeyer that raced through the air. Its burning light analogous to his own exuberance in the air.

Rick's consciousness moved back to the fire pit as a body walked past him into the darkness. Only Kevin and Nancy remained. The rest of the jumpers had disappeared to their own tents or vans in the desert.

Nancy's hands moved in ways that Rick had never seen before as she described strange and different maneuvers performed in the air. The sky now owned her whole being in such a way that she would never find complete release. This wonderful world had trapped her like the rest of them.

Rick lifted the can to his mouth to take in the last of the beer. He dropped the can into the pit and the drops from the can sizzled on the cooling embers. He turned toward the darkness where his tent waited.

Tomorrow would bring other skydives.

Chapter 9

Vicki cocked her ear up from under the hood of her truck to listen to the sound of the vehicle coming down the airport road. After a moment, she recognized the vehicle's engine as belonging to Bob's van.

Vicki's attention went back to her engine as she worked to remove the fan belts. As the second belt came off the pulleys, she heard light footsteps approach from her left. She rose from under the hood, the open-ended wrench gripped tight in her hand. She relaxed as Carrie came into sight with a knapsack over her left shoulder and a towel in her arms.

"Hi, Vicki. Whatcha you doing?"

"Just changing the fan belts."

"They break on you?"

"No. I do this every year so they won't wear out."

Carrie looked down into the engine cavity.

"Need any help?"

"You could hand me the new belts out of that bag over there."

Carrie threw her towel over her shoulder, walked to the bag, and reached inside. She held the two belts up and looked at them for a second. She handed one to Vicki. "Here's the rear one."

Vicki looked at Carrie. "How'd you know that?"

"My father taught me to work on cars before he let me get a driver's license. He said that I needed to know how to fix simple things like flat tires or fan belts if they broke on the road. We lived in the mountains so service stations were few and far between."

Vicki took the belt from Carrie. "I'm impressed. Most women only know how to stand on the side of the road and act helpless until a man stops."

Carrie laughed. "That's what my father used to say. He also taught me how to hunt and fish. I was the only girl of four kids, so I don't think he knew how to relate to me any other way. How did you learn to work on trucks?"

"My father and mother ran a service station when I was growing up. I began to work at it when I was ten."

"Do they still have it?"

The sides of her mouth turned downward as the thought of her parents and little brother crossed her mind. "No. They died when I was sixteen."

"I'm sorry."

"That's okay. It was a long time ago and I've gotten used to being alone."

Carrie fidgeted for a second. "Well, I better go get a shower before the hot water runs out."

Carrie headed toward the Rec. Hall while Vicki started to place the new belt on the pulleys. Vicki stopped working on the engine and straightened up. "Carrie, if you ever need to take a shower and it's too crowded over there; you can take one in my RV. That is as long as you don't mind cat fur."

Carrie smiled. "Thanks. I might take you up on that someday."

Carrie continued her walk while Vicki turned back toward her truck engine. She hesitated before her hands reached under the hood. She looked toward Carrie's receding figure and smiled.

Rick and Vicki walked into the hangar, their open canopies slung over their shoulders. Vicki carried her camera helmet in the crook of her left arm. Stopping at the packing ledge, she gently set the helmet down, being careful to place it away from the edge. She moved back to where Rick had laid out his canopy and threw hers out next to his as Rick straightened his canopy tabs.

Vicki started to remove her coveralls. "What did you think of that one?"

"I think I figured out what's causing the side to side motion of the camera. When you fly your body, you're using your arms to turn.

That's shifting your shoulders and hence your head. I think it might work better if you tried holding your arms still and turn with your legs."

Dropping her coveralls on the floor, Vicki moved down toward her container to set her brakes. "How do you turn with your legs? I was taught to turn by moving my arms."

"It's a technique that Judy and Kevin showed me on some of the jumps we've been doing. You can turn faster with less side movement. I can show you how on one of the benches, then we could go up so you try it in the air."

"Sounds good."

Judy walked up holding a green jumpsuit. "Hey Vicki. Why don't you see if this will fit you?"

Vicki held the jumpsuit up to her body. The leg cuffs touched the ground and the Velcro-closed wrist cuffs hung past Vicki's free hand.

Judy looked her over. "Close enough. Since it looks like you're going to keep jumping, I brought this down for you to check out. I wore this jumpsuit when I first began jumping. After I got pregnant with Susie, I could never fit into it again. It may be a little long, but Robert could shorten the arms and legs."

Vicki held the jumpsuit out in front of her to look it over. Small Velcro-closed pockets lined the belly and the thighs. "What are these little pockets for?"

"You can put one pound shot bags in them to bring your mass up. Most women have more body fat then men so their surface to mass ratio is lower. Rather than having to work hard to keep up with the men, you just put some extra weight in them so you fall faster. I doubt if you'll need any since I don't think you have any fat on you anywhere except your boobs. But, I'll throw in a dozen shot bags. I've collected quite a few over the years."

"Mind if I try it on?"

"Sure, go ahead."

Vicki slipped it on. She zipped the long

front zipper up and the jumpsuit snugged around her body. She then pushed the forearm material up enough so the wrist cuff Velcro could mate. The legs were about 3 inches too long. When she arched, the jumpsuit, while snug, did provide enough flexibility for movement into her practiced body positions. "How much you want for it?"

"Go see what Robert will charge for redoing the legs and ask him what he thinks it's worth. I'll take whatever he says. You can even pay me in jump tickets. That's where the money will go anyway. You can keep it until you decide."

"Okay, Thanks. I'll let you know."

Vicki was sitting at the picnic bench in the hangar as the sunset load prepared for their jump. Carrie talked to Bob as he and Rick suited up. As the men headed to the dirt dive, she walked over and sat down beside Vicki.

"You're not jumping on the sunset load?"

"I ran out of money for the day. Also, the

experience on that load is way above mine. Judy asked me if I wanted to take my camera up and video them, but I'm not ready to do it with a lot of people. I've only done it with Rick so far."

"What's he like to jump with?"

"He's pretty good. He knows a lot and has helped me with my camera flying. I'm actually getting the shots I want thanks to his input."

"Bob and Rick argue, playfully of course, around the campfire all the time about who's the better skydiver."

"I think Rick's the better of the two," Vicki said. "But Bob has a better time jumping. He seems to enjoy every jump. Rick always pushes himself to do everything better and faster."

"If I ever start jumping, I think I'd rather do it just to have fun."

"Are you thinking about jumping?"

Carrie leaned in close to Vicki. "Don't tell Bob, but I am thinking about it. I just haven't made up my mind yet. It does seem like fun."

"I'm sure that Bob would like that. I'll bet he's worried that you will get tired of hanging around and he'll end up having to choose between you and jumping."

"Which way do you think he'd choose?"

"I don't really know, but I'll tell you this. Most of the time that question gets asked, the jumpers are here the next weekend and the girlfriends aren't."

"Well, I guess I better start jumping or at least not get tired of hanging around."

The manifest speaker came to life calling the sunset load to the airplanes. Rick and Bob walked over to the picnic table. Bob bent down and kissed Carrie lightly on the lips. "See you later, Babe."

"Okay," Carrie said. "Have fun."

"Have a good one," Vicki said to Rick. "Don't forget to pull."

"Thanks," Rick said. "I plan to. Have a good one that is." The four all smiled as the men turned toward the hangar doors and the waiting airplanes.

"I'm going to go let my cat out for a little before dark. You want to watch the jumps from my place?"

"Sure."

Vicki led Carrie through the tool room and out the back door toward her RV. As the sun touched the horizon, the trademark Arizona rays burst forth across the sky.

Vicki gazed toward the rays. "Now that's pretty. The sun will probably be down before they jump."

"Bob told me that when they jump at this time of day, the sun is still up at altitude and they get to watch it set while they are in free-fall."

The two women stopped walking as the airplanes lined up on the runway for takeoff. The Twin Beech rolled first, its round engines thundering like a long line of Harley Davidson motorcycles. The less powerful sound of the Cessna provided an anticlimax to the roll of the Beech. Both airplanes disappeared into the setting sun before the women resumed their slow walk.

"Where are you from?" Vicki asked.

"I'm from a little town in New Mexico called Gold Hill."

"How did you end up here?"

Carrie smiled. "I didn't want to date a cousin."

Vicki stopped short. "What?"

Carrie laughed. "It's really a joke, but it has some truth. Gold Hill is an old mining town where hardly no one ever leaves. There has been so much intermarrying that you have to ask about someone's family relationship to you before you go out with him. You don't want to end up kissing one of your cousins. The truth is, I just didn't want to stay there to be a miner's wife. I knew there was more to the world than what that town had to offer. Plus, my father is the union president, so anyone that wanted to date me had to put up with that."

They reached the RV. Carrie sat on one of the lounge chairs while Vicki went in to get

Buster. Vicki hooked him to his long leash and let him loose to explore. Buster immediately walked over to Carrie and began to sniff her feet.

"Don't mind him. He'll leave you alone in a minute."

Vicki sat down in her lounge chair and scanned the sky for the airplanes. Buster left Carrie's legs as he moved toward new smells on the concrete.

"How about you?" Carrie asked. "How'd you end up here?"

"Basically, I didn't want to live in Phoenix and work at Desert Airlines. That's where most of the people that graduate from PAMI go to work. It just wasn't for me."

"I can understand that. Phoenix looked too big for my tastes. In addition, Daddy was able to get me a job through the Telephone Company Union in Tucson. He didn't like me leaving, but once I convinced him that I was going no matter what, he accepted it. He got me my job and helped me get an apartment by co-signing the lease."

"That was nice of him."

"I don't know if he was being nice or just wanted to be able to have a say in where I lived. He's used to getting his way in the county. I wouldn't doubt that he has arranged for union people in Tucson to keep an eye on me. That's one reason that I never let Bob spend the night. The first time Bob comes out of my place in the morning, I bet Daddy will know about it in an hour."

"Wow! You really think he'd do that."

"I love my Daddy, but he is control freak. Out here is one of the few places I don't think he can check up on me. That's one thing about here, you can see strangers coming from a mile away. I still set up my own tent at the campsite for appearance's sake. I wouldn't want Daddy to get mad at Bob."

The distinctive sound of the Twin Beech filtered though the air from the east. Vicki settled back into the lounge chair. "Sounds like jump run."

As the two women looked for the airplane far above, Carrie asked. "How about you? When did you get your first place?"

Vicki's eyes remained fixed on the approaching airplane. "I moved back into my parents' house right after my eighteenth birthday."

"How did that work out for you?"

Vicki voice fell into a saddening tone. "Well, I'm here now."

They both went silent as the jumpers above exited the airplanes. Carrie focused on the jumpers as they fell closer to the earth. Vicki focused on her memories as she pulled on Buster's leash to move him toward her. Then she cradled him in her arms.

Vicki slipped the video cassette out of the player as she turned off the TV. The four jumpers that she had just videoed headed out of the room high-fiving each other. "Thanks Vicki," several said as they exited the room. Vicki checked the counter on the player and noted the setting. She would transfer the dive to the jumpers' personal tapes later in her RV. Vicki inserted the cassette into the camera on her helmet and closed the cover just as Nancy and Frank walked into the room.

"Vicki," Nancy said. "We want to talk about hiring you to video us on some jumps."

"Sure, as long as the dive isn't too big. I've only done up to six jumpers on one load so far. I don't want to go bigger than that for a while yet."

"It would just be Nancy and me," Frank said. "We're working on a routine for the Two-Way Freestyle Competition in California next Spring. They have video people we can hire when we jump there, but we need more practice. Plus, we want to keep our routine secret until the competition."

"We fall faster than the normal speed when we're vertical," Nancy said. "It might take some getting used to. We could go try a jump to see what you think."

"Okay. I can always put some shot bags in

my jumpsuit pockets to fall faster."

"We'll pay for your jumps and ten dollars extra each time for the video. That's what we pay the video people in California."

Let's go try one and see what happens."

Vicki, Nancy, and Frank dropped their gear on the hangar floor and then walked into the video room. Vicki turned on the TV, removed the cassette out of the camera, pushed it into the player, and hit the rewind button.

"I don't think I got much at all after the exit. I just couldn't keep up with the two of you."

Vicki pushed play and the three watched the TV. Nancy and Frank's forms appeared on the screen as they climbed out of the Cessna. They rocked in unison for the exit, their mouths calling a count drowned out by the wind. A few seconds of their bodies in free-fall flashed on the screen before they fell away from the camera. The rest of the video showed only shots of the ground with momentary glimpses of the two.

"Diving, I could catch up to you. But as soon as I went to frame you, I slowed down and you fell away."

"How many pounds of weights did you use?" Frank said.

"Just five. I can put up to fifteen in the pockets of my jumpsuit. Let's try again first thing tomorrow morning. If that doesn't work maybe Robert can make a weight vest or something that can carry more."

"Sounds good," Nancy said.

Nancy and Frank headed out the door. Vicki pushed rewind and, when the tape stopped, pushed play again. The scenes repeated themselves on the screen.

Carrie walked through the door. "Whatcha watching?"

"It's an attempt at filming Nancy and Frank doing that crazy Freestyle stuff. I've never gone so fast in my life."

"Where are they? I don't see them on the screen."

"Just watch. You'll see two little bodies pass by the camera every few seconds. I think I got what I did more from luck then skill. See, there they go."

The video ended and Vicki shut the TV off. "Just when I thought I was getting a handle on this camera jumping stuff."

"You'll figure it out. You're stubborn like that."

Vicki smiled. "What an enduring quality to have people know you for."

Carrie giggled. "Listen, the real reason I came in is to ask you if you're free next month on the weekend of the 21st."

"I'm not going anywhere. I'll be here jumping most likely unless the winds are up. Why?"

"Keep it a secret for now. Bob and I are getting married. We're announcing it tonight at the fire."

"Well congratulations. Are you going to get married here?"

"We're going to go to Gold Hill. My

mother wants me to have the wedding in a church with a big reception. I would rather just go elope in Vegas, but Bob doesn't want my father mad at him. So, to Gold Hill we will go."

"Anything I can do to help?"

"I'd really like you to come to the wedding. Rick is going to be Bob's best man so he'll be there. You wouldn't have to be in the wedding or anything like that, I have plenty of cousins for bridesmaids. I'd just really like you there."

"Thanks for the offer, but I'm really not good in strange crowds. I can barely handle Manuel's at times."

"I figured you might say that but I had to ask. How about if I let you jump into the reception?"

"Tempting, but the answer is still no."

Chapter 10

As a break came in the traffic, Rick turned the van to the east and then folded the visor down to shield his eyes from the morning sun. Carrie looked out the passenger window as Bob snored softly in the back. Friday morning traffic remained heavy going into the city, but lightened as they got past the Air Force base. The edge of the city disappeared into a stark desert filled with scrub oak and stunted mesquite trees. The temperature, cool now, would spike into triple digits by the afternoon. The van would roll into Gold Hill and the shelter of the mountains before then.

"Why do we have to be there so early?" Rick asked. "I thought the rehearsal isn't until five o'clock."

"Mom just wants lots of time for the final fitting of the dress. You know, in case the seamstress needs to make any alterations. You won't be bored though. I've got my little brother set up to give the two of you a tour of the mine."

"That sounds cool. Will that cute cousin of yours, Joan, be around?"

"She's going to be my Maid of Honor, but I'd watch out for that one if I were you."

"Why? Don't you think I can handle her?"

"Let me tell you a little about the women in Gold Hill. The mines in the towns are stagnant. They're still being worked, but not expanding. Nobody is moving into town. There's no new blood. When someone like you who's young, working, and single shows up, the women in town will break their necks trying to latch onto you. They'll try every trick in the book."

"Aren't there enough guys in town?"

"There are single guys there, but there's been so much family intermarrying over the years that when you think about dating someone you have to talk family first. You have to make sure that you're not a first or second cousin. Actually, being second cousins isn't a deal breaker. Lots of second cousins in town marry."

Rick smiled. "Is that why you left? The thought of having three-eyed babies with your first cousin twice removed?"

Carrie giggled. "Partly that. The main reason was I didn't want to be a miner's wife stuck in that town forever. I knew it wasn't for me."

"Sounds scary. I'll remember to watch myself around her."

"Not just her. I'm talking about all of the women there. I mean, they're nice and all. Just keep your eyes open."

"Still sounds scary.""

"It's not so bad. They may tie you to a bed to keep you around, but they wouldn't do anything like break your legs. How would you drive them to the Farmer's Market for Saturday gossip?"

Rick smiled as he returned his full attention to the road. The freeway continued on its straight journey with only the slight curves and dips of Benson to provide variety. Texas Canyon rolled into view with its formations of huge boulders stacked upon each other on both sides of the freeway. It looked like a giant child had played there eons ago and never cleaned up. The rocks fell into the rearview mirror as Rick steered onto roadways he had not yet traveled. The town of Wilcox came and went.

The desert rose again and then flattened before him as though a bulldozer had scraped the land clean. The sparse vegetation, visible fifty miles before, had ended with only the occasional patch of brush showing where water found its way to the surface. The color of the land had also morphed from the tans of Tucson to a muted red. The ground had bled out its color with only a remnant of the damage left due to the constant scouring of the wind. No signs of life, save the fellow travelers in the other cars and trucks on the road, existed in this place.

"What a bunch of nothing," Rick said. "I hope your hometown is better than this. Otherwise those women you talked about might be more desperate than you imply."

"Gold Hill is in the mountains further up on the right. It's the area that Geronimo roamed and fought. He even attacked Gold Hill once."

"Neat," Rick said. His eyes roamed the surrounding land and out to the mountains in the distance as he looked for places that Geronimo and his band may once have hidden. The van began to climb a long slow rise toward a mountain pass. Rick turned his head at the sound of a long horn blast from a train on its way down from the top of the ridge on tracks parallel to the highway. A large sign came into view just off the right side of the road. The Zia of the State of New Mexico in bright orange against a yellow background announced the border.

Rick exited the freeway ten miles past the next town and pointed the van up the road to the south toward the mountains. The land rose and soon stunted oak and juniper trees formed a barrier on each side. They blocked the long-range views so prevalent earlier. He piloted the van higher and higher into the hills, evidenced by the occasional glimpse through the trees at the desert far below in the distance.

Bob moved from the rear until his head stuck between the seats. "Are we there yet?"

Carrie leaned over and kissed him on the cheek. "Almost honey. It's about ten more miles to the town. Rick, make sure that you watch your speed. The county makes a lot of its money off speeding tickets given to tourists."

Rick's eyes flashed down to the speedometer and his foot lifted from the gas pedal just as he heard the quick hit of a siren behind him. A glance in the rearview mirror confirmed a police car with its lights flashing.

"Now you tell me."

Rick pulled the van onto the shoulder, shut

down the engine, and rolled down the window.

The sheriff's deputy walked to the open window with his hand on his holstered pistol. His mirrored sunglasses hid the true direction of his stare. He made a quick glance into the rear of the van.

"Afternoon sir. I need to see your License, Registration, and Proof of Insurance."

Carrie spoke before Rick could move for his wallet. "Hi Johnnie. Look time no see"

The deputy's head shifted to the left ever so slightly and made no other movement for a moment. His right hand stayed fixed on the top of the grip of his holstered pistol as his left hand came up to his face and removed the sunglasses. He squinted across the van. A smile moved onto his face as his hand dropped from his pistol

"Carrie? Carrie Murphy? Is that you? I haven't seen you since high school. What are you doing back here?"

Carrie held up her hand and displayed her

engagement ring. "I'm getting married tomorrow." She pointed at Bob and then to Rick. "This is my fiancé and this is his best man."

"That's great," the deputy said. He reached through the window and shook first Rick's hand and then Bob's. "The name's Johnnie Rodriquez. Carrie and I went to school together. You're a lucky man to have caught that one."

"Thanks," Bob said.

"You say hello to your family for me and give them my best."

"I will."

With a quick headshake to Bob and Rick, the deputy turned toward the rear of the van. He stopped, returned the sunglasses to his face, and came back to the window. Rick saw himself in the mirrored lenses.

"Please watch your speed while you're in the county. Drive safety and have a nice day." He disappeared from the window.

Rick kept his vision focused in the side

mirror until the deputy got into his car and pulled onto the highway.

"Thanks."

"No problem. I figured he wouldn't give you a ticket with me in the van. The sheriff is a friend of my father and will probably be at the wedding. If it had been one of the State guys that stopped us you'd be spending your jump money on a fine."

Rick eased the van back onto the highway and accelerated to below the speed limit. Soon they passed the first of the mountains of overburden from the mine. Rick looked out the side window as trucks the size of houses lumbered by on the service road that ran next to the highway. The trucks carried rocks the size of the van piled to almost overflowing.

"That is big," Rick said.

"Everything about the mines are big," Carrie said. "Wait until you meet my father."

Rick looked over at Carrie expecting to see a laugh, but Carrie and Bob just looked at each other with smiles on their faces.

As Carrie gave directions, Rick guided the van thru the business district. A minute later, they climbed a road toward a group of houses whose porches all faced the mine pit on the opposite hill.

Rick parked as close to the house as the line of cars in front of it allowed. Carrie jerked open the passenger door and ran from the van toward the house. A small woman burst out of the screen door of the house followed by the largest man Rick had ever seen in his life.

"Is that Carrie's father?"

"Yup," Bob said. "He's pretty huge, huh?"

Rick and Bob headed up the sidewalk to the threesome. Carrie and her mother still had their arms around each other while the father waited off to the side with a cigar clenched between his teeth. The father turned as the two approached. He nodded at Bob with no hint of a smile.

"Bob, I see you made it here okay."

He looked straight at Rick. "You must be Rick."

He pulled the cigar out of his mouth with his left hand as he offered his right hand to Rick. Rick extended his hand and the man's long thick fingers wrapped around his entire hand. The man squeezed so tight that it brought pain that caught Rick by surprise. Rick held his face stolid though he wanted to scream and pull his hand away. The man's eyes' twinkled as a half-smile came over his face.

"Daddy," Carrie said. "Stop that."

The pressure on Rick's hand relaxed into a normal handshake.

He looked over at Carrie. "Just saying hello, Angel." His grip held fast as he looked back at Rick. "Name's Murphy, Patrick Murphy. I'm Carrie's father."

"Pleased to meet you, Mr. Murphy, sir," Rick said as the huge hand released him from its death grip.

The cigar went back into Mr. Murphy's mouth as he spoke through it. "Let's get inside. Bob, your parents are already here along with most of Carrie's bridesmaids." He turned back toward Rick. "You ought to check out some of those girls. They're right pretty."

He headed into the house, ducking his head and twisting his shoulders as he went through the door.

Carrie smiled at Rick. "Sorry about that. I guess I should have warned you about him."

"Yea," Rick said as he rubbed his hand. "Anything else I should be worried about besides the police, the women here, or your father?"

"That's about it. I'll let you know if I think of anything else." She grabbed Bob's hand and hurried toward the door.

Rick went through introductions of all the people in the house. The County Sheriff, Randy Hernandez, introduced himself and commented to Rick about speeding in the county. The friendliest person in the group, outside of Joan, was Carrie's brother Mick. He had the same eyes and nose shape as Carrie along with the same hair, a thick red mass that hung over his ears.

"I'm supposed to take you two on a tour of the mine to get you out of the way while mom and the ladies finish up the wedding stuff," Mick said. "Or we could just go to a bar if you'd rather."

Bob answered. "I think the mine tour would be best."

"Will we get to be near those big trucks?" Rick said.

"Sure. I can even let you climb into one."

"Now that would be cool."

Rick placed his burger and fries on the table where his open beer sat. His assigned seat at the rehearsal dinner had been between Mick and a bridesmaid whose name he could not remember, but Joan had switched places with her. Bob and Carrie sat across the table between Carrie's two older brothers. While Mick and Carrie got their looks from their mother, these men resembled their father. Their massive shoulders wedged the couple into place like prison guards in control of their charges.

Joan slid into her seat with a plate. Rick smiled as she went on about her classes at the local college and her job at the mine offices. As she talked, her hand pawed Rick's arm like an angler working to set a hook. Every time he looked across the table, Carrie smiled at him. She winked once.

Patrick Murphy's voice boomed from the head of the table. Rick used the opportunity to turn his head from Joan. The cigar lay unlit in the ashtray, but his left hand gestured toward Bob and Carrie like it remained between his fingers.

"Have you two talked about the opportunity I told you about at the mine?" Mr. Murphy said. "It's a good job with lots of advancement potential. I could talk to the mine manager on my way home."

Mick leaned into Rick and whispered. "This ought to be good. Carrie would never agree to come back."

"Thank you for the offer sir," Bob said. "But Carrie and I both like Tucson and our jobs there. Plus, living here would be too far from the drop zone."

Mrs. Murphy broke into the conversation. "You certainly can't be considering continuing to do that foolishness. You're getting married to our daughter."

"Really Bob," Patrick Murphy said. "You're going to have more responsibilities now. You're going to need to think about starting a family. Carrie's not going to want you running off every weekend to risk your life for no reason."

Rick lifted his beer to his lips just as Carrie pushed her chair back and stood. Her hands pressed against the top of the table. "Stop it both of you. I would never ask Bob to stop jumping. In fact, as soon as we get back from our honeymoon, I'm going to take the first jump course myself."

The table went silent. Rick spit out his sip of beer into the bottle still pressed against his lips. His eyes widened as he looked at Bob for confirmation. A wide-eyed shoulder shrug signified Bob's own surprise. A gentle poke in the ribs from Mick broke Rick's stare toward the couple. Mick's face had a grin with a chuckle behind it.

"Told you this would be good," he whispered. "Carrie used to pull announcements like this all the time while we were growing up. I remember when she told the parents that she had bought a motorcycle. That was hilarious."

"Carrie, you can't be serious," Patrick Murphy said. "You can't—"

"Stop it," Carrie said. "This dinner is about the wedding tomorrow, so please talk about that instead of trying to plan our lives for us."

She sat down and picked up her fork. Rick glanced up the table at Patrick Murphy. His face remained set in a grimace directed solely at Bob as Mrs. Murphy's jaw remained slack while she looked at her husband. Patrick Murphy broke his stare with a pull on his beer. The table remained void of conversation with only the clink of silverware in the air. Joan continued to paw Rick's arm.

Rick slipped out the side door of the building and walked toward the end that faced the mine. The activity across the valley rumbled with a ceaseless fury causing a cloud of dust that stood out against the bright arc lights. He sat down on a bench cloaked in darkness to watch as haul trucks moved slowly up the wide dusty roads across the valley. Though he knew their size, from here that scene reminded him of a tinker toy set he had once owned.

The side door creaked open and Joan's whispered voice called out. "Rick? Are you out here, Rickie?"

Rick hunched down to further blend into the darkness. After a few moments, the door creaked again. No footsteps sounded and Rick relaxed as his gaze returned to the activity across the valley.

Off to Rick's right, one of the double doors to the patio opened. Carrie stepped out with her arm resting in the crook of her father's as it would be when they walked down the aisle the next day. Patrick Murphy faced her and placed his hands into hers.

"Please tell me you're joking about this parachuting stuff, Carrie."

"No Daddy. I'm not."

"But why? I bet that Bob put you up to this."

"It wasn't Bob. You should know me better than that. I don't do things because someone else thinks I should. That's like when you blamed Frank Bartlett when I bought that motorcycle."

"Then why do you want to do it?"

"Daddy, skydivers are the happiest people I've ever met. They laugh all the time. There's always a spring in their step, and they always have a smile on their faces. There's a bumper sticker that many of the jumpers have on their cars. It says Skydivers know why the birds sing. I want to find out why they sing. Maybe I'll only do one jump; maybe I'll do a thousand. But it will be because I want to, not because someone else wants me to."

Patrick Murphy's eyes glistened with moisture. "I just don't want to see you get hurt or..."

"I'll be fine Daddy."

"Angel, I never could control you, even as a little girl. Heck, I still think of you as my little girl."

"I'll always be your angel, Daddy. However, I'm not your little girl anymore. I'm a grown woman that you're going to give away tomorrow. When you give me away, you have to let go. You're going to have to let Bob and me find our own path."

"I'll try angel."

He wrapped his arms around her and hugged her. Rick doubted that the squeeze matched the power of his handshake. The two separated and walked together back through the doors.

Rick heard the side door creak again before Joan's voice penetrated the darkness. "Rick, are you out here?"

Bob and Rick sat in the waiting room in the basement of the church. The room was empty except for two chairs and a small folding table. A cross hung on the otherwise blank walls while a single fluorescent fixture hummed a yellow glow over the stark surroundings. A beam of light streamed into the room through a ground level window too small for a person to climb out. Rick pulled on the collar of the tuxedo like a condemned man trying to loosen the rope. Bob got up to stand in front of the mirror every few minutes to adjust his bow tie and straighten his vest.

The door opened and the minister poked his head into the room. "Hope you're ready. The limo just pulled up."

Bob looked at Rick. "Let's do this." Bob headed toward the door that the minister had left open. He stopped as his hand grabbed the doorframe and turned back toward Rick. “You got the rings?”

“They're in my vest pocket.”

“Make sure. I don’t want to give Carrie’s father any reason to be upset.”

Rick dug into his vest pocket and brought out the two plain gold bands. He held them up in front of Bob’s eyes. “See.”

“Thanks. Any last words of wisdom?”

“Yea. Don’t say yup instead of I do. That might piss him off.” Both men chuckled.

Bob and Rick followed the minister up the back stairs into the main chapel. They moved into their places on the left side of the altar. Quiet organ music filled the open space enough to mute the light conversation murmur from the guests. The only people that Rick recognized on the groom’s side were Bob’s parents. The ushers had evenly divided the rest of the guests between the pews on both sides.

The organ finished the filler song and began the Processional March with a loud flourish. The Bridesmaids and Ushers came with their slow halting walk. The Bridesmaids smiled and looked around at the guests as they passed. They nodded occasionally to a friend or family member. The ushers, all brothers of Carrie's, walked mostly stolid, never shifting the focus of their hard stares from Bob's direction. The last usher, Mick, broke that tradition as he smiled almost to the point of laughter while he made his way forward with a bridesmaid on his arm. When he got to the altar, he shook hands with Bob and then Rick before he moved into his place next to Rick. Joan, as Maid of Honor, walked alone next up the aisle. As she moved a step at a time, she glanced around and smiled at the guests. Every few seconds, she would let her eyes settle on Rick. Rick looked toward Bob or around the room. He only met Joan's glances half the time.

When Joan reached the altar and got into place, the organist stopped the Processional March and with a flourish, started into the

Bride's March. The guests all rose and turned their attention toward the back of the church. Carrie and her father entered the chapel in a slow walk. Patrick Murphy trailed Carrie by a half step as if he wanted to hold back and not let his daughter go. The crowd smiled and turned forward as father and daughter made their way past them up the aisle.

Rick let out a muffled chuckle as Carrie got closer. A quick glance at Patrick Murphy confirmed that he had not detected the noise.

Mick leaned in and whispered, "What's so funny?"

"I just realized that I've never seen Carrie in a dress before," Rick whispered back. "Plus, she's wearing tennis shoes under her wedding dress."

Mick looked forward and then leaned back toward Rick. "That's Carrie."

The wedding party turned toward the center as Bob took Carrie's arm from an unsmiling Patrick Murphy.

A light hand tapped on the door. Rick felt around the strange surroundings for the bedside lamp until he found the button above his head and pushed it. The mounted light filled the small motel room with a worn glow.

The hand tapped again as a voice whispered through the door. "Rick? Oh, Rickie. Are you awake?"

Rick lay in the bed for a moment as he hoped the voice would go away. The room did not have a balcony to drop from nor a window that would open wide enough to crawl out. No escape existed from the voice on the other side of the door. Rick's mind climbed from the slumber induced by the reception food and drink. He knew he had to face the voice.

He made his way across the floor with a halting step like one of the bridesmaids moving up the aisle. His eyes checked that the deadbolt was set while his hand slid the safety catch over the protruding knob. Rick moved his eye over the peephole. He kept it a slight distance away lest a hand might reach through it to pull him to the other side. Joan's distorted image came through the lens, a champagne bottle in one hand with the other hand poised to knock again.

"What do you want, Joan?"

"I missed you after Bob and Carrie left. Thought you might like a little nightcap to celebrate the wedding."

His mind raced for a response. "Thanks, but I really need to go lie back down. I've been on the floor next to crapper since I got back. I guess I drank a little too much already."

"Okay. Would you like me to help you get into bed? I can be a pretty good nurse."

"Ah—no thanks. I just really need to get some sleep."

"I'll stop by in the morning, say about seven. Hopefully you'll be feeling better. We could go get some brunch or something before you have to leave."

"Sounds good. I really got to go lie down."

"Okay. Bye. I'll see you in the morning."

Rick kept his eye to the peephole as Joan's figure moved out of sight down the hall. He climbed back to the bed and looked at the alarm clock. His eyes focused on the red display as his mind calculated the time he had before seven o'clock rolled around. He picked up the clock and fingered the alarm settings. As the alarm display counted down to five o'clock, breakfast in Wilcox flashed into his mind. He would be safe at the drop zone before noon. A lunchtime skydive with Vicki sounded better than whatever kind of brunch Joan had in mind.

Chapter 11

Vicki laid back in her lounge chair as the sun disappeared below the horizon letting the sky complete its transformation from a crimson red to a darkening purple. The first of the skydivers of the weekend turned their vehicles down the airport road. Each one headed toward their own well-known parking places or campsites. Kevin parked next to the classroom where his folding cot waited in the back. Nancy and Frank parked their car on the shady side of the Rec. Hall. The desire to be near the bathrooms overwhelmed the problem of the noise of the party by the fire. Other jumpers had staked out campsites in the outlying desert as their home away from home. A well-known engine sound came issuing forth as it approached down the road. The van turned and Bob parked at a building pad several over from Vicki.

As the last of the sky light faded, a flashlight moved toward Vicki from where Bob had parked his van. A second flashlight beam struck out toward the Rec. Hall. Vicki gathered her dinner dishes as she prepared to go inside to escape the intrusion into her evening. She really did not want to leave the outside since the air remained warm and still, just the type of night that brought out the flying bugs Buster jumped and twirled at in an attempt at capture one. With no TV, Buster provided her evening entertainment.

As the flashlight got closer, Carrie's voice traveled through the darkness. "Hi Vicki."

Calmness returned to Vicki as her friend's voice reached her ears. "Hi Carrie. Pull up a chair."

Vicki set her dishes down and settled back into the lounge chair. Carrie mounted the concrete pad and plopped down in the other one of Vicki's folding chairs. She turned the flashlight off as stillness returned to the air. The rotating beacon activated and the splashes of light illuminated the bugs for the waiting Buster. He jumped over Vicki's chair at an unseen adversary.

Carrie pulled two beers from her jacket pocket and offered one to Vicki. The two clinked bottles.

"Here's to a wonderful weekend," Carrie said.

"You got that right," Vicki said.

The two sipped their beers as they settled back in their chairs. Vicki pulled Buster's lease back as he tried to jump up on Carrie's lap and wrestled him onto hers.

Carrie sat silent for a few minutes. She then turned toward Vicki. "I've got a couple of favors to ask of you."

"Sure. What do you need?"

"Tomorrow I'll be doing my graduation jump. Would you take pictures while I suit up and when I land? I want to send some to my parents back in New Mexico. They still don't like the idea of my jumping, but I figure that if I keep sending them pictures maybe they will get used to the idea."

"No problem," Vicki said. "I'd be happy to. I'll even set up the camera on the Cessna to take pictures of your exit."

"Thanks." Carrie swallowed another sip of her beer. "There's one other thing. I'd like you to come with us to Manuel's for dinner and to the fire party afterwards."

Vicki hesitated as she slowly sipped her beer. "I don't know about that."

"Please? I know you don't ever come to the parties at the fire, but I'd really like you to be there for my graduation celebration. Bob is going to drive. He's promised not to drink anything until we get back here."

Vicki looked at Carrie in the dim flashes of light afforded by the beacon. Vicki's hand shook as she drained her beer and placed the empty on the ground. She clutched Buster tightly. Her friendship with Carrie conflicted with the terrors of her past. Vicki wrestled with the thought of confiding in Carrie. Carrie had become enough of a close friend to deserve an explanation for her refusal. Her fears and skeletons had stayed hidden so long. Vicki had come so far to get away from them, but they still followed her everywhere she went.

She sat quietly in thought as the rotating beacon cast its alternating flashes. The night lay silent and peacefulness filtered into the air. Finally, she came to a decision. She knew she had to confide in Carrie. Carrie was a true friend, her only one. Maybe letting Carrie know everything would help her stop being afraid, jerking at every noise of the night. Vicki had kept it bottled up inside her, which had not worked. Maybe letting it out would. Vicki reached for her cooler and pulled out another beer. She twisted the cap off and lifted the bottle to her lips for a long swallow before she finally spoke. "There's a reason I don't hang out at the restaurant or party at the fire with everybody. I've never told this to anyone around here. You've got to promise never to tell anyone."

Carrie's eyes widened as she fixed them on Vicki. "I promise.

Vicki swigged her beer again. "It happened about four months before I left Casper."

"I told you we'd see you later," Eddie said with a grin. He reached down and roughly kissed her on the lips. "Now, let's have some fun."

Vicki, a grimace set into her face, transferred her weight to the balls of her feet as she tensed her calf muscles. She stared into Eddie's eyes as she waited for the mistake she knew would come. Drunks always make mistakes.

Bud kept a tight hold on Vicki's lower arms as Eddie unbuttoned her flannel.

Vicki tensed her shoulders and balled her fists.

"Relax. You're going to enjoy this," Eddie said with a wink. "Don't struggle and everything will be just fine."

He pulled her shirt open and roughly

fondled her breasts. "Just how I remember them, nice and firm." His hands left her breasts as he began to unbuckle the belt of her jeans.

Bud moved his hands from Vicki's forearms to her breasts. "I want some of that. This might be better than the last one."

Vicki acted. Her right hand went to the crotch of Bud's khakis. She grabbed and pulled upward, squeezing with all her might. At the same instant that she squeezed, she kicked her left leg out and connected with Eddie's crotch. Bud sank to the ground as he tried to remove Vicki's hand. He screamed as something popped. Eddie staggered back, his hands tight to his crotch.

Eddie started back toward her, his hands still on his crotch. "You bitch!"

Vicki maintained her grip on Bud. When the distance looked correct, she kicked upward and her left foot connected with Eddie's nose. The blow sent him over backwards into the bushes. Vicki released

Bud, turned, and drove her fist into his nose. Blood spurted through the air as his head thudded when it hit the sidewalk. Vicki turned to face Eddie again.

Eddie had rolled onto his stomach and was slowly getting to his knees. Vicki kicked her leg up into the soft tissue of his stomach. He fell sideways over on to his back. Then, he slowly sat up and struggled to regain his feet. Vicki swung into a roundhouse kick that connected with his nose. Blood splattered across the bushes to the wall. He fell onto his back again. Vicki moved within reach and grabbed the front of Eddie's shirt with her right hand. She lifted him slightly as she brought her left arm around in a hooking swing. Her fist collided with his jaw.

Her hand still holding Eddie's shirt, she turned her head back toward Bud. He had regained his feet and moved toward her in a stagger. Vicki dropped Eddie and closed the distance between her and Bud. She launched into another roundhouse kick that hit Bud squarely on the jaw. He fell over and remained down. Vicki turned back toward Eddie. A moan came from his bloody form as he tried to turn onto his stomach. Vicki maintained a fighting stance while she shifted her eyes back and forth between the two men. Alternating red and blue lights cast the scene in a surrealistic atmosphere.

Hands grabbed Vicki's shoulders from behind. Without hesitation, Vicki kicked her foot backwards into the knee of her latest attacker. The hands released her and she stepped two paces forward. She flew into another roundhouse kick that connected with the jaw of the attacker. The jaw moved a notch as the head snapped sideways. The badge on the man's chest reflected the porch light as he fell backwards onto the grass. Another police officer crouched behind the now prone officer with a pistol in her hands.

"Don't move. I don't want to shoot you."

Vicki did not move but her body trembled.

"Lay down on the ground with your arms

straight out."

Vicki sank to her knees and then to her chest. Her shaking arms stretched out as the cool grass chilled her exposed breasts. Her torso rose and fell as her rapid breathing released the tension from the fight. The figure moved behind her.

"Place your hands behind your back."

Handcuffs tightened around her wrists. The officer grabbed Vicki's shoulders to lift her from the ground. She pushed Vicki toward a police car and placed her roughly in the back seat. Other police cars and ambulances arrived as Vicki sat slouched, her shirt still unbuttoned.

After the ambulances had left, a man in a suit opened the back door of the police car. A badge on a lanyard hung around his neck. He took one look at Vicki before closing the door.

"Officer Jones. Please come here."

"Yes, Detective?"

"Please button the shirt on your prisoner so

I can talk to her."

"Sorry. In all the excitement, I was more interested in my partner than her."

"Just do it."

The officer opened the door of the car and roughly fastened the buttons on Vicki's shirt. She left the door open. "All done, Detective. Have at her."

The Detective knelt down next to the open door. "What's your name Miss?"

"Vicki."

"Well, Vicki, would you like to tell me what happened here tonight?"

"They tried to rape me. I stopped them."

"Are you saying the officer tried to rape you?"

"No, just Eddie and Bud."

"Why did you attack the officer?"

"He grabbed me from behind. I thought he was one of them."

"The two men tell a different story. They said you invited them over to party. When they showed up without any drugs, you went berserk and started beating them. They want to press assault charges on you."

"That's crazy. I don't do drugs."

"Well, Vicki, what I've got here right now is a he said, she said on that. However, what I do have is an assault on a police officer. The officer here is going to arrest you for that. I will have her take you to the hospital for an examination before she takes you to county lockup for booking."

"What? They tried to rape me."

"And you hit an officer in the performance of his duties. You're going to jail for that."

He shut the car door. He hesitated outside before reopening the door. "Where did you learn to fight like that?"

"I've been taking kick boxing lessons at my uncle's gym since I was eight."

"Well, you can tell your uncle his training worked. You broke the officer's jaw."

"So you went to jail?"

"Yes."

Vicki directed her eyes away from Carrie and she stared into the darkness. "I stayed there for the night. In the morning, my uncle bailed me out. My aunt was with him so I told them what happened. He believed me, she didn't. She called me a trouble-making whore. I got out of the car at a stoplight and walked the rest of the way home."

"I hired a lawyer and we met with the County Attorney. I told the County Attorney my side of the story. She seemed to believe me. She said she would check it out and get back to us."

"Did she?"

Vicki drained the rest of the beer and grabbed another one from the cooler. She opened it and swallowed a swig. She continued to stare into the night. "I guess she did try. She called us back in and said that though she believed me, she wouldn't pursue charges against Eddie and Bud. Eddie had gotten his friends at the bar to tell the detectives that I was a girl that wouldn't say no if you brought a few beers or drugs around. They made me sound like a real slut."

Vicki turned and faced Carrie. She slammed her beer on the table. "Hell, Carrie. I'm not a virgin, but I'm also not a slut. I've only been with two guys in my whole life. The first guy was in high school. We did it in the back seat of his father's Cadillac. He never called me after that. The second was Eddie. We went out for two months until I had a pregnancy scare. I didn't see him after that for three months until the night he attacked me."

Vicki drank deeply from her beer again. "Anyway, the County Attorney agreed to one year probation deal for the assault on a police officer charge. The Trust my parents left me also had to reimburse the county for the officer's medical treatment and lost wages."

"So that ended it?"

"No it didn't end there. Eddie and Bud kept driving by the station and my house at night. They had friends of theirs tell me that they were looking to finish our little party. I didn't feel safe. I kept all the blinds in the house drawn and a pistol by my bed. I cringed every time the old house creaked. Business at the station went down because I wouldn't work at night. Then I found out that my aunt had told every woman she knew in the town not to let their husbands bring their trucks to me. She told them that I would just try to seduce them. It was the last straw. I knew I had to leave."

"What did you do?" Carrie asked while Vicki swallowed another swig from her beer.

"I went to Mr. Gallagher, the Trustee at the bank, and told him I wanted to move. I asked him to sell the house and the Trust's interest in the station. I didn't know where I was going, but I had to leave. He was a real lifesaver. He arranged for the Trust to buy this RV for me, gave me money to live on, and said that if I needed it, he would arrange for more. The only stipulation that he put on me was that I had to either get a job within six months or start school. So one morning I loaded my tools into the back of my truck and hitched it to the RV. I left Casper in my rear view mirror. I chanced upon the Prescott Mechanic's school passing through there one day and decided to enroll."

"And then you ended up here?"

"Yes, thanks to Mr. West and Mr. Sparks."

"But nothing's happened to you since, has it?"

"No. But in Prescott and even here at first, I couldn't go out at night. I kept feeling that Eddie would show up one day and finish what he started. Anytime I hear a strange car engine coming down the airport road at night I hide or run for the RV until I'm sure it's not Eddie. Every time I look at Dan's sunglasses, I see Bud's face behind them. I listen for footsteps behind me. I listen for voices from the past. I tune everything else out."

"But Vicki," Carrie said. "The skydivers and pilots here are your friends; they would never do anything to you or let anyone else do anything."

"I though Eddie and Bud were my friends too. Hell, I even thought at one time that Eddie loved me. But they became the Demons of Casper to me. They're with me every day. Every time I see someone in my side vision, I think it's one of them. I tense and am ready to strike out when footsteps come up behind me. I'm afraid I'm going to hit someone one day. I still work out and train three nights a week. I have to be ready to protect myself all the time. I'm sorry, but it's just too hard to trust anyone."

"I'm your friend."

"I believe that, otherwise I don't think I could have told you all this. I haven't been able to bring myself to trust any men aside from Mr. West and Mr. Sparks. I can work okay and hang around during skydiving, but once the sun starts going down, I have to get some place that I feel is safe. Being around the fire with a bunch of drunken guys just doesn't work for me."

"How about Rick and Bob, don't you think

they're your friends?"

"I don't know. They're fun to skydive with or talk to about jumping and airplanes, but I can't take a chance. Next time I may not be as quick or lucky."

Carrie moved over to Vicki, knelt down, and hugged her. "Thanks for telling me. I am your friend. The fact that you told me everything shows that you think so too. Let me try to help."

"I'm not sure that I want help. You deserved an explanation. Maybe I just needed to talk to someone about the story. It's hard keeping it bottled up inside. You're the only person I trust not to judge me."

"Listen, why don't you think about coming over to our campsite tonight to visit. Bob and Rick don't drink a lot on Friday nights, maybe just a beer. We could talk skydiving or get Rick to talk about his motorcycle trips that he used to take before he started jumping. Bob used to waterski a lot before he began jumping. He has a lot of funny stories about that. Come on, it will be fun. I'll walk you back to your RV when you're ready."

"I'll think about it. How long do you stay up?"

"We usually turn in about 10 or so. Rick and Bob like to get up with the sun."

"Okay. Maybe I'll come over."

"Please think about tomorrow night too. I'll tell Bob and Rick that they can't drink until after we walk you back here when you're ready to leave."

"I'll think about that too."

"I hope you stop by." Carrie turned toward the darkness toggling on the flashlight as she stepped off the concrete pad.

Carrie's light grew smaller as she moved down the path. Part of the burden had lifted from Vicki's shoulders with a small glimmer of hope burning in her heart. A visit to their campsite would be a small step for her, but it would also be a safe one. She could get back to the safety of the RV whenever she wanted. She sipped the last of her beer as she made up her mind to do it.

Vicki made her way down the path to the campsite with a practiced ease that did not require a flashlight. The solitude at the airport in the dark still night offered the same peacefulness as the joy she had under canopy. Only the rotating beacon broke the darkness. Vicki always timed her movements to the darkness between the alternating flashes.

When people were on the airport, Vicki moved from tree to cactus to tree between the flashes, her presence hid from everyone. Vicki had not told Carrie that some Saturday nights she would stand outside the light of the fire to watch the party. She had almost summoned up the courage several times to join the party, but her nerve abated before her feet moved her into the light. Vicki had also stood outside of Carrie's campsite on some Friday nights almost ready to walk in to visit.

The specter of Eddie always stopped her. His face stuck in her mind. The thought of another attack always froze her from being able to move forward. Maybe a visit tonight would help change that. Maybe conversation around their campfire would break the grip the Demons of Casper had on her. Her step bounced a little higher as she looked toward the campsite fire with the hope that it represented. Vicki slowed as she got near the campsite and moved off the path to a well-known mesquite tree. Here Vicki could see and hear everything at the campsite. It also provided the invisibility that she needed for the moment.

She had stopped there many times before the nerve to announce her presence and walk on into the firelight eluded her. She had always remained in the darkness with her fears and memories. She would then slowly back away, ever mindful of the flashes of the rotating beacon, to retreat to the familiarity of her RV.

The flickering fire light of the campsite showed the three friends as they relaxed on their folding chairs. Rick sat on the edge of his as he told a story that the other two had undoubtedly heard before. They would blurt out the next line of the story time after time until Rick finally threw up his hands and sank back into his chair. The scene looked peaceful and safe to Vicki. Another surge of hope hit her heart. She began to step away from the tree to move toward the light.

A shout of "Hello" came from the left in the direction of the Rec. Hall. Vicki slipped back into the darkness while she tensed her body for action. Her feeling of hope vanished as the adrenaline of fear replaced it.

Two shapes approached the campsite on the path from the Rec. Hall. Rick yelled "Hello" toward the approaching figures. The beams of two flashlights swung back and forth across the path spilling into the desert. One of the beams occasionally hit the tree that hid Vicki. Kevin and George moved into the light of the fire and they switched their flashlights off. Vicki slowly backed away from the tree and turned toward her RV. Moving cautiously through the patchwork of trees and cacti, she resisted the familiarity of the path. The rotating beacon flashed both guidance and danger as she worked to hide her movements. She remained anonymous in the night.

Reaching the RV, she unlocked the door and then bolted it closed behind her. She grabbed Buster as she retreated to the back of her bed, her breathing hard and fast. As her heart calmed, what had just happened flashed through her mind.

As she thought about it, she realized that it was just a case of bad timing. Certainly, Kevin and George's appearance at the campsite had been a surprise to Carrie also.

She had to trust Carrie. She had to. She needed to.

Vicki moved from her bed to the door. Unbolting it, she stepped out into the cool night air. Laughter floated across clear desert night from Bob and Rick's campsite. Vicki thought for a moment about heading back over there, but then sat down in her lounge chair just to listen.

As the laughter continued to fill the otherwise silent night, Vicki decided she would take Carrie up on her offer of a ride to dinner and attend the party at the fire with them afterwards. Maybe it was time to stop being afraid and Carrie was the one that could help her. She would tell Carrie the next morning.

Chapter 12

Rick carried his parachute gear into the hangar as the sun climbed into the morning sky. The hangar bustled with jumpers. Some were standing in line at the manifest counter while a steady stream passed by the snack bar window purchasing breakfast burritos. Jumpers ate sitting on the packing ledge or at the various picnic tables spread around hangar. Sally moved around the hangar as she refilled coffee cups and orange juice glasses while chatting with the jumpers.

Carrie and Bob sat at one of the tables on the other side of the hangar as they ate their own burritos. Sitting across from them, Kevin made animated skydiving motions with his hands. As Rick crossed the hangar toward them, Kevin's hands slapped down on the table and the three of them burst out laughing. Bob grabbed his napkin to wipe his mouth.

His laugh had sprayed pieces of egg, tortilla, and chorizo across the table, narrowly missing Kevin. Carrie looked sideways at Bob as she used her own napkin to wipe the table clean.

Rick sat down next to Kevin and spoke at Carrie. "Have you got any more of those or did I snooze?"

She reached down into a cooler on the floor next to her, pulled out a foil wrapped burrito, and tossed it over to Rick. "You almost snoozed. With Kevin mooching breakfast and Bob spraying out most of his, I'm surprised there's any left at all."

Sally walked over to the group and sat down next Carrie. "So today's the big day. How are you doing?"

"Fine. I bribed Kevin with beer last night and burritos this morning to sign me off no matter how bad I do on these last two jumps."

Sally turned toward Kevin. "Are the bribes working?"

Kevin swallowed the last of his burrito. "Sure enough. I told her last night that as long as she doesn't break something, I'll sign her off."

"That's not a nice thing to say," Sally said. She looked over at Carrie. "Don't listen to these clowns Carrie. I'm sure you'll do just fine."

"Oh, I'm not worried. Everything has gone great on my jumps so far. I know that Kevin's just kidding."

Kevin smiled. "Carrie's doing great but I have to pull her string somewhat. Otherwise, her head will get too big to get out the door of the plane. After today, she, Bob, and Rick can go up together to have fun until she's ready to really get serious about learning advanced skydiving."

The manifest loudspeaker came to life announcing the first load of the day in the Cessna. Carrie got up. "I'm on the second Cessna load for my last high jump with George as my jumpmaster. I'm going to go suit up and get with him."

"Okay," Bob said. "Rick and I are on the

first Beech load so we'll probably be in the air when you get back down. You can tell us all about it when we get land."

Carrie leaned down and kissed Bob on the cheek. "Have fun Honey." She turned toward the student gear room.

Rick smiled at Bob. "So who are we jumping with, Honey?"

Bob turned toward Rick with his own smile on his face. "Don't go there fool."

Kevin broke up their banter. "Come on you two. Let's go get dirt diving for the load."

Rick and Bob traveled side by side under their canopies about fifty feet apart as they approached the landing area. A light wind blew from the west. Bob pulled on both of his steering toggles equally to flare the canopy as he got close to the ground, but misjudged and had to run to keep from falling down. As his canopy collapsed to the ground, he gathered it into his arms. Rick had landed his own canopy with no movement forward or back as his feet touched the ground. He quickly spun around and gathered his canopy into his arms before it settled to the ground. Carrie ran toward then smiling.

"She looks happy," Bob said. "I guess her jump went well."

Carrie grabbed Bob and hugged him tight. "I did great on my jump! George cleared me for my graduation dive."

Bob kissed Carrie. "That's wonderful, Honey. When are you going up for it?"

"George has us on Cessna load seven. I've got about a ten minutes before I have to get ready."

"Okay, let us drop our gear in the hangar and you can tell us about your jump."

"Ok! I'm going to go tell Vicki. This is so neat! See you in a bit."

She ran off toward the hangar, almost skipping. Her ponytail bounced off her back.

"You know Bob, she may just kill you with love tonight."

"You're right. But what a way to go."

Bob and Rick quickly dropped their gear in the hangar. They stripped out of their jumpsuits by their gear bags. Carrie sat on the packing ledge with her student jumpsuit on and her ponytail bound up inside the plaid scarf she wore during jumps. Vicki was sitting on the ledge next to her. Rick walked over to the two women while Bob dropped his jumpsuit on top of his gear bag.

Bob picked up a small colorfully wrapped package and carried it over to Carrie. "Here, I got you a little something for your graduation."

Carrie tore into the box. Inside, a new Teal scarf lay folded. "You are too sweet. It's wonderful. Thank you so much." She kissed Bob heavily on the mouth.

"Get a room," Vicki said.

Carrie just smiled, grabbed Bob's hand, and placed the box in it. "Hold on to this for me for now. I'm going up soon so I don't want to untie this one. I'll wear that one after I graduate."

"Sure." He put the box in his pocket.

Carrie retook Bob's hand. "Vicki set up the camera on the strut of the Cessna to take pictures of my graduation jump exit. Isn't that cool?"

"I set it on burst mode so you'll get a sequence. You can pick out the best one for enlargement."

"That will be neat. Maybe I'll frame several of the sequence to send to my parents."

Bob grimaced. "Please don't do anything that's going to get your father angry with me. I still think he doesn't like that we got married."

"He's fine," Carrie said. "Forget about him. Also, Vicki said she would ride with us to Manuel's for dinner and also go to the graduation celebration at the fire. Have you told Rick about the deal?"

"Glad you're coming with us, Vicki," Bob said.

Rick cocked his head. "What Deal?"

"I'll tell you later."

"What Deal?"

"Don't worry about it. Go take care of that other thing."

"What other thing?" Carrie said.

Don't worry about it," Rick said. He turned toward Vicki. "Can I talk to you for a minute outside?"

Vicki hopped off the ledge. "Sure."

She followed Rick out to the parking lot to Bob's van parked next to the hangar.

Rick stopped next to the van. "Bob bought Carrie a new Teal colored rig. I bought her a Teal jumpsuit, helmet, and goggles to match. We're going to set it up on a lounge chair next to the van at the student landing area so that when she lands she'll see it. We'd like to get some pictures of her face when she sees it set out on the lounge chair."

"Sure, I'll do it. I guess the scarf was just an afterthought."

"Actually no. We figured that Carrie would expect Bob to get her something so we decided the scarf would help with the surprise for the real stuff."

The manifest speaker blared into life. "Cessna load seven, get it on. Airplane is on the way down. Jumpmaster George, student Chris, student Sammy, and Graduation Carrie. Cessna load seven, get it on."

"I guess we better get back in to see her off," Vicki said.

Carrie had the student free-fall rig on when they walked back into the hangar. Bob was standing next to her talking softly with her student helmet and goggles in his hands. Vicki grabbed her camera and moved around the two snapping pictures from all angles.

George pulled Carrie aside to perform the equipment safety check. He slapped her on the backpack when he finished. "You're good to go. Wait here while I finish checking Chris and Sammy."

Bob handed her the helmet and goggles. "Have fun. We'll be out at the student landing area waiting for you."

Carrie lightly kissed Bob on the cheek.

"Thanks for everything. I've never been so happy."

"Wait until after this jump," Vicki said. "Then you'll really be happy."

George walked by with his other students in tow. "Airplane's taxing in, let's go!" Carrie turned to follow him. She stopped, looked back, and waved softly to Bob.

As the small group exited the hangar, Bob turned to Rick. "Let's do it! I can't wait until she gets down and sees her new stuff."

"Did you ask Kevin what trick they were going to play on her?" Rick asked.

"Yup. He said they weren't going to do anything. He figured that we had filled her head with so many horror stories that she would be nervous enough."

The airplane had taxied away by the time Rick and Bob got to the van. Bob slipped into the driver's seat while Rick got into the back. He folded the back seat up and pulled out Carrie's new gear from the storage space beneath it. He piled it on the floor before he climbed into the passenger seat.

When they got to the student landing area, Rick and Bob set out the three lounge chairs. They laid Carrie's new gear out on the center one. Vicki could get a good shot of her face from the open side door of the van. Vicki pulled up in her pickup truck as they finished the setup. The two men settled into the lounge chairs on each side.

"I've got to get a picture of this. This is so funny." She clicked several shots.

The three listened for the Cessna as they waited at the empty landing area. The birds fluttered between the mesquite trees singing their cheerful songs. A light breeze blew in from the west causing the windsock to bulge half-filled. The shaft squeaking on the rusty support seemed to answer the singing birds.

Vicki walked out into the center of the landing area, ready to move to whatever part Carrie would land. Her camera hung by a lanyard looped around her neck, primed to shoot the landing.

"So what's this deal you're supposed to tell me about?" Rick said as he scanned the sky.

"Not much really," Bob said. "Carrie said that the only way Vicki would come to Manuel's and the fire party with us was if you and I didn't have anything to drink until after we walked her back to her RV when she was ready to leave."

"Where did that come from?"

"I don't know. Carrie said she had talked to Vicki last night when we got here and that's what she promised Vicki. You okay with that?"

"Sure. If that's what it takes to get Vicki to come along with us, no problem. I know it will make Carrie happy."

"Thanks."

The engine of the Cessna filtered down from the sky. Rick leaned his head back to find it in the air above. He spotted it. "Jump Run."

"Where is it?" Bob asked.

"Slightly southeast turning west about a quarter mile out,"

"Got it."

The plane passed south of them on a westward heading. As it got overhead, the engine sound diminished as the pilot throttled the engine back. A figure appeared in the air beneath the airplane.

"She's out," Bob yelled.

The distance from the figure to the airplane increased second by second. The airplane's engine did not resume its normal sound.

"Shouldn't she have pulled by now?" Rick said.

"She probably just had a little trouble getting stable right out the door so she's holding her arch until it feels right," Bob said.

A second figure fell from the airplane. "I wonder what that is all about."

Vicki yelled from across the landing area. "The pilot hasn't throttled the engine back up. Maybe something's wrong with the airplane. They might be bailing out for real."

The first figure continued pick up speed as the second figure slowly closed the distance to the first. No one else appeared in the sky from the airplane. The engine of the airplane stayed subdued as the two figures in free fall approached the earth.

After a few more seconds, Rick realized something was definitely wrong. The two figures were lower to the ground than he had ever seen anyone before in free fall. The second figure continued its slow advance toward the first. The first figure, clearly visible as it fell lower and lower, showed itself to be a spinning body on its back.

“Pull, Carrie—Pull,” Rick yelled. “Don’t try to stop the flat spin, just Pull!”

Bob jumped out of the lounge chair. “Shit! Pull Carrie. Pull!”

The first body fell closer to the ground. A cracking rustling sound filled the air as the body spun faster and faster.

“Pull!” Rick yelled. “Damn it. Pull.”

Vicki screamed from the center of the clearing. “Pull!”

A definitive hard crack sounded across the

open air as a square canopy opened above the second body. The canopy colors identified the jumper as George, the jumpmaster. His canopy hung in the sky, no turns or spins came from it.

Bob sank to his knees. He turned his face toward the ground. He moaned. "No, no, no."

Rick's eyes stayed transfixed on the body as it fell closer and closer to the ground. The sharp rustling sound of the flapping jumpsuit grew louder every second that passed. The noise became deafening as the body approached the top of the trees.

"PULL!" Rick screamed once more as the body disappeared behind the mesquite trees. A moment later, a sickening thud echoed across the landing area. All became silent except for Bob's constant moaning. "No, no, no." None of the three moved as the horrible truth sank in.

Vicki reacted first as she ran to her pickup, jumped into it, and started the engine.

She called out to Rick, "Stay with Bob."

A rooster tail of sand flew as she peeled out and raced south through the landing area toward the trees that the spinning body had disappeared behind.

Chapter 13

Vicki reached the south edge of the cleared landing area but kept the truck moving in as straight of a line as possible. She weaved her way around the mesquite trees and Saguaro cacti while she ran over smaller bushes. The truck slid around a thick hedge of Indigo plants. The engine stalled as Vicki pushed down the emergency brake.

A pilot chute, half inflated by the light breeze, lay visible just to the left in a small clearing 20 yards away. Vicki raced out of the cab toward the white nylon. As she approached the clearing, another pilot chute and two deployment bags became visible. The pilot chutes radiated out at different angles and the fabric of two parachutes spread out across the desert floor. The parachute packs were still strapped to Carrie's motionless body. Vicki stopped in her tracks as she brought her hand to her mouth with a gasp.

Vicki then slowly moved to within a few yards of the prone figure. The body lay facedown with the head twisted to one side. An eye, as dull as the desert sand, stared out toward Vicki and announced that no life remained. Vicki sank down to her knees, not sure of what to do, too stunned to move. She stared at the face of her friend as time stopped.

Time began again as Harry called her name from beyond the bushes. "Vicki, where are you? Have you found anything?"

Words struggled out as Vicki did all she could to hold back the flood of tears that welled inside of her. "She's over here. Come around the hedge."

The sound of Harry's truck broke the desert stillness. The engine sound grew louder and then came to a sudden stop. Doors opened behind her and footsteps loomed as a momentary wave of fear struck at her as the movement rustled behind her.

The fear subsided only as she heard Sally's voice. "O-Shit."

Sally knelt next to her and put her arm around Vicki's shoulder. Vicki wrapped her own arm around Sally and held tight. Tears gushed from their eyes.

Harry walked slowly toward the body, bent over, and placed his fingers on the neck over the carotid artery. His lips tightened as his eyes misted over. He rose and looked skyward. He stayed silent for a minute before he turned and walked back to the women.

Kevin called from the other side of the hedge. "Harry, where are you?"

Harry wiped his eyes with the palms of his hands. "Kevin. I need you to go back to the hangar and get Robert out here as quick as you can. You better come back with him."

Harry stopped for a moment as he breathed a deep breath. "Who do you have there with you?"

"Mike and Judy are here."

"Mike. I'd like you to go back to the edge

of the Student landing area to keep anyone else from coming down here. Judy, would you please go tell Dan to tie down the Cessna away from the hangar and keep everyone away from it. Then guide the police back to here when they arrive."

The jumpers answered back "Sure." Car doors slammed and the vehicle pulled away. The noise echoed across the quiet desert air.

The two women stayed on their knees as they silently held each other.

"Sally, you better take the truck back to Bob's van. You will have to let him and Rick know. It would probably be best if they just stayed there until the police have a chance to talk to them. Tell them I'll talk to them as soon as I can."

Sally helped Vicki slowly to her feet and held her hands. "Are you going to be okay? You want to come with me?"

"I need Vicki to stay here with me," Harry said. "The police will want to talk to her since she was the first to find the body."

Vicki looked at Sally. "I'll be okay. Bob and Rick need to know."

"Okay," Sally hugged Vicki tight. She then turned, walked to the truck, and backed it away.

Harry looked at Vicki. "Are you doing okay?".

She looked over at the body. "Not really. I was just talking to her before she got on the plane. It all seems just so–so sudden."

The sudden loss of her own family flooded her mind. Tears flowed from her eyes as she started to gasp and convulse.

Harry held her loosely, lightly patting her on her back. After Vicki regained control, she slowly pulled away from Harry. She stared across the clearing at the body. "Shouldn't we cover her up with something?"

"It's better if we don't touch the body or disturb the scene at all. The police need to do their job to figure out what happened."

"Okay. I just wish there was something I could do for her."

"I'm sorry Vicki. There's nothing we can do for her now."

A vehicle pulled up on the other side of the hedge and car doors slammed. Robert and Kevin ran around the edge of the hedge. They stopped suddenly when the body came into view.

"Damn," Robert said.

Kevin stared across the desert.

In the distance, sirens howled. The sound of the sirens grew louder by the minute and contrasted to the silence that the group maintained. A police car pulled around the hedge with Judy in the front seat beside the officer. The officer got out and looked across at the body.

"Anybody check for a pulse?"

"I did," Harry said. "There's none."

The officer said something into his shoulder mounted radio mike and then got some yellow tape out of his trunk. Other police cars pulled in and officers moved to secure the scene. A Police Sergeant moved up next to the Harry. He nodded to the group.

"Afternoon Harry. It looks like bad happenings here."

Harry nodded his head slightly. "Yea."

The Sergeant separated Harry and the others from each other to take their statements as EMS personnel arrived with the siren blaring and lights flashing. Confirmation that Carrie was dead came quickly from them and they left silent.

The Sergeant interviewed Vicki and then told her to wait in the pickup truck. Vicki sat in the truck with nothing to do but look out onto the clearing and watch the police as they measured distances and snapped pictures. The clearing was strangely familiar to Vicki. Nausea came to her throat as she realized the clearing had been the one she had landed in on her first free-fall jump. Once a place of freedom and joy, it had now become a place of horror.

After about a half hour, a hearse, with County Coroner stenciled on the doors, pulled into the clearing and two men got out. They opened the rear doors, pulled out a gurney, and rolled it toward Carrie's body. Stopped it about 20 feet away, they left it as they walked slowly forward while they pulled on latex gloves. One of the men snapped pictures of the body and the surrounding area. Then they slowly rolled Carrie over and snapped more pictures. One of them waved Robert over. As Robert pointed to different items on the parachute harness, they snapped more pictures. They carefully unbuckled the leg and chest straps. When all the straps were undone, Robert moved back over to Harry. The two men from the Coroner's hearse gently pulled the shoulder straps of the harness down and freed Carrie's arms. One of them walked over to the gurney and picked up a large black bag from it. As he moved back toward Carrie's body, he unfolded it.

The sight of the body bag hit Vicki in the gut. She buried her face into her hands, unwilling to watch her friend get shoved into a bag. The tears flowed freely until her body was drained and she could only sob quietly. Several vehicle doors shut and an engine started. When she finally looked up, the hearse had disappeared.

Two police officers lifted the parachute equipment into a large paper evidence bag. Robert gestured to the police officers as they handled the equipment. With the gear bagged up, Robert and the Sergeant walked the area slowly. Robert pointed several times to the ground and the Sergeant placed a numbered cone at each spot. The police snapped more pictures before they gathered the items by the numbered cones into little bags. When the officers had finished their collections, the Sergeant walked back over to Harry and spoke. Harry then walked over to Vicki's pickup.

He opened the passenger door. "Are you okay to drive? We need to head back to the hangar."

Vicki sat up straight in the seat. "Yea."

She wiped her eyes with her hands as Harry got in the passenger side. Vicki backed around as soon as the Sergeant's car cleared the path. She followed the police car out of the desert back into the Student Landing Area. The area was as empty as a tomb with Bob's van gone. The vehicles reached the concrete apron before turning toward the hangar. The police car pulled up next to several others that surrounded the Cessna.

Harry pointed toward the Cessna. "Park next to them. Sergeant Ortiz needs you to show him how to remove your camera from the strut. He needs to take it with him to get the pictures developed as part of his investigation."

"Take my camera?"

"You'll get it back, most likely tomorrow. He just needs to get control of the film. Don't worry, it's all normal."

"Okay." Vicki started to open the door. She stopped and turned her head toward Harry. "You've had to do this before, haven't you?"

"Yes. Twice. This is the first student fatality."

The Sergeant led her to the yellow police tape that surrounded Cessna. He lifted the tape so that Vicki could slip under it. Together, they moved up to the strut with the attached camera.

"Tell me how this thing works."

"There's a button mounted on the pilot's yoke that he presses when he wants to take a picture. I set the camera on burst mode this time so it would take six shots each time he pressed the button. If he wanted to shoot continuously, he would just hold the button down until he wanted to stop."

"Is the camera still turned on?"

Vicki looked at the camera switch. "Yes, it is."

"Can you tell how many shots he took?"

"There is a counter next to the manual trigger on the top."

The Sergeant looked at the counter. "The arrow is pointing toward the number 12."

"That means he hit the button twice."

"Can you set the camera to take a single picture?"

"Yes."

"Please do it."

Vicki moved the selector from 'burst' to 'single'.

The Sergeant motioned to one of his officers. "Get me the next evidence cone in sequence."

He turned toward Vicki. "Would you please climb into the pilot's seat and take a picture when I tell you too?"

Vicki started climbing into the pilot's seat. A wave of nausea swept over her as she climbed over the same spot that Carrie had been alive an hour before. She sat in the seat, shaking slightly, while the Sergeant waited for an evidence cone.

The Sergeant placed the evidence cone on the ground next to the wheel. "If this is placed here, will it show up in the picture?"

"It would be better if you moved it back

about three feet. The camera sees the doorway but mainly shoots the person as they exit into the air."

"How about over here?"

"That's good."

The Sergeant stepped away from the cone. "Go ahead and take the picture."

Vicki hit the button once and quickly released it. The shutter activated. Vicki knew at that moment that whatever had happened on jump run would be on the roll of film.

"Thanks," the Sergeant said. "Now, how do you disconnect this to get it off?"

"Can I get out and show you?"

"I'm sorry, of course."

Vicki climbed out of the Cessna until she stood next to the strut. She pointed to the off/on switch. "Turn that to off." Vicki then pointed to the electric trigger connector. "Unscrew the knurled knob until the connector drops out. Then, loosen the wing nut on the cover plate and lift it. Next, you twist the little handle on the mounting arm and the camera will come loose. Keep your hand on the camera or it will drop"

The Sergeant removed the camera and placed it in an evidence bag. He sealed the bag, then wrote on the flap before tearing a numbered tag from the edge.

"This is your receipt for the camera. You'll need to surrender it to get the camera back. Thanks for your help. I'll get this back to you as soon as it is released. It should be tomorrow or the next day."

The Sergeant looked over at Harry. "Ok Harry. You can have your airplanes and the airport back. I'll give you a call when I know something."

"Thanks Ray. You take care. Give my best to Betty."

The police cars moved in a line across the apron and around the hangar. Their engines faded down the airport road. All became silent across the airport.

Harry turned to Vicki. "Come on, let's go get a cup of coffee." They climbed back into the pickup truck and drove slowly toward the hangar.

The hangar contained few skydivers. Those that were there stood in small groups talking in subdued conversations. Several of the women held tissues as they wiped their eyes. Sally stood by the closed door of the office with Kevin. She broke off from Kevin as Harry and Vicki walked toward her. Sally hugged Harry tight and then Vicki. She wiped her eyes with the palms of her hands.

"Bob's in the office. He wanted to call Carrie's parents and his own so I said he could use your phone. Rick's in there with him."

"Good," Harry said. "How're they doing?"

"Rick seems to be handling it okay. But I think that's because he's trying to help Bob. Rick came out after Bob talked to Carrie's father. Her father didn't handle it well. He called Bob a murderer and said he'd see him in hell."

"Shit."

Harry looked up at the ceiling for a few

seconds. When he looked back down, his eyes were misty and his face looked older. His mind then seemed to shake out of it.

“I doubt if anyone is going to want to jump anymore today and I really don’t feel like launching any airplanes. Let's shut down. We’ll see what tomorrow brings. Sally, you had better keep an eye on Bob and Rick. Vicki, see if you can find some help and get the airplanes tied down. I’ll go close down manifest.”

The P.A. speaker came to life. “Harry, please come to manifest. You have a phone call.”

Harry headed toward manifest. Dan, the Cessna pilot, sat at a picnic table so Vicki headed over to him. Sally returned to her vigil outside the office door.

Vicki walked into the hangar after tying down the airplanes with Dan. Harry and Sally talked by the door to the office.

Harry turned to Vicki as she approached.

"The phone call was the Sheriff of Lee County, NM. Carrie's father called him and told him that Bob killed Carrie. He's coming out here tomorrow with her father to see what's going on. I called the local Sheriff. He told me to call him if they show up."

"Does the Sheriff think they're going to cause trouble?" Vicki said.

"He's not sure. He said he'll handle them."

The door to the office opened and Rick slowly backed out. He looked haggled with his eyes puffy and red. After he closed the door behind him, he looked around for a moment as if to gather his thoughts before he turned toward Sally.

"Bob's finished his calls. He's lying on the couch just staring at the ceiling. He really doesn't seem to know what to do. I've talked him into coming back to my apartment for the night to get him away from here and so he doesn't have to deal with his and Carrie's place."

Harry nodded his head slightly in

agreement. "That would probably be a good idea based on Carrie's father's reaction."

Harry told Rick about the phone call from the Lee County Sheriff.

"Why don't you keep him at your place for a few days? I'll let the local sheriff's office know where he is if they need him."

"Okay. I have some vacation coming that I can take this week off to help him out. I'll go straighten up the van, get my tent, and then come back to get him."

"We'll go sit with him until you're ready," Sally said.

Rick walked toward the hangar door. Vicki started after him. "I'll give you a hand."

Within minutes, they had stored the new parachute gear away in the under seat storage space. They drove to the campsite where Rick took down his tent, throwing it unfolded in the back of the van. Vicki loaded the coolers and cooking supplies also into the back of the van. Shortly, they headed back toward the hangar.

"Why don't you pull up to the back door? We can go through there to Harry's office so Bob doesn't have to go out on the hangar floor."

Rick turned the van. "Good idea."

Vicki, Sally, and Harry watched silently as Rick pulled the van away to head down the airport road. As the sound of the tires against the pavement faded, the unnatural silence of the normally bustling Saturday afternoon provided an eerie backdrop to the almost empty parking lot. The few remaining jumpers congregated in a small group by their cars. George sat next to the cold unlit fire pit by himself as he drew on the ground with a stick.

"I better go over to talk to him," Harry said. "He's never been near a fatality before or even had one of his students get hurt."

"Would you like me to come too?" Sally asked.

"No. This is something I better do myself."

He turned and walked toward the solitary man.

Sally touched Vicki on the shoulder. "Would you like to come over to the house for some tea or a beer?"

"Thanks, but I think I just want to go be with Buster right now."

"Okay. But feel free to come over later if you change your mind."

Vicki nodded before turning toward her RV. She got Buster out on his leash and held him while she lay on her lounge chair. As the hours went by, Vicki thought of Carrie and then of her own family's deaths. She cried until her eyes were dry and empty like spent shells. As the sun set in the west, the sky turned a crimson red with the evening rays filling to the opposite horizon. Darkness enveloped Vicki as she continued to hold Buster tight.

Vicki awoke on the lounge chair as the sun came up on a clear blue sky. The winds were light and the birds fluttered from tree to tree. Buster meowed as he kneaded his front claws on Vicki's chest.

Vicki grabbed him gently. "Stop that, it hurts." She placed him on her stomach and he meowed again. "I'm sorry, you must be hungry. I forgot to feed you last night."

Putting Buster under her arm, she carried him into the RV and filled his bowl. She made a cup of tea while he gobbled his food and then petted him as he cleaned his face and paws.

"I guess it's back to you and me again, buddy."

She had dwelled thru the night on the events of the day with the lesson that she had learned many years ago rolling through her mind. She had to live past this moment to keep her life together.

"I guess I better get ready for the day."

Vicki changed clothes, ate some cereal, and then headed to the hangar. As she walked around the corner onto the concrete apron, the world seemed almost normal. Bill, the Sunday Cessna pilot, stood on a ladder pre-flighting the airplane. Inside the hangar, jumpers moved around in their normal morning routines. Some jumpers only jumped one day during a normal weekend and few of the jumpers present today had been there the day before. Those that had been there talked quietly to the groups of the Sunday jumpers.

Judy had come back from the day before and she walked over to Vicki. "Hi Vicki. Would you like to make a jump? We've got a three way that could expand to four."

"Thanks, but I'm not really over what happened yesterday."

"Okay. If you change your mind, let me know. You might find that a jump would really help." She headed toward her group. She stopped and turned to face Vicki. "Or if you'd just like to talk, let me know."

"Thanks."

Judy resumed her path toward her friends. As she departed, Vicki remembered again the lesson that came when her family had died.

I have to keep living.

Vicki yelled across the hangar. "Judy, wait. I'd like to go. Let me go get my gear out of the shop."

Vicki settled deep into her harness for landing as she turned her canopy toward the main landing area. The tranquility of the five minutes of canopy flying with no one around relaxed her and swept aside the thoughts of the day before. Only the sound of the rustling parachute fabric disturbed the air around her. When she flared her canopy, her movement stopped just as her feet touched the ground, presenting a momentary appearance of weightlessness to her body. Vicki spun around to her left, collapsed her canopy, and was gathering her lines as Judy walked up.

"Good One!"

"Yes ma'am," Vicki responded enthusiastically.

Judy waited while Vicki finished gathering

her canopy. The two walked across the concrete apron toward the hangar.

"Want to do another one?" Judy said.

"Yea! That would be great!"

A police car sat parked in front of the hangar with an unfamiliar blue pickup truck parked behind it. A young man leaned against the pickup truck, his face vaguely familiar to Vicki.

"Maybe I better see what's going on before I commit."

"I understand. Let me know."

The printing on the side the police car identified it as from the Lee County Sheriff's Department. A man's voice came loudly from inside the hangar.

"No, I don't want to go into your God-Damned office to talk! I want answers and I want them now! Where is that murdering asshole Bob? I know he's not at the apartment."

Vicki entered the hangar. A huge man with a cowboy hat and a cigar in his hand towered over Harry in the center of the hangar. His face contorted as his neck muscles bulged. His wild eyes looked they were going to strike out like snake's fangs. He moved the cigar in his hand like a dagger toward Harry's face.

Harry kept his face turned upward toward the huge man's face. Harry's eyes, eyes that had handled a hundred life-threatening situations in cockpits around the world, were calm and relaxed. His voice spoke in a normal tone with words constantly cut short by the huge man's screams.

A police officer waited behind the huge man and slowly scanned the hangar. His eyes shifted left and right like a sentry stationed to ensure that no one interfered with the huge man. His thumb rested on his belt as his fingers strummed the handle of his holstered pistol. The jumpers in the hangar stood frozen against the walls. The manifester had the telephone to her ear.

The huge man continued his rant. "You either tell me what I want to know or I'm going to have you and everyone else associated with the pile of shit airport arrested by the sheriff and taken to jail for hindering an investigation."

Vicki dropped her gear onto the floor. The man in the police uniform glanced in her direction and motioned with his hands for her to move to the wall with the rest of the jumpers. Vicki tensed as she rose to the balls of her feet, her arms shaking with a desire to strike out to protect her boss.

A voice thundered from the direction of the hangar doors. "Stand down!"

Vicki turned toward the voice. A short thin man in a police uniform strode purposely across the hangar toward Harry and the huge man. His heels clicked as he moved quickly across the concrete floor. No pistol belt surrounded his waist and the patch affixed to his shoulder showed the Pinal County Sheriff's Department emblem. Two other police officers stood next to police cars just outside the hangar doors.

The thin man positioned himself between the huge man and Harry. "No one's going to jail except you if you don't calm down."

The huge man looked back at the police officer standing behind him. "Do something!"

The police officer straightened himself slightly. "I'm Sheriff Hernandez of Lee County. We are here to investigate the suspicious death of this man's daughter. I plan on interviewing—"

"Shut up! I'm Sheriff Gomez of Pinal County. This is my jurisdiction. Any investigations are my responsibility. If you or anyone else from your county continues to question anyone here, they will be arrested for interfering with a police investigation. That includes you."

Sheriff Hernandez softened his stance. "I didn't mean to step on your toes or your jurisdiction, Sheriff. This is Patrick Murphy. His daughter was killed here yesterday and he just wants some answers."

"The hell you didn't want to step on my

jurisdiction," Sheriff Gomez said. "Otherwise, you would have come to my office in Florence rather than sneaking in the back roads through Globe."

Sheriff Hernandez placed his hand on his belt. His fingers strummed the grip of his pistol.

"Take your hand away from your weapon or I will disarm you and you will go to jail," Sheriff Gomez said.

Sheriff Hernandez dropped his hand to his side.

Patrick Murphy turned to Sheriff Hernandez. "Stop this pussy footing around or you'll never win another election."

"Mr. Murphy," Sheriff Gomez said. "You will direct your comments to me or I will order you out of this county. Now you and your party go stand over by my deputies. I will be with you in a moment."

His unwavering eyes stayed in a firm gaze toward the huge man.

Patrick Murphy looked menacingly at

Sheriff Gomez for a moment. He then flicked his head toward Sheriff Hernandez.

"Come on."

Sheriff Hernandez trailed him out the hangar doors.

After the men got out of earshot, Sheriff Gomez turned to Harry. "Sorry about that. I got here as soon as I could. I figured after that call you got yesterday that they may try to sneak in, so I posted a deputy in an unmarked car down by Oracle Junction to keep an eye out for them. He followed them all the way here and waited in the parking lot for me."

"Thanks," Harry said. "I had manifest call 911 as soon as they came through the doors so I figured you or somebody would be here quick."

"What I'm going to do now is go talk to them outside. I will take them up to where we recovered the body to see the site. I will answer what questions I can now and promise them a copy of my report. Then I will tell them that they are to leave the airport not come back without my permission. If they do show up, call me and I'll arrest them for trespassing."

"Thanks. We'll let you know. Anything you can tell us yet."

"Not officially yet. However, unofficially it looks like it will be deemed an accident. The physical evidence is corroborating the witness statements. We are still waiting on the toxicology reports and the report from the parachute riggers down at Davis-Monthan on the equipment. However, given Robert's history, I don't think the rig is a possible cause of the incident. I should be able to tell you more tomorrow. Now, let me go get rid of these guys."

He turned and marched toward the doors. He stopped after several steps, turned, and came back to Harry. "Do you know where the victim's husband is?"

"Yes. He's in Tucson staying with a friend."

"He's not at his home?"

"No."

"Better tell him to stay away from his place until these guys leave the state. It would probably be best for all if he did not run into this guy. I'll call you when they've left."

"Okay," Harry said. "I'll get word to him."

"Thanks," Sheriff Gomez said. He walked away.

Vicki walked over to Harry. "That was intense."

"Yea," Harry said. "I wasn't really sure what was going to happen there. I understand grief, but that guy is scary."

Footsteps approached them from the side. The third man of the group from New Mexico walked up to them.

Harry stared at the man for a moment. "Can I help you?"

"Sheriff Gomez said I could wait here while they went out to where Carrie died. I'm sorry for all that. My name is Mick Murphy and Carrie is, uh, was my sister. My father is not handling it well. Anyway, I just wanted to apologize for him."

Harry stuck out his hand. "No problem. My name's Harry Sparks. This is Vicki, my mechanic."

Mick shook Harry's hand and then Vicki's. "So you're Vicki. My sister used to write me all the time and mentioned you often. In fact, after she started dating Bob, she wrote me that she had met a mechanic that she liked and they were becoming friends. I thought she had stopped dating Bob and had started dating the mechanic. Then she started writing about her friend Vicki. It wasn't until the night before her wedding that I talked to her and was able to put two and two together. Anyway, I just want to thank you for being her friend."

The tears started to well inside Vicki again. "Thank you."

"Is Bob or Rick around? I'd like to give them my condolences."

Harry spoke. "No. They left yesterday. I don't really know where they are."

"Okay. I met them both at the wedding.

They both seemed like really good people. I know that Carrie loved Bob and he loved her. She spoke of Rick often in her letters as a good friend. When you see them, please give them both my best."

"I will," Harry said.

"Well, I better go wait outside in the truck for them to get back. I doubt if they are going to stay around after getting back with the Sheriff. Thank you."

He turned toward the hangar doors.

Vicki called out. "Mick!" He stopped. "You're right. They did both love each other."

Mick slowly nodded his head then continued his slow walk to the truck. He waited by it until the police cars returned and then followed the Lee County Sheriff's car down the road.

Late Monday morning, Vicki worked unscrewing the inspection panels on the Cessna. The routine of opening the panels made the job systematic and allowed her mind to drift to happier times rather than dwell on the horrors of the weekend. As she unscrewed the last of the panels on underside of the right wing, an unfamiliar engine sound came from the front of the hangar. She looked toward the doors as Sheriff Gomez exited his police cruiser. After he removed something out of the backseat of his car, he marched into the hangar. Harry stepped out of his office. Vicki rested her forearms on the top of the wing with her head beneath it as the two men approached each other. They talked before they turned to face Vicki.

Harry called over. “Vicki, could you come over here a minute?”

Vicki placed her screwdriver and the cup of screws on the floor of the Cessna cabin and walked toward the two men. “What’s up?”

The Sheriff held out an evidence bag. “My Sergeant said that this camera belongs to you. Would you please inspect it to see that it is in the same condition as it was when he removed it as evidence?”

Vicki opened the bag, pulled the camera out, and looked it over. The film counter pointed to zero so she opened the back. The inside lay empty.

"The film was kept because the negatives are part of the physical evidence of the investigation. Six months after the case is closed you can get them back if you want."

Vicki nodded her head. "Okay." She closed the camera back, turned the camera on, and operated the trigger. The camera's shutter clicked several times flawlessly. She turned it off. "It seems fine."

"Good," Sheriff Gomez said. "I hate when we have to take an expensive piece of equipment like that. I am always afraid someone is going to drop it and damage it. That's why I wanted to get it back as soon as I could."

"Is there any more you can tell us about the investigation?" Harry asked.

The Sheriff glanced over at Vicki.

"Anything you can tell me you can say in

front of Vicki. That will just keep me from having to repeat it and probably getting something wrong."

"Okay. Let's go into your office. I could use a cup of coffee. You may want to get Sally so she can hear everything at the same time. You'd probably get it wrong with her so I'd have to tell it to her all over again."

Vicki and the Sheriff headed into the office while Harry went into the manifest to get Sally. They all grabbed coffee or tea before taking seats. The Sheriff pulled out his notebook, flipped it open, and then thumbed the pages as he scanned them.

He finally stopped turning pages. "The reports are getting typed up right now for my signature. The Coroner ruled the death accidental with no further action recommended. Here is the best we can figure out about what happened."

"Mrs. Smith stayed seated on the floor of the airplane until it turned toward the airport. When the pilot called out that they were turning on jump run, she got to her knees. She did an equipment check on herself that the jumpmaster witnessed. When the pilot nodded to her to open the door, she did so. She then turned her body ninety degrees to the right so that she faced the open doorway. When she made this turn, her right foot went behind the rear of the right mount of the pilot's seat. The student jumper sitting in the rear witnessed this. He was watching her feet to make sure that he kept his out of her way. Mrs. Smith then provided several flight corrections to the pilot and then called for him to reduce power on the engine. She launched herself into the air by pushing against the pilot's seat mount with her left foot. When her left leg fully extended, the trapped right foot stuck and her forward motion stopped with her torso outside the airplane. The wind caught her and her head was driven into the side of the airplane."

He looked over at Vicki. "Pictures from your camera caught the launch sequence in six frames."

He continued. "We found paint on her helmet that matches the color of the airplane and there are nicks on the right side of the airplane the approximate distance that her torso would have reached with the foot trapped. She apparently became unconscious by the blow to the head, her foot relaxed, and then it slipped out from behind the seat. She then fell away from the airplane in an uncontrolled manner. The jumpmaster did not realize something was wrong until she had fallen too far for him to do anything."

Harry interrupted. "I had to have a long talk with him Saturday afternoon. He was really broken up about it. He feels it was his fault."

The Sheriff pursed his lips and continued. "Mrs. Smith fell in an uncontrolled manner upside down and most likely unconscious until she impacted the earth. Upon impact, the closing loops of the parachute containers broke so both the main and reserve pilot chutes were released. The body apparently bounced several feet in the air, turned over, and struck the ground again several feet south of the original impact point. It came to rest facedown. The pilot chutes continued in motion until they reached the end of their connecting straps and then fell to the earth. That coincides with how we found the body. Anyway, the case of death was massive trauma consistent with a high-speed impact. Toxicology came back negative and the equipment was cleared from fault by the riggers at Davis-Monthan."

He folded his notebook, placing it back in his shirt pocket. "I'll send you a copy of my report and the Coroners' report later today."

"Have you heard any more from the father," Harry asked.

"No. They spent the night at the motel in town but checked out this morning. I expected them to be at my office this morning raising hell. Have you heard from the husband?"

"No," Harry said. "Not since I called him

about the confrontation here with Carrie's father. I decided to wait to call again until I heard something from you."

The phone in the manifest rang.

"I'll get that," Vicki said. She walked through the door joining the office to the manifest and picked up the receiver.

"Florence Airport."

"Hello," the voice on the other end said. "This is the Pinal County Coroner's office. I'm trying to reach Sheriff Gomez."

"He's here. Just a minute, I'll get him."

Vicki walked back into the office. "Sheriff, it's for you. It's the Coroner's office."

The Sheriff's half of the conversation came through the open doorway. "Sheriff Gomez."... "He did?"... "That is strange."... "Send it over to my office and I'll take care of it."... "Okay, Thanks."... "Goodbye."

The Sheriff walked back into the office but did not sit down. "Carrie's father showed up at the Coroner's office this morning along with a hearse from a mortuary in Gold Hill.

They had an out-of-state-disposition permit signed by a judge in Lee County. Mr. Murphy hounded the Coroner until he released the body to transport for burial in NM. When the father signed for the personal effects, he tore open the envelope, removed the wedding ring, and threw it in the trash. The attendant retrieved it after they left. I will hold on to it until it the husband can pick it up if he wants it. The attendant also heard the father say something to another man about how he needed to get to Tucson. You had better get a hold of Mr. Smith and suggest that he keep a low profile for another day or two. I'll see what I can do about finding out when they have left the state. Mr. Smith can see a lawyer about getting her remains back."

"Wow," Harry said. "Thanks. I'll call them right now."

"Let me know what he says."

The Sheriff marched out of the office toward his patrol car, his heels clicking across the empty hangar.

Chapter 14

Rick muted the already quiet TV and grabbed the ringing phone before the noise had a chance to disturb Bob. Nothing on weekday TV interested him, but it provided a distraction while he waited for Bob to wake up. The two of them had stayed up until almost four in the morning talking about Carrie. This was the first sleep Bob had been able to get since Carrie's death.

Rick spoke softly. "Hello."

"Rick, this is Harry down at the Airport. How's it going up there?"

"It's going as best as could be expected. I finally got Bob to go to bed in the spare room. I think he's sleeping, but I haven't checked."

"Well, when he gets up there's a few things you should tell him or you can have him call the Pinal County Sheriff if you'd rather."

Harry told Rick what would be in the

Sheriff's report on the accident.

"I'll tell him. It's probably better if hears it from me rather than from someone he doesn't know."

"Okay. There's a few of other things you need to tell him. Carrie's father got her body released to him and it's on the way back to Gold Hill."

"What?"

"Yea. My reaction exactly. In addition, when Carrie's father signed for the personal effects, he threw away her wedding ring. The Sheriff has it and Bob can get it from him."

"Okay."

"Also, Carrie's father mentioned at the Coroner's office that they had to get down to Tucson. Sheriff Gomez thought it might be a good idea if Bob stayed away from his apartment for a few days more until he's sure that they have left the state."

"Does he think Bob's in danger?"

"I don't know. But based on how Carrie's father acted down here, I'd just play it safe."

"They don't know where I live. I'll get him to stay here for a while longer. I don't think he's really anxious to go home to an empty apartment anytime soon anyway."

"Okay. Stay in touch."

"Will do."

Rick hung up the phone. He picked up the remote to unmute the TV as Bob's voice drifted down the hall.

"Who was that?"

Bob appeared from the darkness of the hallway. Disheveled hair topped his head. Sleep creases marked his three-day-old blue jeans and t-shirt.

"That was Harry. Let me fix you a cup of coffee then I'll tell you what he said."

Rick went over everything that Harry had told him as Bob sipped his coffee. When Rick told him that Carrie's father had taken her body back to Gold Hill, Bob slammed his coffee on the table and rose from the chair.

"That asshole! He didn't have the right to do that. We ought to just head over there and get it sent back."

"Maybe you better do what Sheriff Gomez suggested and get a lawyer involved. I don't know about you, but Carrie's father scares me. I really don't know what he's capable of."

Bob sat back down in the chair. "You're right. He isn't someone that I want to confront without some sort of help around. I'll call a lawyer to see what can be done."

"Why don't you just plan on staying here for at least a few more days until you get everything sorted out? I've got the whole week off so I can help you with whatever you need."

"Thanks buddy. I don't know how I would get through this without your help."

"No problem, man. Listen, why don't you take a shower and change clothes. Then, we'll get something to eat. You haven't eaten anything since Saturday."

"That sounds good. I am starting to get hungry. I need to stop by the apartment to get some more clothes though."

"Do you think you should go there? Remember what the Sheriff said."

"We'll take your car. That way if we see anyone there, we can just pass on by and go back later."

"That'll work."

Not a word transpired between the two men on the drive. Bob wore one of Rick's baseball caps instead of his normal cowboy hat to disguise his presence in the car.

The apartment sat near one of the complex's entrances. Rick pulled in at the entrance furthest from the apartment so they could drive by and quickly exit if needed. As they drove through the parking lot, they scanned the vehicles for unfamiliar ones. A large blue pickup truck with New Mexico plates was parked close to the apartment. A figure waited in the driver's seat. Rick pointed it out to Bob as he continued driving out onto the street. He headed away at normal speed and turned left at the light. No vehicle followed them through the turn, so Rick pulled into a gas station down the block and stopped.

"Well," Rick said. "What do you think we should do?"

"I don't think that is Mr. Murphy's truck. I think it's her brother Mick's. Let's drive by again to see if it's him. We'll look for anyone else hanging around there. If it's just her brother, we'll stop. Anytime I talked to him on the phone when he called Carrie, he seemed okay."

"All right. Let's check the lot over real good and make sure that there is no one else there."

The two drove through the parking lot twice more from different directions until they were convinced that no one but Mick waited. Rick pulled up in front of the pickup truck, left the motor running, and stood by his door. Bob got out but remained by the passenger door. Mick slowly got out of the cab and headed toward Bob.

"Hi Bob," Mick said. "I'm glad I was finally

able to catch up with you." His eyes glazed over as he grabbed Bob in a bear hug. "I'm so sorry." He burst into tears and sobbed uncontrollably.

Rick reached into the back seat of the car and pulled out his lineman's hammer. He clutched it tight as he scanned the parking lot for danger. Rick circled Mick's truck as he searched for any movement. Rick relaxed his grip on his hammer when no ambush materialized.

"I'll park the car," Rick said.

Bob nodded okay. Mick still held him as he sobbed. Rick returned the hammer to the back seat before he moved the car into a space. By the time he got back to them, the men had separated and were leaning against the hood of Mick's truck. Mick and Rick shook hands then hugged loosely, patting each other on the back.

Mick wiped his eyes, looked to the sky, and waited a moment to calm down. "Sorry about that. I've been with my father for the last two days and he's so full of anger that I couldn't let anything out. I'm really sorry for you about Carrie. I know that you loved her and she loved you. I'm sorry for me too. I'm really going to miss her." He hesitated for a moment. "But that's not why I'm here. I need to warn you about what my father is doing."

"What's that?" Bob said.

"My father came by here this morning with a truck and several of his union guys. He was on the lease so he got the manager to open up the apartment. They took all of the furniture and Carrie's things, loaded them into the truck, and headed back to Gold Hill. I told him I wasn't going to have anything to do with it and was heading back home. But I parked around the corner to warn you if you showed up."

Bob turned to Rick. "That does it. We're going to Gold Hill, get that stuff back, and bring Carrie back here to spread her ashes over the drop zone."

Mick grabbed Bob's arm. "Don't do that.

That's exactly what he wants you to do. He blames you for taking Carrie away from him. He wants you to come to Lee County. The Sheriff will arrest you as soon as you get there and say he found drugs in your car."

"What?" Rick said.

"Listen," Mick continued. "The Sheriff doesn't care about you or the Law. All he cares about is the upcoming election. My father can bring in the whole union vote for him. Besides the Sheriff, several judges and county commissioners owe their jobs to my father. You can't go there. You'll go to jail for a long time. I wouldn't be surprised if my father arranged for you to be killed in prison. I wouldn't put anything past him."

"What do you think I should do?" Bob asked.

"Stay away. As long as you're over here he can't get to you." His voice softened as his eyes became watery again. "Do it for Carrie, Bob. If she were here, she'd tell you that everything from that apartment and even her corpse isn't worth the trouble my father could cause you. Let her go."

Bob stared at Mick and seemed to deflate. "You're right. I can't fight that. I can't fight anything right now. Thanks."

"I've got to start heading back," Mick said. "I just needed to warn you about my father." He hugged Bob again, nodded to Rick, and got into his truck. He pulled away out to the street.

"Let's go check the apartment to see what we have to deal with," Bob said.

The two walked up the stairs and Bob unlocked the apartment door. The door swung open to a hollow sound. A pile of papers sat in the center of the otherwise empty living room. As the two moved further in, the pile of papers turned into ripped up pictures taken out of the frames. However, not all of the pieces of the pictures were there. Every piece of picture on the floor only showed Bob. Bob stooped down and handled several of the pieces. He looked at each one as if reconstructing the whole photo in his mind. He stood, still carrying one of the pieces, and began to move through the apartment. Rick followed as he first glanced left, then right rapidly for any danger left behind to surprise them.

They walked into the kitchen. Every cabinet door stood open, the shelves empty. Only water marks where dishes once dried delivered memories of life. Bob opened the refrigerator and the light displayed a stark white bareness. He hurried into the bedroom with Rick close behind. The bedroom, empty of furniture, echoed their footsteps across the hardwood floors. The contents of Bob's bedside table lay in a loose pile on the floor. The closet door stood open with only Bob's clothes still on the hangars. A pile of Bob's underwear and socks remained where the dresser had been.

They moved into the bathroom. Bob's razor and toothbrush sat alone on the counter. The medicine cabinet hung open, only Bob's items on the shelves. Vacant towel racks and the missing toilet seat cover defined the rest of the room.

Bob finally spoke. "Look at it Rick, they even took the toilet paper."

He sank toward the floor. Rick caught him, moved him back into the living room, and settled him onto the floor with his back against the wall. Rick knelt next to him with his hand on Bob's shoulder. The front door creaked.

A voice sounded from the front door. "Hello?"

Rick moved toward the door, muscles tense, ready to protect his friend. A man in coveralls, with Galaxy Apartments sewn over the pocket, waited in the open doorway. A clipboard hung loosely from his hand.

"Hi. The apartment manager sent me over to check the apartment. He said the renter moved out. I need to inspect it and change the locks."

Rick explained about Carrie's death and

how the father stole everything. "Anyway you can give Bob a little time to get his stuff out?"

"Sure. I'll tell the manager that the apartment is okay, but they're still moving stuff out. I'll come back in a few hours."

"Thanks."

The man nodded and walked away while Rick went back in. Bob, his back still to the wall, had several pieces of the ripped pictures in his hands. Tears flowed down his cheeks. He looked at Rick as he held up one of the torn pictures.

"Remember this one? You snapped it of us that day we all went to Tombstone. Carrie was holding a fake rifle to my head." He dropped the ragged photo and picked up another. "This one was taken by Vicki at the drop zone the day after Carrie asked me to marry her. Now they're gone, all gone."

Rick sat down on the floor next to Bob. Bob continued to go through the torn pictures and commented on each one. His comments stopped as he let the pieces drop from his hands. He sank closer to the floor while he cradled his head in his hands. Soft sobs filtered through his fingers. Finally, he stopped and wiped his eyes with the palms of his hands. "What am I going to do Rick? I've got no place to live, no place to go, nothing left."

"You can move into my place."

"Are you sure?"

"Of course. You can stay there as long as you want."

The tears came again. Bob managed a weak, "Thanks."

"Come on. Let's go find some boxes to pack your stuff in."

Music filled the void as Rick waited in the van at the parking lot of the Sheriff's office in Florence. Patrol cars came and went from the rear parking lot. Rick wondered what caused so much activity for such a sparsely populated county. A patrol car shot from the rear of the building with its lights flashing and siren blaring before it turned south to race away down the street. Rick's gaze left the side mirror as movement at the front of the building entered his peripheral vision. The door swung open and Bob came into the sunlight. He walked toward the van with a large envelope in his hands. As he climbed into the driver's seat, he threw the envelope over to Rick.

"That's the Sheriff's Report with a copy of the Coroner's Report. I haven't looked at them, but the Sheriff talked to me. He pretty much said the same thing that you said Harry told you."

"I really don't want to look at it," Rick said. "Want me to put it in the back?"

"Yup. That'll work."

"How about the ring?"

"It's in my pocket. Funny thing though, it looked fine. I expected it to be bent or something." Bob started the van and then shut it off. "One more thing. The Sheriff said that his sources told him that the Lee County

Sheriff was back in his office on Monday afternoon. They must have headed home right after clearing out the apartment. I guess they're waiting for me to come to them."

"Are we going there?"

"I'm not. I'm going to listen to Mick on this one. I think I just have to deal with what I have here."

"Good. I didn't really want to have to watch your back in jail."

Bob started the engine again. "Let's go home."

He pulled out of the lot and turned south. As they headed down the highway toward Tucson, they came upon the sign that pointed to the airport.

"Want to stop in to say hello?" Rick said.

"Not yet."

The van turned onto the airport road Thursday evening as the last rays of the sun disappeared into the purple sky. Bob parked as close to the cold and empty fire pit as he could.

Rick, sitting in the passenger's seat, turned toward Bob. "You sure you want to do this?"

"I have to. I can't keep seeing this stuff and hold it together."

"You could send it down to one of the Florida drop zones. They could sell it and you'd never see it again out here."

"I can't take that chance. Skydiving is too small of a universe. It would show up in the hands of a visitor and I'd lose it."

"Okay. I'll go over to the Airport office to tell the Harry that we're out here so he won't get worried."

"Just tell him we're going to have a fire and that I need some alone time. I don't want anyone else out here for this."

Rick nodded his head, got out of the van, and headed toward the hangar. The main hangar lights still burned with additional lights showing through the office windows. Rick walked toward the familiar concrete of the airport apron. He could walk the path blindfolded, but tonight he stepped slowly, carefully, almost like a stranger. The desert night loomed all around while the stillness of the normally bustling drop zone added a sense of peculiarity to an already abnormal night. Rick glanced toward Vicki's darkened RV before he returned his attention toward the hangar as the lights in it began to go dark.

The last of the interior lights went out as Rick's feet hit the concrete, only a single flood light stayed lit at the front. Harry, Sally, and Vicki walked out the almost closed hangar doors and turned toward the house.

"Hey, Harry," Rick yelled.

The three of them stopped, turned around toward Rick, and then waited while he walked up. Harry offered Rick his right hand as Rick approached. Rick grabbed it and Harry pulled him into a tight hug, patting him on the back with his left hand.

"How are you doing?" Harry said as the two separated.

"Okay. I just never want to have to go

through this again."

Sally gave Rick a motherly hug. "We've been so worried about you and Bob," she said as she stepped back next to Harry.

Vicki and Rick stared at each other. Rick knew what the situation called for, yet was hesitant to act upon it. Vicki finally approached Rick and the two hugged like cousins at a wedding. Shoulders tight and stomachs apart, the embrace lasting only a moment. Vicki's hand followed Rick's arm down to his hand as they separated. A slight squeeze of his fingers came from her hand before she retreated into her own space. Rick turned his gaze toward Harry.

"I just wanted to let you know that Bob and I are going to have a fire at the pit. Bob wanted to get away from town for the evening to spend a little time alone. I wouldn't let him go out by himself, so I suggested a little fire time. I hope that's okay."

"Sure, no problem. How's he doing?"

Rick stayed silent for a few seconds.

"Better."

"Give him our best."

The two women nodded in agreement.

Sally grasped Harry's hand. "I hope we'll see you Saturday, Rick."

She pulled Harry toward their house while Vicki followed them. Rick turned back toward the fire pit. As he stepped off the concrete and back onto the desert sands, he dreaded the return to the pit. A thought came to him that if he just turned around, went to shoot the breeze with Harry and have a beer, Carrie's death would go away. It just would not have happened so he would not have to deal with it. His friend would not have to deal with it. Everyone would be happy and laugh again. However, Rick walked on with the reality that his friend needed him.

By the time Rick got back to the fire pit, Bob already had a good size blaze going. Flames licked the evening sky while sparks sailed away into the darkness. Bob pulled Carrie's parachute equipment from the back of the van, set it on the ground next to the pit, and began to open it up. Rick reached into the van and grabbed the jumpsuit he had bought for Carrie. He reached back into the van for the helmet before he walked over next to Bob.

Bob fluffed the canopies before he gathered them into his arms. He crept up to the fire's edge. In one heave, he threw the canopies into the flames. The nylon started to melt and dense smoke rose from the pit. A tiny flame shown on the edge of the nylon, then the mass burst into heavy flames. The heat drove the two away from the edge of the pit. As the initial flare-up subsided, Rick approached the pit, threw the jumpsuit into the fire, and then threw the helmet in. The flames grew and the heat drove both of them back again. The helmet sat on the flames for a moment before it erupted into a column of fire like a spirit moving toward heaven.

Bob looked at the flames for a minute. "Goodbye Carrie."

He then reached into his pocket and

brought out Carrie's wedding ring. Removing the wedding ring from his finger, he placed both of them into his right hand. He drew back his arm to toss them into the fire, but stopped in mid-throw. He brought the arm down, opened his hand, and stared at the rings. The fire light reflecting on the gold bands created another spot of light in the darkness. Bob slowly placed his ring back on his finger. He continued to stare at Carrie's ring in the light of the flames. Reaching around his neck, he removed the chain holding his old dog tags. He methodically unsnapped the chain, placed the end through the ring, and snapped it closed. He replaced the chain around his neck to its normal resting place.

Bob turned from the fire and climbed into the passenger seat of the van. The firelight through the windshield revealed tears flowing down his cheeks. Rick turned his gaze and stared down into the fire while tears came from his own eyes. The hurt of his friend left him helpless. He wished he could do more.

Vicki hid in the shadows of the nearby mesquite tree, just beyond the reach of the firelight. As she held Buster close to her chest, she remained still, the fire in the pit tonight providing no welcoming banter. In the darkness, she petted the softly purring Buster while tears flowed from her eyes.

No movement came as the pyre burned the sacrifice to ashes. Each person stayed in their own little part of the world until the fire died embers. Rick turned on the hose to kill the embers and white steam rose into the night sky as the pit hissed and popped. He scooped dirt over the wet ashes to cover any buckles or snaps left from Carrie's gear before he stacked new wood into the pit. The evidence of the night would remain hidden. No inquisitive eye would gaze into the emptiness of that now special pit. The next person there would just start a fire.

The van drove slowly away and the

taillights disappeared as the engine sound faded into the distance. Vicki moved from her spot behind the tree and walked to the side of the still warm pit. She stared down into the black void. A few embers missed by the hosing popped as water found them. She shifted Buster into one arm as she knelt down. Picking up a small handful of the desert sand, she extended her arm over the pit and slowly let the grains trickle away. As the last grains dropped, she hugged Buster tightly and began a slow walk back to her darkened trailer.

Saturday morning, Rick awoke as the sun rose over the mountains. The morning birds sang and the temperature climbed from its dawn low. The sound of Bob's van bit through the desert air as it approached from the road and pulled next to Rick's tent.

Bob called from outside the tent. "Wake up sleepy head. We've got a skydive to make."

"Okay. Just a minute."

Rick zipped open his tent and stuck his

head out. Bob sat on the lounge chair as he sipped on a large cup of coffee. Another large cup with a lid sat on the ground next to the tent.

"Black. Just like you like it." Bob continued to sip his coffee while Rick slowly extracted himself from the tent.

"Hard night?" Bob asked.

"Yea. There was me, Kevin, and two twelve packs."

Bob smiled. "Can't leave you alone for a second, can I? Are you going to be okay to jump?"

Rick hesitated for a second. He should ask Bob that question rather than the other way around.

"Yea. As long as it's not too hard of a jump."

"It's going to be easy. One formation. You and me. My treat."

"Okay, let me go brush my teeth and get some clean clothes on. I'll meet you in the hangar in fifteen minutes."

"Okay. I'll go manifest an airplane."

Rick moved slowly as he got ready. His head did not hurt, but his balance did seem a little off. When he walked into the hangar a half hour later, Bob sat on the packing ledge in his jumpsuit, his gear piled next to him. Rick dropped his gear, grabbed his jumpsuit, and looked over at Bob while he slipped himself into it.

Jumping down from the ledge, Bob started an equipment check. He methodically ran his hands along each side before opening each flap as Rick had seen him do before every jump. Rick was doing his own equipment check when Harry walked up with a load sheet in his hand.

He knelt down next to Rick and quietly spoke. "Bob manifested you and him on the first load. He paid for the whole airplane. He said he wanted the two of you to have a private jump. Does he seem alright to you?"

"He seems okay. His equipment checks look normal. He still hasn't told me what we're doing though."

"I'm flying the load. I want you next to the door. If anything seems wrong to either of us, you protect the latch and I'll bring us down fast."

"Okay. But right now he seems fine."

Rick stood up, pulled his harness over his shoulders, and stepped into his leg straps. He walked over to Bob.

"What's the dive?"

"It's a secret. I'll tell you in the airplane on the way up." Bob turned toward the open hangar doors and headed to the airplane behind Harry. Rick tightened his leg straps and then grabbed his helmet.

As the plane climbed through nine thousand feet, Bob moved forward on his knees until he came up behind Rick. Rick had knelt next to the door during the entire climb with his hand tight on the latch. Bob tapped Rick on the shoulder as stuck his clenched fist in front of Rick's face. The end of the Teal scarf that Bob had given to Carrie stuck out of the top of his fist.

Bob put his mouth next to Rick's ear and shouted over the engine noise. "You and I are saying goodbye to Carrie. We'll exit with a normal count. You fly to me and take my arms. Then take your hand and grab the end of the scarf that will be sticking out of my fist. I'll loosen my grip so you can pull out the scarf until most of it is flapping in the wind. When we get to seven thousand feet, I'll give a headshake. You release your end of the scarf. I'll wait a few seconds before I let go. Then turn, track, and pull high. We'll ride the morning breezes and face the rising sun. Got it?"

Rick nodded yes. He glanced over to Harry, smiled, and relaxed his death grip on the door latch.

Harry turned the airplane to the left. "Jump Run."

Rick looked back at Bob and then turned the door latch. The door swung up on its hinges as the familiar cold wind filled the cabin. Rick looked out and down at the ground. Harry had placed them on a perfect jump run. Rick waited about 30 seconds before he called out. “Cut.” He turned toward Bob. “Let’s Skydive.” Rick climbed out the door onto the step with Bob close behind.

The exit went flawlessly. Soon Rick and Bob faced each other in free-fall with Rick holding Bob’s arms. Rick slowly moved his hand over Bob’s hand. He drew the loose end of the scarf out until the scarf blew into an inverted U shape as it was extended to its full length and flapping violently in the wind. The two friends looked at each other and then at the scarf as they dropped through the air toward the ground. At seven thousand feet, Bob nodded his head and Rick released the scarf. Bob waited a few seconds before he opened his fist. As the scarf shot up out of sight in a flash, Bob turned to track.

A twinge of nervousness came over Rick as he did his own turn and moved into the track position. His fears ended as he looked back between his legs at Bob's canopy opening. He quickly pulled and his canopy opened a couple of hundred feet below Bob's. Rick turned to face the rising sun and the heat of it touched his face.

"Goodbye Carrie," Rick said to the wind. "Loved you."

The two friends landed within seconds of each other and walked together to the hangar. The Saturday contingent of jumpers had arrived filling the cavernous hangar with the normal amount of noise and laughter. As Rick and Bob entered the hangar, the noise level dropped. People turned to watch Bob as he laid his gear on the floor. While the two packed side by side, the noise in the hangar rose but not to the previous level as jumpers spoke close to each other. Rick noticed the change and looked over at Bob to see if he had noticed anything, but Bob just continued to pack his gear. Bob closed his container and then looped his pull-up cord on his belt.

He hefted the parachute container onto his shoulder. “I’m going to walk around for a while. I don’t think I’ll do any more jumps today.”

“Are you going to hang around for dinner?”

“I don’t know. I just need to walk.”

“Want some company?”

“No, I need to walk alone for a while. You’ve got skydives to do. I’ll see you at the campsite later.”

“Okay, I’ll be here.”

Bob gathered the rest of his gear before he walked alone out the hangar doors.

As the sun went down, Rick headed over to their campsite with his container over his shoulder. He had his jumpsuit, helmet, and goggles in his arms. Bob lay stretched out on one of the lounge chairs, a beer in his hand.

“Good jumps?”

“Great. I did two more fun jumps before helping Kevin suit up his first jump students.

He said that the Conference Director is coming out from California next weekend, so I can take the test to finish my jumpmaster rating. I'm going to talk to him about it at the restaurant tonight. Are you ready to head over there?"

"You go ahead. I don't feel like eating there tonight. Maybe I'll head over in a little to get something to go."

"Are you sure?"

"Yup. I need a break. I think everyone else does too."

Rick realized that his friend had seen the stares along with the whispering. "Why don't we both get something to go and just have a fire here?

"No, you head on in. I'll come over to the fire pit later when everyone gets back."

"You sure?"

"Yup. I need to do this my way."

"Okay," Rick said. "I'm going catch a ride with Kevin. See you later."

Bob nodded at Rick and went back to his

beer.

When Rick and Kevin got back to the airport, they walked up to the fire pit as the flames began to rise high into the sky. The coolers overflowed with the beer from all the jumpers that owed for one reason or another. Within a half hour all of the jumpers were back from the restaurant and the party roared in full swing.

From the edge of the shadows cast by the flickering flames, Bob approached the group. He stopped by the coolers, grabbed a beer, opened it, and surveyed the crowd. He swallowed a long swig as he moved toward the fire. Jumpers in the crowd noticed him. They motioned to others of his approach. The normal dim of the party slackened as more jumpers turned to stare.

Bob reached the chair that Kevin used as a dais. He stopped for a moment, looked around, lifted his beer to his lips, and drained it. He threw the empty can into the fire as he mounted the chair. The jumpers went silent and the crackling fire provided the only sound. The firelight and the alternating white and green flashes of the beacon lit Bob's face.

Bob spoke in a firm voice. "This morning, I heard people whispering that it was too soon for me to be back here jumping. Well, I want to ask you, where the hell else would I be? I've always heard that in times of tragedy, you should look to your family for comfort. Over the last two years, you people have become my family." He looked over at Rick. "Some of you have become the brothers and sisters that I never had. I couldn't think of any other place to be or any other people to be with right now."

"So please everyone, let's not be silent and avoid the subject. Let's not pretend that Carrie's not dead. She is. I've lost something very dear to me. A lot of you have lost that same thing. So tonight, please celebrate Carrie's life with me and her life here. I want to laugh, I want to cry, and I want to hear everything that anyone has to say about who she was to them."

Bob then fell silent while the fire continued to crackle. The crowd of jumpers remained still. Not a beer moved. Rick pulled himself off the ground, walked over to the coolers, and grabbed two beers. He moved over to where Bob remained standing on the chair, opened both beers, and handed one to Bob. As tears came down his face, he raised his free hand to Bob's shoulder.

"I loved her too, man. She was the sister I never had."

Judy moved from the edge of the crowd and stopped in front of Bob. She spoke in a voice barely audible above the sound of the fire.

"She was always nice to me."

Over the next few seconds, a floodgate appeared to have opened as people crowded around Bob and shouted words about Carrie, tears on many faces. They all extended their arms to touch Bob. The scene turned into a huge group hug as everyone in the crowd placed their arms around each other and closed their eyes. All fell silent once more.

From the edge of the darkness, a figure slowly moved into the firelight. Vicki hesitantly approached the silent crowd of jumpers and placed her own arms out into the group. One hand touched Bob as the other touched Rick. She closed her eyes. After a minute, she silently moved away from the firelight and faded back into the darkness.

Chapter 15

As the sun slipped below the horizon, Vicki moved the lower cowl of the Cessna into position below the engine. The warmth of the spring sun faded and a chill swept into the hangar. Buster lay upside down on the dash of the cockpit, his eyes tiny slits, but open enough to take in all that happened around him. A familiar engine sound hit Vicki's ears and brought a smile to her face.

A minute later, a voice came from the hangar door opening. "Would you like some help?"

Buster's head perked up. Vicki turned to face the voice. "I'd love some."

Rick grabbed the left side of the cowl while Vicki lifted the right side. Together they slipped it into position. The side holes lined up and snapped into place. Vicki screwed in the top camloc on her side and then handed the screwdriver to Rick. He seated the top one on his side.

He handed the screwdriver back. "There you go."

Vicki methodically seated and engaged the rest of the camlocs. Rick handed her the bolts and wrenches as she lay on her back to hook up the cowl-flap rods. Together they placed the top cowl into position. Vicki secured the camlocs on it.

"What were you doing to this?"

"Just cleaning the plugs and checking the torque on the cylinder nuts. Monthly stuff."

Rick reached his hand into the cabin to tickle Buster's head. From his shirt pocket, he produced a coffee creamer. Buster jumped to the floor and meowed around Rick's legs. Rick popped the top as he placed the creamer on the floor. Buster attacked it with his fast pink tongue.

"You know you've spoiled him with those things. He won't even drink my cereal milk anymore."

"He seems to like the French Vanilla the best. Maybe I should buy a box so you could give him some during the week."

"Let's not. They're fattening and he's big enough already. I can barely breathe when he gets on my chest at night. Want to help me push this out?"

"Sure," Rick said as he grabbed the strut.

Vicki hooked the tow bar up and maneuvered the front wheel as Rick pushed and pulled to get the Cessna out of the hangar. They slowly rolled it across the apron to the line of airplane tie downs. Rick ran the chain through the strut attachment on his side while Vicki got the tail and the other wing. She unhooked the tow bar and hoisted it over her shoulder. They slowly walked toward the hangar.

"Are you working this weekend?" she asked.

"Yea. I'm hangar jumpmaster both days. Kevin's doing the first jump course and Mike's out of town. Judy didn't want to work since she'll be doing her 1000th jump tomorrow."

"You've been working a lot over the winter."

"Yea, tell me about it. Since George never came back, things have been tight. I hope that someone else will get their Jumpmaster rating soon so I can get back to doing some fun jumps. I don't think I've done more than 50 fun jumps in the past nine months. How about you? Are you working this weekend?"

"Yeah. I'm videoing Nancy and Frank tomorrow and doing Judy's 1000th at sunset. Nothing is on the schedule for Sunday yet, but I'm sure it will fill up. I'm trying to leave Sunday open for students. As far as fun jumps, I haven't done one since you, Bob, Kevin, and I did that one on New Year's Day. Between videoing skydives and working on the airplanes, I barely have time to do my laundry. The DCs are leaving Monday for Montana so I might be able to swing a day off soon."

"What would you do with a day off?"

"I don't know. I might drive up into the mountains to take some pictures of the spring flowers."

"How about a motorcycle ride to the lakes?"

Vicki stopped walking. "What do you mean?"

"It's warming up nice during the days so I have been thinking of taking a ride up past the lakes and back through the mountains. If you'd like to come along, we could pick up some chicken in Florence to have a picnic by one of the lakes."

Vicki's hand twisted her left pigtail. "I don't know. I'm not really interested in having a date, more like just wanting some time away."

"It wouldn't be like a date, just two friends going for a ride."

Her hand stayed on the pigtail. "I don't know…"

"Come on. It'll be nice. You could bring

your camera and I'll show you some great places to get shots of the hills."

"Well, as long as it's not like a date, okay. But I get to buy the chicken and we have to be back before dark."

"Deal. We'll be back way before dark. I want to get home before the sun goes down and it gets chilly. Any day better for you?"

"I'll have to check with Harry, but Tuesday will probably be good."

"Okay. I'll be here about ten."

The two resumed their walk to the hangar. Nancy and Bob came around the side of the building and headed toward them.

"What's happening with those two?" Vicki asked.

"I'm not really sure. They hang around at the drop zone and talk on the phone a lot, but Bob has never gone up to Phoenix to see her or anything. He did take his wedding ring off New Year's Day after sitting at the fire talking to her the whole night. He wears it now with Carrie's ring on his old dog tag chain."

"That sounds serious."

"I don't know. Bob comes back to the van every night alone. They just seem to talk a lot together."

"What about?

Rick shrugged. "Skydiving whenever I'm around. Nancy keeps talking about that competition next month in California. You've been videoing them a lot. Do you think they'll win?"

"I don't know. The skydives I've videoed look real good to me, but I don't know what any of the other teams are doing. Nancy made me promise not to show the videos to anyone. They want to keep their routine a secret. Only thing I can tell you is that they fall real fast."

Bob and Nancy approached.

"Hi, Vicki," Nancy said. "Are we still on for tomorrow?"

"Yea. I've blocked you out for three jumps. I've got us manifested on a Cessna at eight. I have to do Judy's 1000th at sunset, but everything else is open for now. We can do more on Sunday if nothing else gets in the way. However, I promised to make myself available on Sunday for any students that want video."

"That'll work. We only have four more training weekends before the competition. I hope we can get thirty more training jumps in with maybe 10 of them videoed."

"Hey Rick," Bob said. "I volunteered to drive Nancy and Frank out to California in the van for the meet. You want to tag along?"

"Maybe. I never thought about jumping anywhere else. It could be fun."

"How about you, Vicki?" Nancy said. "Would you like to come out to the competition? You could probably get a video slot at it and make some money."

"No thanks. I'll just stay here."

The group reached the hangar and Vicki left them as she carried the tow bar into the tool room. The manifest PA came to life and Sally's voice sounded across the hangar.

"Rick, could you come see me a moment?"

Rick headed over toward the manifest. Vicki walked out of the tool room and locked the doors behind her. Nancy touched Bob's sleeve as they quietly talked.

"Where's Frank?" Vicki said as she got close to them.

"I left him setting up the tents. He should be over in a minute."

"I just got put on your eight o'clock load," Rick said as he walked up. "A student wants to make two free-fall jumps tomorrow but has to leave by noon. He'll get out at 6500 so he'll be down and clear before you jump. I'll just stay in the airplane and ride it down"

"Would you like to follow us out and watch our routine?" Nancy said.

"Sure. That sounds fun. I even promise not to tell anyone what I see."

"You can pull when we break off and that will keep you out of the way."

"Just remember what I told you," Vicki added as she picked Buster up. "They go real fast."

Rick stoked the small fire at the campsite until the flames renewed their slow dance. The sound of footsteps broke the stillness of the night. Rick picked up the flashlight from the ground and shined it toward the noise. Rick switched it off when Bob appeared out of the darkness.

"I was wondering when you were going to show up."

"Nancy and Frank kept talking about their routine. I didn't understand much of what they were saying, but I guess they did. At the end of the conversation they seemed to agree on something." Bob reached into the cooler and pulled out a beer. "You want one?"

"I'm good."

Bob plopped down in his camp chair and stared into the fire. The night grew still again, broken only by the occasional pop of the burning mesquite wood. A bat flew first past Rick's face then around the firelight before it moved on to better feeding grounds.

"Rick?" Bob said. His eyes never left the dancing flames. "How long should I wait?"

"Wait for what?"

Bob turned toward Rick. "You know, wait until I start seeing someone. Is there a rule about what's proper?"

"I'm the last person you should ask about what any rule is or what's proper. I guess you're talking about dating Nancy."

"Yup. I like being around her a lot and I would like to take it past just being a drop zone buddy. But, then I feel like I'd be disrespecting Carrie. I mean, I don't want to have to not talk about her or pretend she never existed."

"Do you have any idea how Nancy feels?"

"I don't know. It seems like she would like to carry it to the next level, but I think she's waiting for me to make the first move."

Rick swigged his beer. "Well, since you asked, I'll give you my opinion. I think Carrie would want you to move on. You're never going to forget her just like I'm never going to forget her. Nancy knows what the two of had. I don't think she would expect you to pretend Carrie wasn't what she was to you. I'd go for it. If it doesn't work, you can go back to being drop zone buddies again."

"Do you think she would go for it?"

"I think that if you don't try and she starts seeing someone else, you'll be whining next to this fire for months. I don't want to have to listen to that. So go for it."

"Thanks."

Bob raised his bottle and clinked Rick's. The eyes of both men fell back toward the flames of the fire. The full moon rose above the mountains casting a shadowy glow across the desert floor.

Rick reached into the cooler for another beer. "I finally decided to take a chance myself. I asked Vicki to go for a motorcycle ride with me."

"It's about time."

"What do you mean?"

"You've been in love with her forever. I

never have understood why the two of you didn't do anything before. Carrie saw it first and pointed it out to me."

"What are you talking about?"

"Remember when you ran from Gold Hill in the middle of the night to get away from Joan?"

"I didn't run."

"Yes, you did. When Carrie told you that Joan was pissed at you for leaving before brunch, you told us that you decided that a lunchtime skydive with Vicki was better than any brunch that Joan had in mind. You showed your cards then and there."

"Well, Vicki has never seemed to want to do anything with me except skydive. Even when I asked her to go for a ride on the motorcycle, she didn't want to call it a date."

"Maybe the word date brings back a bad memory for her, I don't know. She may not seem to want to do anything with you, but she is going for a ride with you. In addition, she's not doing anything with anyone else. She may have just been waiting for you to say something."

"Maybe you're right."

"I know I'm right. But it'll never work out for you and her."

Rick's heart deflated. "What do you mean?"

"I've seen you drive that motorcycle. As soon as you have gone a hundred yards on it, Vicki will want off and she'll never speak to you again."

Rick grabbed the beer from Bob's hand. "I'm cutting you off. No more beer for you. You're a mean drunk."

The frigid morning air at 11,000 feet blew into the cockpit when Nancy cracked open the door on jump run. She looked out the bottom of the door, pulled it closed, and signaled to Harry with her hand for a five-degree right turn. Nancy held the door closed for another ten seconds before she cracked it open again and gazed down at the ground.

She turned her head to the others and called out, "Ready?"

Rick and Vicki nodded yes. Vicki flipped the tiny switch rubber-banded to her fingers and the red record light lit on her eyesight. After Nancy let the door fly up, Frank quickly backed his way onto the step while he held onto the strut. Nancy grabbed Frank's harness and pulled herself up until her chin rested on his chest strap. She shifted her hands, one at a time, to the bottom of Frank's container, and pulled herself tight against him. To the untrained eye, the two jumpers now looked like one. Vicki positioned herself in the door with her feet braced hard against the pilot's seat supports. Rick remained in the back of the Cessna cabin out of the way.

Vicki's focus transfixed on the two jumpers bound together on the strut as she waited for the slight but unmistakable exit count. Nancy performed the count, but with her head buried in Frank's chest, only her elbow betrayed the cadence. Nancy's elbow moved in and then out. As it started in again and Frank released his grip on the strut, Vicki pushed herself forward into an immediate head down dive. She extended her legs straight into the wind while she positioned her arms pointed slightly behind her. Experience had taught her that this position would keep her head pointed to the ground and push her body toward Nancy and Frank. A second lost at exit meant twenty feet to recover. At the speeds they were going, twenty feet would ruin the video.

Vicki fixed her sight on the two as she let her instinctive flying skills guide her legs and arms. She concentrated on keeping the sight in a fixed position toward them. The enjoyment of the performance waited for the video room. Vicki's framing sight centered on Nancy. Nancy stayed in the center of the shot throughout the dive while she performed ballet moves that went beyond Vicki's understanding. Frank worked around Nancy moving in ways that Vicki likened to something out of a Fred Astaire movie.

Occasionally they linked hands and spun around a common center. Vicki's eye locked into position through the sight. She willed her body to respond to the scene before her. The framing remained solid.

Movement beyond the performers caught Vicki's eye. Her near vision remained locked on target while she processed the extra movement in the shot. As it flashed again across the sight, she realized it was Rick. His body zoomed around the trio in a full track position with his face turned toward the group. He did not close the gap between them as he made pass after pass through the sight.

Frank waved his arms aggressively and turned to track away. Nancy flipped face to earth and instantly rose above Vicki. She assumed a track position also. Vicki flipped into a face to earth body position and reverse arched to slow her descent. She held this shape until instability wavered her. After she looked over her shoulder at Rick's canopy high above her, she gave a quick pull on her soft ripcord and her canopy blossomed.

Freedom and solitude surrounded her. The whirl of the camera vibrated through her helmet before she flipped the switch to shut it off. The rustle of the fabric above her became the only sound. The morning air was clear and crisp. Vicki turned her canopy toward the sun and warmed her face.

Rick turned his canopy on a short final above the experienced landing area. He pulled his steering lines smoothly so his feet touched the ground just as the canopy stopped flying and the orange and brown parachute fell behind him. Vicki touched down close to his landing spot and gathered her canopy into her arms.

Rick pulled his helmet off. "When you said they go fast, you weren't kidding. I couldn't stay down with you. I was able to dive and catch up, but as soon as I tried to fly alongside I went high."

"It's a trip going that fast. We only get about 35 seconds of free-fall time from altitude instead of the normal 60."

"Where did you learn to fly on your head like that? I've never seen flying like that except in a dive."

"Nancy showed me how to do it. She learned it during one of the training camps in California. Some of the teams do routines in a head down position. Flying head down is only way I can stay with them to catch the shot. The first couple of jumps I was orbiting them like you just did."

"So you saw that. Any chance I can get you to cut out that part?"

Vicki giggled as she undid the straps on her helmet. "Don't worry. Nobody will see these until after the competition. You've got a month to redeem yourself."

Nancy and Frank walked up with their canopies in their arms.

"So what did you think, Rick?" Nancy asked.

"What little I could see was neat. I spent most of my time trying to get down closer."

"I'll be glad to show you how to fly head down when the competition is over," Frank said. "Or Vicki may be able to show you."

Vicki finished pulling off her helmet. "I'll show you if we ever have a jump together that doesn't involve work."

Rick fed his pull up cord through the grommet of the outer flap and closed the container. His hands pushed the pin into the closing loop locking the flaps tight then seated the soft ripcord handle in the elastic keeper. Holding the rig up, he twisted it left and right to check that all the flaps mated correctly.

Sally and an unfamiliar woman approached him. "Rick, this is Beth."

Rick stood and shook the woman's outstretched hand.

"She just moved to Phoenix from Virginia and is going to start jumping here. She only has 30 jumps and would like to get some intermediate instruction. If you can do it, I can get the two of you on a Cessna going up in about 45 minutes. Nancy, Frank, and Vicki are on it already."

"Sounds good to me," Rick said. "I've got Judy's 1000th for sunset so I can only do one more instruction jump today."

"That sounds fine," Beth said. "Will you be available to do more tomorrow?"

"We'd have to do them early. There's a large first jump course that I will have to help jumpmaster in the afternoon."

"I can put you on a Cessna at eight in the morning," Sally said. "Nancy and Frank are on it going up on a training jump." Sally turned to Beth. "There's room for one more if you'd be interested in hiring a video person."

"I'd like that. I've never had any video done on me."

"Okay. I'll set it up."

Sally headed back to manifest leaving Rick and Beth alone.

Rick hoisted his rig onto his shoulder. "Do you have your own gear?"

"Yes. I bought it before I moved, but I only

jumped it a couple of times. The weather in Virginia is not good for jumping in the winter. That's the main reason I moved to Arizona. I wanted to skydive more than the weather would let me."

"Okay. Let's go look at your rig and then dirt dive something that will show me where your flying skills are at."

"Please keep it real simple. I've only jumped with other people five times. Like I said, Virginia in the winter is not the best place to jump."

"Your body position was good but you were tensed up," Rick said. "That's understandable for the first jump at a new place. You also need to think about your lower legs more. They were straight up and that's what caused you to back slide. You need to press them down against the wind. Why don't you lie face down on the floor and assume your arch."

Beth laid on the floor in her jumpsuit and

raised her torso into an arch.

"Now press your feet against my hands. Do you feel that back pressure?"

"Yes."

"That's what you should feel in the air. Think about that and we'll work on it more in the morning. The video Vicki will shoot tomorrow will show you a lot."

"Is Vicki that same lady that videoed those two on our load?"

"Yea. And she's real good."

Chapter 16

The Beech and one Cessna sat fueled and ready for the climb to altitude as the 15 jumpers assembled with their gear. The pilots talked to each other off to the side as they moved their hands in pilot speak of the flight to come. Vicki was standing next to the group of jumpers with her camera helmet cradled in her arm as Kevin called out names and pressed jumpers into lineup positions. Kevin placed Rick as first out from the Cessna.

"Where do you want to exit Vicki?" Kevin said.

"Rear-rear Float of the Beech."

"You got it. Okay everyone listen up. What we're doing here is a three-formation 14-way in celebration of Judy's 1000th jump. Judy is last out of the Beech. She gets swooping honors so you Cessna people leave when the Beech goes. Vicki is videoing this for Judy, so don't mug the camera and get in her way. Keep the formations smooth with the transitions flat. Break off altitude is 4,000 feet. Everybody track away except Judy. Vicki will drop down in front of Judy to film her opening. After Judy opens and is extracted, Vicki will open in place. Everyone should be well away by then, so she'll have clear air. Carry your openings down to a normal 2,500 feet. Does anybody have any questions?"

Other than a comment about Judy's taste in beer brands, none came.

"Okay," Kevin continued. "Get your pin checks done and let's board. Stay safe and have fun!"

The jumpers broke into their respective groups as they headed toward the airplanes. Vicki waited to get on the Beech last. She handed her camera helmet to Kevin in the airplane and then climbed in.

Harry stuck his face out the pilot's window of the Beech. "Clear," he yelled before he cranked the right engine. The engine quickly fired up and Harry repeated the process on the left engine. The Twin Beech lumbered down the taxiway as the Cessna followed on the left side. Rick sat in the doorway of the Cessna holding the up-swinging door open as they taxied along. The Beech door was still open as Vicki settled down in the rear of the cabin.

"Kevin," Vicki yelled over the noise of the pulsating engines. "See if it would be ok for us to leave the door open for takeoff so I can video the Cessna."

Kevin turned toward the rearward facing jumpers. "Anybody got a problem with the door staying off for takeoff?" When no one voiced any concern, Kevin yelled to the front. "Check with Harry if we can leave the door open for takeoff."

The forward most jumper tapped Harry on the arm to get his attention. Harry pulled the headset away from his right ear and the jumper spoke into his ear. Harry signaled an "OK" sign with his fingers then replaced the headset.

Vicki handed her camera helmet to Kevin before she shifted herself around so that she sat next to the open doorway. After she secured her seatbelt, Vicki retrieved the camera helmet from Kevin then aimed it out the door toward the Cessna.

She had just gotten the sight set when Harry called from the front, "Everybody ready?"

The jumpers whooped approval as Vicki toggled the record switch.

"Here we go," Harry yelled as he advanced the throttles. The engines roared to a thunderous pitch.

Vicki kept the camera aimed toward the Cessna as the two aircraft rolled faster and faster down the runway. The Cessna lifted off the ground before the Twin Beech, but Dan held it just off the runway while Harry built up the speed he needed for takeoff. The Beech reached takeoff speed and the wheels left the pavement. The rumble of the vibrations died off as the spinning wheels slowed. The Cessna stayed in position as the airplanes climbed next to each other. Vicki filmed the swaying airplane 30 feet away for a minute before switching off the camera. As Kevin maneuvered the door into position, Vicki unbuckled her seatbelt and turned around so that she faced forward. She leaned her rig against the rear bulkhead to settle back for the 30-minute climb to altitude. Her relaxed eyes kept a silent vigil.

As the airplane climbed through 10,000 feet, Vicki handed her helmet to Kevin again then pushed herself to her knees. She reclaimed the helmet from Kevin, strapped it tightly to her head by pulling the dual chinstraps as tight as she could, and then wiggled her head side to side to seat it. Vicki pulled both chinstraps tight again before stowing the loose ends in their keepers. She positioned herself to the right rear of the cabin so that she would be out of the way when Kevin opened the door.

Shortly the call of "Jump run" came back from the front of the airplane. Kevin removed the door, stowing it quickly in the rear. The cool evening air swirled through the opening and bits of dust spun from the cabin floor and out the door when Kevin stuck his head into the slipstream to look for the exit point. Vicki flipped her hand switch to start the camera as she moved herself forward so the camera sight pointed at the Cessna as it flew swaying alongside the Beech. "Cut" and then "Climb Out" came from Kevin as he reached outside the door for the forward handhold to begin pulling himself out.

Vicki reached up, grabbed the rear handhold, and slipped herself out into the rear-rear float position. Her neck muscles automatically tensed as the windblast attacked the camera. She settled into position with her left foot on the step and her right foot hanging free over the abyss. The rest of the jumpers in the other floater positions followed quickly.

When Vicki saw the rock of the count

begin, she dropped her left foot from the step and let herself hang by her right arm so her body would be clear of the exit. Vicki wanted to time her release with Judy's exit through the door to catch the honoree's dive.

The jumpers exploded out the door when the Center Float yelled "Go" and Vicki struggled to keep track of the jumpsuit colors. Tom, dressed in his red jumpsuit, held the position in the lineup in front of Judy. Vicki let go as soon as he appeared in the doorway. This provided the best chance of Judy being in her sight as she exited, but Judy was a split second slower than Vicki had anticipated. Vicki was about 6 feet away from the airplane when Judy appeared through the door. The shot was not what Vicki had planned, but she centered the sight on Judy with both airplanes in the background. Vicki waited until Judy passed below her before she turned and followed her toward the other jumpers diving toward the building formation.

As the two approached the almost

completed formation, Vicki moved above Judy's flight path and positioned herself slightly above and up sun from the group. Judy grabbed the legs of two jumpers and then shook them. Her signal passed through the group by the shakes of other jumpers. After the jumpers released their grips, they rearranged themselves into the next formation. When this maneuver completed, the shaking repeated and the third formation built. Vicki dropped down even with the jumpers as the third formation completed to catch the faces of the happy and laugher-filled jumpers in her sight.

At 4,000 feet, the jumpers released their grips and turned outward to move away for opening. Vicki flew forward and positioned herself four feet in front of Judy where she signaled her with a thumbs up. Judy, after she glanced over her right shoulder, pulled her deployment handle and the pilot chute left her back in a flash with the main canopy following. The blossoming canopy extracted the smiling Judy quickly up out of Vicki's camera sight.

Vicki reached for her own deployment handle as a tug came on her left foot. Her body was spun around and her hands grabbed in vise-like grips. Rick pulled her close and pressed his lips to hers. She violently shook off his grips, balled her hands into fists, and slid backwards away from him. Vicki, her face taut and hard, kept her eyes focused on Rick as she reached for her deployment handle. She released her pilot chute without clearing the air above her. She kept her fists balled in front of her as her main canopy extracted her upward and Rick fell away.

Vicki shook uncontrollably as the Demons of Casper raced through her mind. She came back into the present as she looked beneath her to where Rick's canopy had opened.

She shouted at the top of her lungs. "That jerk!"

Grabbing her steering toggles from their

keepers, she brought the left one to her waist. The canopy dove into a fast spiral.

The pressure on her arm grew as the canopy spun faster and faster. When her arm grew so weary that she could no longer hold that toggle down, she let her left hand go up to the keeper as she brought the right toggle down to her waist hard and fast. The spin reversed and the fast descent kept going. All the time, she kept her eyes on Rick and his progress toward the landing area.

As Rick set up for his landing, Vicki stopped her downward spin and maneuvered her canopy into position behind his. Rick touched down lightly as he flared his canopy with a practiced timing, spun around on his feet, and pulled on his right toggle to spin the canopy into the ground. Vicki transferred both of her steering toggles into her right hand and let her left hand drop to her side. She pulled on the toggles with her right hand to set up her landing path just to the left of Rick, out of the way of his collapsed canopy.

As Rick removed his helmet, he looked up as the rustle of parachute fabric approached to his left. When Vicki came even with him, she flared her canopy with her right hand. Her feet touched ground as she swung her left fist in a roundhouse punch that caught Rick squarely on the jaw. The blow sent him hurtling to the ground onto his back.

"You jerk!" Vicki screamed at him. "Don't you ever get in the way of my deployment again."

Vicki collapsed her canopy and quickly gathered it into her arms. She turned back to Rick, who slowly was working to regain his feet, and sent a kick into his chest which knocked him back to the ground. She moved over his stunned body as he laid face up on the desert sand and knelt down to grab the collar of his jumpsuit. She lifted his upper body slightly from the ground as she looked him square in the eyes.

"What the hell did you think you were doing?" she screamed.

Rick looked up at Vicki's face. His eyes were wide and his mouth was tightly drawn.

He whispered his answer. "I was just trying to have a little fun."

"Fun? You wanted to have some fun?" Spittle hit Rick's face. "I'm not here for you to have fun with my body. If you ever touch me again Eddie, I'll kill you."

Vicki's eyes stayed focused on Rick's face as a total sense of fear emanated from his eyes. She roughly pushed him back down to the ground and stood above him.

"You Jerk!"

She stormed away. As she purposely moved across the concrete, she released the straps to her helmet and pulled it from her head. The camera motor whirled. She flipped the switch to shut it off.

Vicki headed toward the hangar but changed her mind halfway there and angled toward her RV. She needed to calm down and regain control. Her uncle had taught her that the fighter who loses control loses the fight.

She had defiantly lost control. She didn't need to explain anything about why she was upset to the other jumpers. What she needed was to get into her RV and have Buster snuggle in her lap.

Rick remained on the ground as a shadow crossed in front of the sun. He flinched when a hand came toward him.

"Easy man," Bob said. "Let me help you up."

"Thanks." Rick slowly got to his feet as Vicki's form receded on the concrete. He relaxed his tensed stomach muscles.

"What the hell was that all about?" Bob asked.

"I just gave her a surprise kiss pass before opening. I didn't think she would go ballistic."

"Something set her off." Bob's face broke into a slight grin. "Maybe you're just not as good of a kisser as you make out to be."

Rick rubbed his jaw. "That girl packs a punch."

"Let me look at that." Bob swiveled Rick's head left and right. "No real damage, but you're going to have a bruise."

"Do you think anyone else saw?"

Bob's head scanned the other jumpers as they walked in from the jump. No jumpers looked their way as small groups headed toward the hangar.

"Doesn't look like it."

Bob looked toward the hangar and Vicki's receding figure. "Vicki looks like she's heading toward her RV."

"Let's get to the hangar and pack. I'll just tell everyone that I did a face plant on landing. Hopefully, Vicki won't say anything."

Bob grinned. "I won't lie for you. Unless of course there's beer involved."

"Deal."

The two picked up their canopies and headed toward the hangar. They were halfway across the concrete when Rick stopped. "Hey Bob. Who's Eddie?"

"I've never heard that name around here.

Why?"

"Vicki called me Eddie. Then, she threatened to kill me if I ever touched her again."

Vicki wasn't worried that anyone would miss her at the hangar since she had videoed the jump. They would think that she had gone to her RV to copy the tape so that it could be shown in the Rec. hall after dinner. Vicki had about an hour to get herself under control and edit the tape before Judy would come to get it. That would be enough time.

A meowing Buster greeted her at the door. She blocked the opening so that he couldn't get out by rustling her bunched up canopy before she threw it on the couch. She slammed the door shut and rammed the bolt home before placing her helmet on the table. When she released the straps of her harness, she let it fall from her shoulders into a pile on the floor. Vicki scooped Buster up into her arms and retreated into her bedroom, curling into a ball on the back of the bed with Buster held close to her chest. She lightly stroked his head as she held him. His calming purr issued forth.

"Damn. I thought he was different. I thought he was different."

Vicki stayed on the bed long enough for her heart to get steady and the shake in her hands to stop. She lifted Buster high over her head.

"Well, I've still got you and you still have me. What more do we need?"

She placed the cat off to her side, slid off the bed, and made her way into the front. After she stripped off her jumpsuit, she sat at the table where she had left her helmet.

"Let's see what we got here."

Buster jumped up on the table next to her as she hit the rewind button on the camera. When the whirling stopped, she grabbed the cables that came from the VCR, plugged them into the camera, turned on the TV, and punched play. As the video started with the Cessna takeoff roll, she hit the mute button to quiet the wind noise.

She played the tape through once completely, wincing as her fist struck Rick on the chin.

"That had to hurt," she said to the still purring Buster.

She only paused the tape once when Rick's face and his fearful eyes shown close on the screen. She left her seat and moved closer to the TV. "So much fear. Well Buster, I guess that friendship's done. Damn that jerk."

Vicki rewound the tape and then dubbed the copy for Judy but stopped it before Rick entered the scene in the air. She punched the eject button on the VCR, removed the tape, and broke off the erase tab so that it would be safe from the drunken skydivers who would play it over and over tonight as they looked for every time they appeared on the screen. She glanced at the clock on her wall. A half an hour remained before Sally and Harry would stop by to head to the restaurant. She gathered her strength and put on a clean T-shirt.

"I guess I better go see what's going on in the hangar," she said to the now sleeping Buster. "We may not have a job anymore." She reached down, scratched the back of Buster's neck, and headed out the door. Buster yawned before settling his head back on the hand towel that he had claimed as a temporary bed.

When Vicki walked into the hangar from the tool room, everything seemed normal. No one stared at her or pointed. Jumpers worked on packing their rigs as others stood in small groups drinking beer with the normal amounts of laughter and banter. Sally leaned against the manifest counter in a laughter-filled conversation with Tom. Vicki scanned the hangar for Rick, but he was nowhere in sight. Bob was leaning against one of the large open hangar doors talking to several jumpers. Standing with another group of jumpers, Judy laughed along with the others as Kevin moved his hands to accompany a skydiving story. Vicki moved up to Judy and handed her the tape when the story ended.

"Here you go. I edited out all the parts that made you look bad. There's about three seconds left."

Judy looked stunned for a second until she burst out laughing. "Oh, you kidder. Thanks for doing this."

"No problem. How did the post dive go?"

"It went pretty well actually. Kevin didn't have much to say to anyone. I guess with the camera on, everyone behaved themselves in the air. You ought to see Rick though. He's a big bruise on his chin. He said he caught his foot on landing and did a face plant. He'll be hurting in the morning."

"Too bad for him, I guess. I'll see you at the restaurant." Vicki made her way over toward Bob.

Bob acknowledged Vicki with a wave of his beer. He then walked out the hangar doors stopping about ten feet onto the concrete. He kept his eyes fixed on the setting sun as Vicki walked up next to him about five feet away. They both turned slightly toward each other and quietly talked.

"Nice sunset," he said.

Vicki responded with a hesitation in her voice. "Uh…Yeah."

Bob turned to face Vicki. "Rick told me what happened. He's back at the camp nursing his jaw. You really did a number on him. Remind me never to piss you off without a baseball bat in my hands."

"I'm sorry. I really lost it"

"Look, I'm not going to judge what you did. I'm also not going to say anything to anyone and neither is Rick. I don't understand why you did it, but you certainly must have your reasons. Rick does dumb things at times and sometimes they turn around and bite him. I just want you to know that I consider you a friend. Rick is also my friend. I just don't want to have to choose between the two of you. I hope it will pass."

"I don't know, Bob. It's a long story why I'm like I am. I'm not willing to go into it right now."

"I know you told Carrie your story the night before she died."

Vicki's head snapped toward Bob, a firm grimace set on her mouth. "What did she say?"

"She didn't tell me anything really. She just came back to the van and said the two of you had a long talk. She said that you might agree to come to the party at the fire the next night, but that we couldn't drink until after we walked you home. I just figured that something bad had happened in your past involving drunk men. Rick and I were both ready to be teetotalers that night to get you to come along. I think we all lost a dream the day she died."

Vicki turned her head toward the sunset. "You're right about that."

The two of them stood silently as the setting sun formed gold and red rays across the sky. Vicki glanced over at Bob. A tear sat on his cheek. She then realized that tears streaked her own cheeks as she wiped her eyes with the palms of her hands.

Turning her face away from his, she spoke with a sob behind her voice. "I'll see you at the restaurant."

She turned and hurried toward her RV. Vicki raced into it and pulled open the drawer that held her collection of personal pictures. Picture after picture fell to the floor as she rifled through the numerous shots of skydivers, fellow mechanics, sunsets, and pilots. When she came upon the shot she wanted, the one of Carrie and her at the restaurant the night after Carrie's first jump, she held it up into the light while she traced Carrie's face with her finger. She remembered Carrie's over bubbling excitement that night. At that point, they had already begun to be friends, though not as close as they had become by the day she died.

Vicki decided just to ignore Rick at the restaurant. Her issues with Rick would better be handled tomorrow, in private, away from Bob. She would have to deal with Rick in a way that didn't hurt Bob. He had lost enough already and did not need to worry about the two of them.

The Sparks pulled up with a light toot from the horn. A car door opened and Sally's voice called from outside the RV door. "You ready to head to dinner?"

"Yes," Vicki answered. "I'll be out in just a minute."

Vicki splashed some water on her face and went to dry it with the hand towel by the sink. When she put it to her face, cat fur stuck to her wet skin. She playfully threw the towel at Buster and grabbed a clean one out of the linen drawer. As she looked at her face in the mirror, red puffy eyes stared back. She could only hope that no one would notice in the dim light of Manuel's. She scratched Buster on the head before she bounded out the door and into the backseat of the waiting car.

Chapter 17

Bob turned the van into one of the few open spaces in the parking lot of Manuel's. As he shut off the engine, Rick turned to him.

"Can't we just get a to-go order and take it back to the camp site? I really don't want to go in there."

"Relax. I told you that nobody saw Vicki punch you. They all think you just did a face plant on landing. You might take some ribbing for that, but it's nothing that half the people in there haven't done themselves."

"It's not just that. Vicki's in there and I really don't want to face her yet. She was really pissed."

"She looked like she had calmed down when I spoke to her at the hangar. She even said she was sorry for losing it."

"Maybe she said that to you, but I don't know if she'll say that to me. God, I don't know what I was thinking. That was really stupid of me."

"You've done other stupid things before and survived. Just give her some space for a little and some time to let it go. Go buy her a beer and quietly say you're sorry. I don't think she wants people to know she hit you. She'll be cool."

"Okay," Rick said. "I hope you're right. Because let me tell you, when she's pissed, she's scary. I'd rather leave now than face that again."

"Come on. I'm hungry. I'll even only have one beer so you can drink mucho cerveza to keep your jaw from hurting."

The two climbed out of the van and headed for the door of the restaurant.

When Rick pulled the door open, the sights, sounds, and smells of Manuel's embraced him like an old friend. The odor of Cilantro filled the air along with lively Mexican music. The party of a thousand jumps bellowed forth in full swing. The clank of the beer bottles punctuated the room as waitresses in their festive costumes delivered them to the laughing skydivers. The troubles that plagued Rick so far this evening fell away, minimized for the moment. He stepped into the ruckus with a little more bounce in his step. Rick and Bob made their way Judy's table to offer their congratulations.

"Thanks," Judy said. "Grab a beer. We're having a fiesta tonight and everybody drinks for free." The two grabbed beers from the collection on the table. Judy looked intensely at Rick. "How's your jaw doing? It looks like you must have hit it pretty hard on landing."

"It's okay," Rick said. "It hurts a little but the beer will help."

Tom yelled from across the table. "Hey, Rick. You're supposed to stop your canopy before you stop your feet. Didn't anyone ever tell you that?"

"Thanks for the advice. I'll remind you of that next time you blow a landing."

Tom raised his beer in a touché salute to

Rick and turned back to the woman seated next to him.

Rick looked toward the table always reserved for the Sparks. Next to Vicki a seat sat unused. Normally, he would be welcome to sit there, but tonight he knew better so he did not want to press his luck. As Bob had suggested, he would give Vicki some time. Then, he would see what he could do to mend their relationship, whatever it might be, or whatever Vicki would let it become. Her reaction to the kiss remained a mystery to him.

"Why don't you find us a couple of seats?" Rick said to Bob. "I'm going to see if I can start making peace."

Bob glanced at the Sparks' table and nodded to Rick. He turned and waded off through the crowd as Rick turned toward the bar, slowly weaving his way to the counter.

"Whatayahav?" Carlos asked.

"Corona with lime."

Carlos placed it before him as Rick threw a

five on the counter. "Keep the change."

Carlos eyed the bill. "Keep it. Judy's buying all the skydiver beer tonight."

"I'm paying for this one. It's a present."

Carlos slipped the bill into his shirt pocket. "You got it."

Rick slinked toward Vicki at the table. He maneuvered his path so that his approach toward her kept him in her line of sight. After this afternoon's fiasco, he did not want to surprise her. His face could not take another pounding. She glanced up at him before returning her attention to the story that Sally was telling. Rick waited several feet away while Sally finished and the table broke into laughter. He then slowly and carefully placed the beer down in front of Vicki. Vicki stared up at him with a set jaw.

Bending down, he spoke in a low voice only Vicki could hear. "I'm sorry for this afternoon. I hope you'll forgive me. It was stupid."

Vicki raised her left index finger slowly

and motioned Rick closer. With one of the sweetest smiles that Rick had ever seen on her face, she quietly spoke. "I don't want your beer. I want you to leave me alone."

With the smile still on her face, she sipped from her own beer as she turned back toward Sally.

Rick straightened up and started to turn away when Harry spoke. "How's your jaw doing? I heard you had a pretty good face plant on the last jump."

"It still stings," Rick said as his gaze returned to Vicki. "I think it'll sting for a while yet."

Rick nodded a goodbye to Harry and Sally then made his way back across the crowded dining room to find Bob. He looked back at the Sparks' table just in time to see Vicki hand the beer he had left for her to a passing skydiver. Dejected, he turned back into the fray while he resumed the search for his friend. As he walked through the crowd, he nodded to all the jumpers that said hello or commented on the story of his landing. He stopped to talk to no one. He just wanted to sit down, drink another beer, and sulk. Actually, he just wanted to leave, but he doubted that he would be able to talk Bob into that yet.

Rick found Bob seated at a table for eight filled with jumpers. A chair sat empty in a small spot next to him. Rick squeezed into the tiny space.

"Best I could do. When everyone heard Judy was buying, nobody stayed at the airport." Bob lowered his voice. "How'd it go with Vicki?"

"Not too good," Rick whispered. "I'll tell you later."

"I didn't know how long you'd be, so I ordered you a chicken burrito smothered in green."

"Thanks. Any chance I could talk you into getting it to go?"

"No way, Amigo! We're here for the duration. Drink your beer and enjoy the music."

Bob turned back to the jumper on the other side of him. Rick drained his beer then grabbed another from the pile in the center of the table. He hid behind Bob as he nursed the beer. If asked, he blamed his hurting jaw on his unusual quietness. He ate his meal in silence while enduring comments from the teasing jumpers.

"Finally found a way to shut you up."

"Didn't anyone tell you not to fight with Mother Earth?"

"I'm holding a class on landing if you're interested."

Rick accepted the verbal jabs with a painful grin. If the truth came out, he would have to leave, never to return. The other jumpers bantered about their jumps of that day, but his mind stayed on Vicki's comments to him. He hoped Bob was right about her forgiving him. His heart ached at the lost chance of a wonderful thing.

Harry, Sally, and Vicki headed out the door early while Rick remained concealed in his tiny spot. As the door closed behind them, his gut relaxed with the knowledge that he wouldn't run into her heading to the bathroom or as they left. Rick had consumed more than his share of the free beers so his jaw felt no pain, but his heart still ached.

Most of the skydivers cleared out from the restaurant an hour later. Cars left the parking lot in a steady stream as they turned toward the flashing beacon in the distance. Together Rick and Bob avoided the exiting cars as they made their way to the van. Rick moved with a slight stumble and fell into the passenger seat. The van soon left the lights of Florence.

"You want to tell me what Vicki said?"

Rick kept his gaze out the window toward the darkness beyond. "Not much. Just that she doesn't want me near her and wants me to leave her alone. She wouldn't even keep the beer I offered her. She gave it away."

"Well, at least she didn't hit you or yell at you. So, she's not still really mad. And, she only drinks one beer a night, so she would have given it away even if she wasn't mad."

"You always seem to find the good side of things, don't you?"

"It's a gift and a curse."

"If it's all good, how come I still feel so bad?"

The rest of the trip to the campsite stayed quiet save for the rumble of the tires on the chip-sealed roads. When Bob pulled the van into its normal parking place, Rick got out and started to build a fire.

"Aren't you going to the party at the Rec. Hall?" Bob asked.

"I don't know. Right now I think I just want to stare at the flames and dull out."

Bob reached into the cooler, pulled out two beers, and opened both before he set one down by Rick. Sitting down in his chair by the fire, he sipped his beer while he stared at his friend. The yellow flames of the fire grew until they bathed campsite in flickering light. Neither man said anything. They sipped their beers as the sounds of the desert night filtered into the campsite. The noise of the party replaced the sounds of the night as the fire at the Rec. Hall began to rise into the night sky. A tape player boomed out music across the desert air while laughter punctuated the beat. Rick just stared into the flames while he slowly sipped the beer. Bob rose from his seat and moved toward the noise.

"I'm heading to the party. Will I see you over there?"

"Maybe later."

Vicki turned on the TV, sat down at the table, and hit play on the camera. Rick's head came into focus on the screen as he pulled her in to kiss her. The sound of the rushing wind on the tape filled the RV. Vicki pressed the fast forward button and held it down. The images sped past. First, her canopy filled the screen then the spinning earth as she spiraled down. As the spin stopped, Vicki released the fast forward button. Rick's back shown on the screen as he landed his canopy. The ground got closer on the screen as the tape caught him removing his helmet. Then his face filled the screen.

Vicki's fist appeared from the left and connected with his exposed jaw.

Her voice came over the speaker. "You jerk! Don't you ever get in the way of my deployment again."

A collapsed canopy passed by the screen and Vicki's hands appeared as they gathered the canopy together. Jerky and unfocused scenes played on until the camera centered on Rick as he lay on the ground. Her hand grabbed him and pulled his face toward the lens.

Vicki hit pause and stared at Rick's face on the screen. A look of bewilderment and fear leapt from the image. She stared at the screen for a full minute and drank in the look of fear on his face with a slight sense of satisfaction before she hit play again. Voices from the tape burst forth.

"What the hell did you think you were

doing?"

"I was just trying to have a little fun."

"Fun? You wanted to have some fun? I'm not here for you to have fun with my body. If you ever touch me again Eddie, I'll kill you."

Vicki's face flushed as she fell back against the bench seat while the words on the tape dug into her brain. She hit pause again. Rick's frightened face froze on the screen. Nausea filled her throat as the real reason for her reaction sunk in. She had assaulted Rick for what Eddie and Bud had tried to do to her. She buried her face in her hands as tears flowed freely from her eyes.

She looked over at the sleeping Buster. "My God! What have I done?"

Rick had kissed her without asking, but he could not have known the problems that would cause. Kiss passes in the air were commonplace with many of the jumpers. With the exception of the kiss, he had not really done anything that he hadn't done before. The kiss was new, but he had surprised her with after-stars in free-fall before. They had both laughed about it on the ground afterwards.

She dropped her head into her hands once more. Her memories focused on how Rick had treated her with respect for the last two years. He had not deserved what she had done. The demons of her past in Casper might have ruined her friendship with Rick, or maybe more. She lifted her head as she realized that the Demons of Casper had not done this, she had done it. She had let them own her.

Vicki spoke to Buster again. "I've got to make this right. Rick deserves better. I have to apologize to him."

Vicki looked at the door to the RV. She would have to open up her soul to him, something she had not done with a man in many years. Vicki raced out of the RV, the door slamming behind her as she headed directly toward Rick's campsite.

She moved quickly with a purpose that focused on the small fire in the distance. The music from the party at the pit barely drowned out her hurried footsteps as her heart beat almost as loud. She took no actions to conceal her presence but moved away from the shadows and the trees. The rotating beacon lit her back with alternating white and green light and her fuzzy shadow preceded her as she neared the campsite. The music from the tape player stopped as the tape came to its end. A twig snapped beneath Vicki's right foot.

A second later, a flashlight beam shined in her face from the other side of the fire. Shielding her eyes with her right hand, she balled her left into a fist. She drew her left arm back as she instinctively went into a fighting stance. The flashlight beam left her face and turned toward the Rec. Hall. A chair clattered as it overturned. The flashlight beam moved wildly away as running footsteps faded into the night before the tape player boomed again.

"Shit!" Vicki said before she slowly turned toward her RV.

Rick looked up from the fire as a shadow crossed his eyes. The rotating beacon revealed the silhouette of a figure heading rapidly toward the campsite. He threw down his beer and grabbed the flashlight next to him. The music from the Rec. Hall went silent. A twig snap came from the direction of the figure. He pointed the flashlight toward the figure as he turned the light on. Vicki's face showed clearly in the light. She raised one hand to shield her eyes and balled her other into a fist as she flexed into a hostile posture. Rick knocked his chair over as he bolted toward the party. The flashlight illuminated the ground in wildly swinging arcs, but Rick ran blindly. He focused only on the fire pit in the distance as he stumbled over small bushes while branches from the mesquite trees slapped his face. The pain was minor compared to the fear.

Rick ran into the light of the fire at the pit. As he got close, several jumpers ran up to the fire and leapt across. No one noticed of his sudden appearance, all eyes stayed focused on the fire leapers. Rick slowed his pace as he glanced behind him. He expected Vicki to be ready to strike, but the space behind him stayed empty of threats. Breathing hard and in short puffs, he made his way to the coolers where he grabbed a beer. He held it to his front unopened, like the head of a hammer prepared to strike. He scanned the crowd for a friendly face before he saw Bob next to Nancy at the far edge of the firelight. The two held hands as they talked close to each other's faces. Rick weaved through the revelry to the safety of his friend. He grabbed Bob by the arm and pulled him away from Nancy.

"Bob, I need to talk to you."

Bob looked into Rick's wide eyes and moved with Rick toward the fire. When they got next to it, Bob closely spoke to Rick. "What's wrong?"

"Vicki was just at the campsite. I think she came to kill me."

"That's crazy talk. She won't hurt you."

"Her arms were raised with her fists balled

up."

"Come on over to the picnic table and calm down. You can hang with us."

"Okay. Maybe I can sleep in the front seat of the van tonight?"

"Sure. If it will make you feel safer. I still think it's nothing."

Judy stumbled toward them as they made their way across the grass. "Hey Rickie, baby. Give me a little hug."

Rick backed slightly away from her. "Hey Judy. Any chance you want to take my eight o'clock instruction jump?"

"Sorry Charlie. I plan on not being in shape to jump until at least noon. If at all." She stumbled away.

Bob made Rick sit at the table as he motioned Nancy over. "Just sit there and drink your beer. I'll stand with you."

Chapter 18

Vicki closed her container as Rick and Bob walked into the hangar. Nancy and Frank danced in the corner practicing their routine. Beth knelt next to Vicki and talked about jumping in Virginia, but Vicki had not heard much of what she had said. Her mind remained fixed on the injustice she had done to Rick. Her attempt at an apology last night had ended in disaster when Rick fled before she could speak. She would have to talk to him today.

This morning.

Vicki closed the last flap and rose to face Rick and Bob. Bob continued to approach while Rick held back in the protective shadow of his friend. Vicki quickly put on a smile.

"Morning Rick. Morning Bob."

"Good Morning," Bob said.

Rick mumbled. "Morning."

Rick positioned himself so that Bob was closer to Vicki, but Bob turned and headed over toward Nancy. This left Rick open and defenseless so he shifted closer to Beth.

"So what's the plan for the jump?" Vicki said.

"Huh, huh, just a two way exit with Beth working on free flying to me."

"Okay," Vicki said. "Let's go dirt dive the exit at the mockup. Plane's ready when we are."

Rick followed Vicki and Beth out of the hangar. At the mockup, Rick arranged the exit order so that Beth would be between him and Vicki. The group ran thru the simple exit and dive several times. The PA came to life as they finished up.

"Cessna load one. Rick, Beth, Vicki, Nancy, and Frank. Get it on. Pilot's at the airplane."

"Beth," Vicki said. "Why don't you go suit up? I need to talk to Rick for a minute."

"Sure," Beth said smiling as she walked away.

Rick stepped away from Vicki, his stance centered on the balls of his feet ready to run.

Vicki saw his tension and she softened her voice. "Please relax Rick. I promise I'm not going to hit you. I just want to talk."

"Okay, so talk."

"Not now. Maybe after this jump we can sit down to talk for a little. There's a few things I need to tell you about me and it will take longer than we have now. Is that okay with you?"

His stance softened. "Yea, sure."

"Let's go have fun on this jump. We'll both feel better when we get down."

Rick followed Vicki into the hangar, but stayed ten feet behind her.

Rick stayed on his knees in the rear of the Cessna the whole ride to altitude. Beth sat with her back to the pilot's seat and Vicki sat facing her in the rear of the Cessna. Frank's back leaned against the instrument panel as Nancy kneeled in front of him. The brother and sister teased each other and joked about their dive. Rick remained silent while he stayed focused toward the front. As the plane passed 9000 feet on its way to jump run, Vicki grabbed Rick's shoulder. Rick stiffened and jerked his head around.

"Help me up, will you?" Vicki yelled above the engine noise.

Rick reached back and lifted his arm for her to grab. He removed his arm as soon as Vicki's knee hit the cabin floor and returned his focus to the front. Vicki bumped into Rick repeatedly as she struggled to seat her helmet in the cramped quarters. Rick jerked around with each touch, each time noting the position of her hands. As the airplane reached 10,000 feet, Rick helped Beth to her knees and performed a final safety check on her gear. Nancy and Frank checked each other's equipment.

"Jump run," Bill yelled.

Nancy looked around the cabin and got a nod from both Vicki and Rick.

"Door," she yelled and turned the latch.

The door lifted open and Nancy stuck her head out into the wind. She signaled a few corrections to the pilot before she called "Cut" and pointed to Frank.

"Climb Out."

Frank slid across the strut to his exit position. Nancy placed her right foot on the step as she gripped Frank's harness. Her left hand reached for his backpack just as a pocket of turbulence rocked the airplane. Nancy faltered in her grip.

Her hand pushed against Frank's soft ripcord and dislodged it before her hand shifted to grip the harness. Frank's pilot chute snaked its way around his pack and caught air.

Frank's face lay on top of Nancy's head as the two prepared for their exit count. The pilot chute dragged the deployment bag out of Frank's container and, as it loosened, he glanced down toward his harness. The bag shot pass Frank's line of vision and his eyes widened as the danger he and his sister faced materialized. Before he could react, the suspension lines went taut as the canopy opened. Frank and the still unsuspecting Nancy disappeared from the strut toward the tail.

The airplane shuddered and pitched wildly to the right as a loud bang reverberated through the cabin. Rick grabbed the edge of the door with his right hand while thrusting his left arm upward to the ceiling to keep himself inside the airplane. He looked through the rear window as Frank's canopy dragged him over the horizontal stabilizer. Frank struck the rear of the elevator and forced it downward so that the tail of the airplane pitched uncontrollably upward.

Bill wrestled the yoke as he tried to regain control. A woman's scream pierced the wind but was cut short as a heavy thud came from the rear of the cockpit. The airplane's motion threw Rick upward to the ceiling and then down to the floor as Frank's body cleared the tail. His damaged canopy spun his body wildly behind the airplane. Rick looked out the door at Nancy as she fell away spinning on her back. The vision of Carrie falling to her death instantly came into his mind. He knew he had to do something and he had to do it fast.

He brought his head back into the cabin. Vicki had wedged her arms against the roof of the cabin while Beth held tight to the back of the pilot's seat. Beth's face was filled with terror. Vicki's only shown deep concern.

Rick looked straight into Vicki's eyes as he shouted, "Look after her!"

Then with the same intensity but with a slight softening of his voice, he yelled, "Please."

He turned toward the door and shouted as he left the airplane.

"Not again!"

Vicki's body violently shifted around as the plane gyrated almost out of control. Bill fought the controls as the airplane bucked and rolled. Vicki pulled herself forward to the door and peered out as she gripped the frame. The tail of the airplane curved to the right and a dent 4 inches deep cut across the front of the stabilizer. A canopy spun behind and below the Cessna. The spin stopped as the jumper cut away from the damaged main before a white reserve appeared.

She scanned lower and located Rick in a steep dive directly below. She shifted her gaze rearward to look for Nancy when a hand grabbed her and pulled her upright. Bill pulled her ear to his mouth.

"Vicki," he screamed. "Grab the student and get out. I'm not sure how long I can keep this thing flying. It feels like the tail is coming off."

Vicki pushed herself to the back of the cabin and grabbed Beth. The airplane bucked and threw Vicki toward the roof. It rolled to the right before it settled level again. Beth held tight to the back of the pilot's seat. Vicki grabbed the top of the seat and pulled her mouth close to Beth's ear.

"We have to bail out. Let go of the seat and exit."

"Are we near the landing area?"

"I don't know. Just get out, open up, and head toward the hangar."

Vicki pulled Beth's fingers loose from the seat and pushed her toward the door as the airplane bucked again. The violent movement threw Vicki to the roof and then to the floor with a heavy thud. She shook her head to clear the stars from her vision as she resumed pushing Beth toward the door. Beth grabbed one of the seatbelts with her hand and held fast. Vicki bit Beth's hand to force a release and pushed her out the door. Vicki got to her knees as she looked at Bill.

"Good Luck," she yelled as she left the airplane.

As Rick hit the air, he spotted the still spinning Nancy far below him at an angle steeper than his experience told him she should be. He brought his arms to his sides while he stuck his legs straight out with his toes pointed. Tucking his chin into his chest, he focused on the Cessna as he fell away. Vicki's face appeared in the doorway for a moment before the airplane moved too far away to make out details.

He used first the Cessna, then the horizon as the reference for his dive and held this position for several seconds until his body extended vertical to the Earth. Rick lifted his head and shot a glance out to where he thought Nancy should be. The empty sky terrified him. He held his body position steady as he searched left, then right. He spotted her to the right of his present direction so he dipped his shoulder to head toward her. Nancy's body did not spin as fast as it had been, but it had taken on the appearance of a rag doll. It flopped off to the left and then off to the right.

The distance between them diminished,

but not fast enough. Rick tucked his chin back into his chest to resume his vertical dive. The hope of a few more feet per second filled his heart and he began to count in an attempt to bring control to his wildly active mind. He could no longer process time. He focused his thoughts on the out-of-control body somewhere beneath him.

Rick brought his head up when he reached the count of four and regained sight of Nancy. Her body grew larger by the second as it flopped across his course. He lifted his shoulders to adjust his angle of descent toward her as he studied the body's wild gyrations. Her legs caught air, flew upwards, and her torso went down. Her body fell faster until the legs lost their air causing the body to flop back level again. Her arms flailed uncontrolled into the airstream and then across her body. Rick's dive brought him closer and closer to his target.

Something in the back of his mind said *Pull.*

Rick brought his arms forward while relaxing his legs. The wind blew them loosely as he slowed his approach at Nancy. If he did not stop in time, he would slip below her without having time to recover. His legs moved first in tension and then relaxed as he slowed until he pulled even with the unstable form. Blood spread from Nancy's mouth across her face. Rick kept his eyes fixed on her arms as his body, without thought, reacted to the gyrations caused by the lack of any control in her limbs.

Something in the back of his mind yelled *Pull!*

He hovered five feet from her for several seconds to study the motion of her arms. He did not want to get in the way of a deploying reserve. That could be deadly to both of them. He focused his eyes intently for a sign of control by the flopping arms, but decided that the air rushing by is what caused the movement.

Something in the back of his mind

screamed *Pull!*

Rick moved toward the body, his arms and legs working without thought to match the rag doll movements. His gaze remained fixed on her arms with their motion near the reserve ripcord. He needed to be prepared to abandon his approach in a split second if the white of a pilot chute appeared. He closed to four feet, then three, then two.

As he looked across the remaining distance toward her body, the horizon in his far vision looked wrong. It was further up then it had ever been before. Suddenly, he realized the danger. He had absolutely no idea how high above the ground they were. He had broken the first rule of skydiving and had lost track of altitude.

His mind screamed *PULL!*

As his eyes stayed fixed on Nancy's flopping body, an urge to grab his reserve ripcord coursed through his veins. He fought that urge away and screamed to the air around him.

"NOT AGAIN!"

Rick stuck his legs straight out driving his body directly into Nancy's as he grabbed her harness with his hands. He flipped over her body, reached for her reserve ripcord, and yanked it clear in one motion. The pilot chute leapt from Nancy's back as Rick continued to hold her body stable and then the bag lifted off her back. The suspension lines trailed loosely until the canopy hit the air and filled the sky above them. Nancy's body ripped upward from Rick's grip.

Rick brought eyes to his chest along with his left hand. He grabbed his own reserve ripcord and yanked it. The cable cleared the guide tube in an instant. Rick glanced at the ground as he returned to his arch. The leaves on a mesquite tree waved in the breeze and a jackrabbit's brown eyes stared back at him.

His harness loosened. His legs swung forward of his body as the canopy fully inflated and jerked at his shoulders. Rick looked past his toes toward the horizon as the waving tops of the mesquite trees raced by.

Darkness engulfed him.

Chapter 19

Vicki pulled her ripcord as her feet cleared the edge of the door. The airplane descended in jerky movements away from her but Bill did not bail out after her. She watched the airplane for a few seconds more and then turned her attention to the air beneath her. Vicki moved her gaze a little at a time as she mumbled, "Come on! Come on!"

A flash of white showed below and she zeroed her eyes on a reserve parachute swinging so near the ground that it almost touched its shadow. A second later, another flash of white blossomed and then almost instantly collapsed to the side.

Vicki's heart sank.

She located Beth under canopy below her and to the south. Beth's canopy faced east as it moved away from the drop zone. Frank's reserve hung like a white beacon high over the drop zone. No other canopies flew in the sky. The Cessna had disappeared but no smoke rose from the desert. Vicki looked back to the spot that the reserves had landed. Cars and trucks raced across the desert floor toward them. A flash of lights on the airport road caught her eye as several police cars and ambulances raced toward the scene. She pulled down on her left toggle and started into a spiral to get to where the reserves had landed.

Beth's canopy came into view as Vicki completed the first spiral. Rick's last words before he jumped came to her as the blue and red canopy flashed by a second time.

Look after her. Please.

Vicki stopped her spiral, zigzagged behind Beth, and matched her flight path.

Vicki's mind raced as images of Rick crossed her mind. Not the Rick that kissed her without her permission, but the Rick who petted Buster and brought him creamers. Not the Rick who partied hard every Saturday night at the Cantina and the fire, but the Rick who tried to give her Burritos from Manuel's on Friday nights. The Rick who soiled his hands when he helped her clean her tools. The Rick who landed next to her on a bad spot so she would not have to walk in alone. The Rick who surprised her with ten jump tickets at Christmas. The Rick who helped her push airplanes out of the hangar. The Rick who packed her parachute when she had too little time between jumps. The Rick who she trusted with Buster's life.

Tears came to her eyes as she realized what she had lost. They rolled out the sides of her eyes before flying away on the wind. She turned her head to look at the cars and flashing lights that headed to the spot in the desert where the two white canopies lay half-inflated in the breeze. Her tears continued to fly into the wind.

Vicki and Beth walked through the open desert with their canopies in their arms.

Vicki's helmet swung loosely from her elbow. Her eyes were red and puffy.

"I'm sorry about making us land so far out," Beth said. "I thought that big barn was the hangar."

"Don't worry about it. It's happened before."

"What do you think that helicopter was all about?"

"I don't know."

"Was one of them your boyfriend?"

"Yes, uh, no, uh, I don't know. They were all good friends."

"Do you think they're alright?"

"I don't know. Let's just keep moving."

The throaty rumble of the Beech engines sounded in the distance as the airplane headed in their direction. The trees and vegetation nearby opened up into a clearing and Vicki pushed Beth toward it.

"Get in the clearing and lay your canopy out. I hear the Twin Beech. They must be looking for us."

A minute later, the Twin Beech flew by headed east. It flew on for another minute and then reversed direction, the course closer to them this time. It flew past them to the west about a mile before it reversed course a second time. As it leveled out, the sound of the engines dropped and the airplane descended heading straight for them. The Beech leveled out a hundred feet above the ground and began to circle their position while a figure crouched in the open doorway.

Vicki waved her arms above her head. "Wave your arms so they know we're okay"

The Beech pilot rocked the wings in response as it continued to circle them. It leveled out after about five minutes and disappeared to the west. Vicki picked up her canopy and helmet.

"Pick your stuff up. I hear the truck."

The truck pulled up next to them several minutes later. Sally and Judy jumped out.

Judy ran to Vicki. "Are you two okay?"

Her duty to Rick completed, Vicki's lip

trembled as she leaned on the trunk of a tree for support while her tough exterior failed.

"How's Rick?"

"He's okay," Judy said. She reached out and held Vicki close. "They're all okay. Rick had about a quarter-second canopy ride and got knocked out for a minute by the landing, but his rig cushioned the blunt of the impact. The Medics drove Rick to the clinic in Florence to check him out, but he'll be back later. Frank had a few cuts, line burns, and bruises, but he's fine. Nancy was unconscious when the medics arrived, but she woke up while they were working on her. They airlifted her to Tucson General for X-rays. She might have a concussion. Her helmet was cracked and pushed in."

A wave of relief came over Vicki and she collapsed to the desert floor. Tears flowed down her cheeks as her voice sobbed.

"I was so afraid."

Judy helped Vicki to her feet. "Come on. Let's get you into the truck and back to the hangar."

Vicki wiped her eyes with the sleeve of her jumpsuit. "How about Bill and the airplane?"

"Bill landed it," Sally said. "Harry doesn't understand how he did it, but he did. The impact of Nancy and Frank hitting the tail almost ripped it off. Also, there's a big dent in the leading edge where Nancy's head hit."

Vicki walked around the damaged Cessna for the third time. It sat broken in the rear of the hangar. The tail skewed ten degrees. Rips in the aluminum skin ran vertically along the right side. The fuselage rippled all along the left side from tail to wing strut. A large dent disrupted the smooth lines of the leading edge on the right stabilizer. Vicki grabbed it for the second time and jiggled it up and down. What had been solid in the morning now moved six inches both ways.

"It's a mess," Harry said as he walked up. "There's only one bolt of the original eight holding the stabilizer on, the rest sheared off.

Bill should have bailed out."

"Can it be fixed?"

"No. We can salvage the wings, instruments, the engine, but the fuselage is ruined. There's also a few parts we can keep like the in-flight door, but the rest of it is beer can material. We'll start dismantling it as soon as the FAA gets out to make their report."

"Will you get another one?"

"Of course. It'll take me a month or so to find one and another month for you to convert it to a jump plane. We'll just make due until then."

Vicki's ears perked up as a known engine sound pulled up to the front of the hangar.

"It's Rick," a voice called.

Vicki made her way around the Cessna and toward the front of the hangar. A crowd of jumpers massed by the doors and surrounded Rick as he climbed out of Bob's van. Hands extended and shook his as others padded him on the back. Rick scanned the hangar until his eyes focused on Vicki. He moved deliberately through the crowd toward her. The rambunctious crowd parted as Rick approached Vicki then surrounded them both as the two faced each other.

"Are you okay?" Rick said. "I was worried about you."

Vicki's eyes misted. "You were worried about me? You're the one that had the quarter-second canopy ride."

"But I left you in a broken airplane with my student to take care of. I'm sorry."

Before Vicki could respond, Kevin's voice came through the crowd. "Welcome back Rick."

The command voice that had presided over hundreds of parties at the fire pit silenced the crowd. Jumpers parted as Kevin came into the throng. Rick and Vicki turned toward the approaching figure as he stopped three feet in front of Rick.

Kevin nodded toward Vicki before looking back at Rick. "I've got a few questions for you. That is, if you don't mind answering them."

"Sure," Rick said with a smile. "Go for it."

"First, do you want on the sunset load? I saved a slot for you."

"Yea. I'll go. Has Robert repacked my rig?"

"Don't worry about that. You can borrow my spare."

"Thanks."

"Next question, did you lose track of altitude?"

Rick cast his eyes to the floor. "Yea."

"That was stupid."

"I know."

"Last question. Had you realized that you had lost track of altitude before you pulled Nancy's reserve?"

"Yea."

"But you did it anyway?"

Rick looked up and straight into Kevin's eyes. "Yes."

"Now that, my boy, was righteous." Kevin brought his hands together and began a slow clap. More and more jumpers picked up the clap until the hangar became a thundering shell as voices hooted and called out congratulations. Vicki clapped enthusiastically with the crowd.

Over the thunderous rhythm, the PA came to life. "Sunset load. Let's get it on. Kevin plus fourteen. Airplanes are ready to go. Sunset load. Get it on."

The jumpers assembled by the airplanes with their gear as Kevin worked the adjustments on his loaner rig to fit it to Rick's torso. He finally patted Rick on the back.

"That's got it."

"Okay everyone," Kevin called out. "Listen up. We've had enough excitement for one day. This is going to be a one-formation jump. Simple round. Hold it until 6000 feet. Pull high and enjoy the sunset." He turned toward Rick. "You have exit order rights on this one. Where do you want to go?"

"I'll ride by the door of the Cessna, hang from the strut, and leave last."

"You got it," Kevin said as he turned

toward the group of jumpers. "Rick's got swooping rights on this load. Everyone else gets into the formation and waits for him." He turned to Vicki. "Where you want to exit?"

"Rear-rear float on the Beech."

"Okay," Kevin said. "Vicki's rear-rear. Everyone else take a slot. I'll go front float."

The jumpers claimed positions in the lineup and several practice run outs later, Kevin called the jumpers to go to their airplanes. As Rick started for the Cessna, Vicki grabbed his hand.

"Rick, can I talk to you for a moment."

"Sure."

"Listen, we never got a chance to talk earlier. I'm really sorry that I went off on you. Would you come by my RV after this, maybe have a beer with me so we can talk a little?"

"I'd love to, but right after I get down, I've got to take Bob's van down to Tucson General and pick him up. He drove Nancy and Frank's car down there for them."

Her free hand twisted her left pigtail.

"Okay. Well, how about if you bring your motorcycle up here on Tuesday. We could get some chicken in Florence and go have a picnic by one of the lakes. You know, kinda like a date."

Rick smiled. "Like a date?"

"Yea, like a date."

"I'd like that."

"Okay. I'll see you about ten."

"It's a date."

The airplane engines began to crank and came to life with mighty roars. Rick and Vicki turned toward their individual airplanes, but Vicki stopped and grabbed Rick's hand again. She squeezed it tight as she pulled his ear to her mouth.

"Please don't mess this up."

Rick looked into her eyes. "The date or the skydive?"

"Both."

Rick squeezed Vicki's hand. "Deal."

He smiled, turned, and headed to the Cessna. Vicki's heart beat happily as she handed her helmet to Kevin as she climbed into the Beech.

Vicki tightened the chip straps on her helmet as the Beech climbed through 9,000 feet while the Cessna flew thirty feet away. Vicki slid over next to Kevin and pulled his ear to her mouth.

"Would you please spot low in the door? I need to communicate with the Cessna before exit."

Kevin signaled her with a thumb up. The airplane continued its climb past the normal exit altitude of 10,500 feet. As Vicki's altimeter showed 12,500 feet, the call came back from the front.

"Jump Run."

Kevin pulled the door and stowed it in the rear. He stayed low as his head went out the door. Vicki moved to the upper part of the door and stuck the palm of her hand out with his fingers pointed upward to get the attention of the Cessna jumpers. She then pointed to the

Cessna, then to herself, then blew a kiss toward the Cessna to let Rick know that she wanted to do a kiss pass after the formation.

Four hands appeared in the Cessna's open door with their thumbs pointed to the sky. Vicki giggled at the reaction from the Cessna as she stuck her hand out in a fist with her thumb pointed down. She then stuck one finger in the air to designate the exit position of the jumper the message was for.

First position.

Rick.

This time three thumbs pointed down, only one pointed up, Rick's.

"Cut, Climb out," came the call from Kevin.

Vicki pulled back to clear the door. Her fingers went automatically to the camera switch and toggled it on. Kevin swung out into the front float position as Vicki followed into the rear-rear float position, but she paid no attention to the jumpers on the Beech. Her camera sight zeroed in on Rick as he worked his way out onto the strut of the Cessna. She hung from the bar by her right arm, her left arm back, ready to fly. The jumpers started the count as Vicki framed Rick in her sight.

On "Go," the Beech rocked as the jumpers piled out in tight formation. The three other jumpers on the Cessna rolled out the door into their dives. Rick hung on, his head turned toward the Beech. After a few seconds more, he released his grip and started a right turn as he fell from the airplane. Vicki released her grip as she straightened her legs. She side-slipped toward Rick as he set his body into a dive. Vicki kept the sight fixed on him as she drove herself toward him.

They met halfway across the sky with Rick pointed downhill and Vicki pointed up. Vicki turned left to maintain the frame on Rick. He barrel-rolled as he passed her, a smile plastered on his face. She fell in place behind him following his path to the formation. Vicki set up above the group with the whole assemblage framed as Rick grasped two arms, gave a shake, and entered the formation last. The formation fell perfectly round and stable toward the approaching earth.

Kevin nodded his head and waved off at 6,000 feet. Most members of the group turned outward and placed their bodies into relaxed tracks. Rick stayed. Vicki relaxed her arch so she fell into place in front of him as she moved slowly forward until their hands met and their fingers intertwined. Vicki pulled Rick in to her lips and closed her eyes. As their lips touched, the Demons of Casper worked to raise their ugly heads. Vicki pressed Rick's lips tighter to hers and the love in her heart for Rick dispatched the Demons to the pit they belonged. Only the vision of Rick filled her mind.

Their lips and fingers separated at 4,000 feet. Vicki turned to track and centered the setting sun in her sight as the rays of Arizona filled the sky.

Tomorrow, the rising sun would welcome forth a new day with the same rays. The birds would sing their morning song of freedom.

Vicki would hear those birds sing.

Excerpt from

Book 2 of
The Vertical Speed Chronicles

THE DEMONS OF CASPER

Chapter 1

Only two people were still lifting weights Saturday evening as the three men walked into the gym. Eb Fox came out of his office just as the door buzzer stopped when the third man cleared the electric eye.

"Evening Harvey."

"Evening. You got the office ready?"

"Yes. All piled up and ready to go. I took the important stuff home to keep until you finish recarpeting it and get the furniture back in."

"I should be able to have it ready for you by Tuesday, but let's say Wednesday."

"Okay. I'll get those last two out of here so that you can get to work." Eb walked away toward the two weight lifters.

Harvey led Bud and Sam into the office.

"Clear everything out of here and put it on the floor area that I stripped the tile off of last night. When you're done, you can take off. I won't need you again until Monday evening. We'll move more of the gym equipment around then."

Bud and Sam nodded their heads with disinterest as Bud let his eye wander around the room. The eye movement was not lost on Harvey.

"And don't get any ideas Bud. I told Eb to take anything valuable out and lock everything else up. Just clear the room and try not to damage the walls." Harvey left the two in the office.

Bud walked around the desk, pulled out the swivel chair, and plopped down in it. "Go on out and get the hand truck. I'll start getting the small stuff together."

"Yea. Right. I'll bet you'll still be sitting in that chair when I get back."

"Just get the hand truck."

Sam left the room and the door buzzer

sounded. Bud tried pulling on a couple of the drawers only to find them locked as promised. He stood and let his eyes wander over the box of staplers, tape, pads of paper, invoices, and mail piled in the box on top of the desk. His eyes widened as he read the return address of the letter on top of the pile. He glanced up at the door before reaching into the box and pulling the already opened letter out. He stuffed the letter into his shirt pocket just as the door buzzer sounded again. A few seconds later, Sam rolled the hand truck into the room.

Bud grabbed the box from the desk. "Come on. Let's get this done. I've got somewhere I need to be later."

"What got your ass in gear? We get paid by the hour. I'm not interested in rushing faster than I have too."

"Well I am. So get moving."

Later that night, Bud cruised by the Cattleman's Bar and Grill. He finally spotted the car he had been searching all over the town for. The car, a 1975 GTO, was Eddie's pride and joy. Bud parked in the rear of the lot between two widely spaced light poles. Pulling the letter out of his shirt pocket, he flicked on the overhead light to read the return address one more time. A smile crept over his face.

He pulled out the three pages of neatly written script and read them slowly. His lips moved as he took in the words. When he had finished, he carefully folded the pages along their original creases and stuck them back into the envelope. Another smile crept onto his face as he leaned back on the seat. This would fix everything between him and Eddie. Eddie might even give him some free coke in addition to settling his outstanding debt.

Bud got out of the truck and headed toward the door of the bar. He side-stepped to avoid a staggering couple and caught the door before it closed. As he stepped into the dim light of the room, he searched the bar and then the booths with his eyes until he spotted Eddie. With a purpose, Bud moved through the crowd toward the booth where Eddie sat engrossed in a conversation with two women. The women giggled as Eddie delivered what must have been the punchline to a joke.

As Bud approached, Eddie looked up from the women and frowned at the approaching figure. He sipped slowly from his beer, his eyes staring toward Bud with no hint of warmth.

Bud stopped two feet from the booth. "Evening Eddie. Got a minute? I'd like to have a word with you."

Eddie looked down at Bud's hand and then back toward his face. "I don't see any money in your hand, so I doubt that I'm going to be interested in anything you have to say."

Bud leaned down. He spoke quietly so that only Eddie could hear. "You'll like this. You might even want to let me have a little taste for free for what I have to say."

"I told you before. You're not getting

anymore until you pay what you owe. And you're never going to get any more credit."

Bud moved his mouth closer to Eddie's ear and spoke even quieter. "You'll like what I have to say. You might even thank me. Hell, you might even let me hang with you again."

Eddie cocked his head slightly toward Bud's. "Now what could you know that I would be interested in?"

Bud moved his mouth to Eddie's ear. "I know where Vicki is." He moved back slightly so that he could see Eddie's face.

Eddie remained stoic. Then, his eyes widened and a grin moved across his face. He turned toward the two women. "Why don't the two of you go up to the bar for a few minutes? I've got some business to discuss with Bud."

Bud stood straight up. "Not here, let's go out to my truck."

Eddie nodded and pulled himself from the booth. Together the two men headed out the door.

With a smile on his face, Eddie laid the pages of the letter into his lap and looked out the windshield. Bud held a small mirror up toward Eddie. Two lines of white powder lay stretched across the glass surface. Eddie looked back toward Bud and shook his head.

"You go ahead and do both. I want to think for a minute."

Bud shifted the mirror into one hand and moved the rolled up twenty toward his nose. "Sure. No problem." With a quick snort, one line disappeared into his left nostril. Several seconds later, the second line went into his other nostril.

Eddie lifted the pages of the letter off his lap and began to reread them. He stopped several times to go back over certain passages. When he finished, he carefully folded the pages along the original crease lines and stuffed it back into the envelope. He held it out to Bud.

"Put this in a safe place. When you go back

to the gym to move the furniture back into the office, put it back where you found it."

Bud took the letter and placed it in his shirt pocket. "So we square?"

Eddie nodded. "Yea. We're square. In fact..." He dug into his jacket pocket and brought out two small paper packets. "Here's a couple more grams for your troubles. Don't mention that letter to anyone."

As Bud reached for the packets, Eddie continued. "We're square, but you still don't get anymore credit."

Bud took the packets and pushed them down into his pocket. "So what you going to do? You going after her?"

Eddie turned his head and stared out the windshield again. "Yea. I need to finish our business with her." He turned his head back toward Bud. "Correction. We need to finish our business with her."

A grin crept over Bud's face. "That sounds good. I've always wanted another chance to do her." His grin turned into a frown. "Only we better knock her out first or at least tie her up."

"Yea."

"So when you want to do it?"

"Not sure right now. From what's in that letter, I think there's a bigger opportunity we need to explore first. I need to call Carlos and talk to him about it."

"What do you mean?"

"Carlos told me that ever since the Feds put that radar balloon in the air between Phoenix and Tucson, he hasn't been able to sneak any plane loads of coke across the border. Plus, the dirt airfields he used to land at have been torn up by the Fed's bulldozers. Everything now has to come across the border on people's backs. That's why the price has gone up so much recently."

"I don't think Vicki will help you and Carlos bring in coke."

"I don't either. But it sounds like Vicki's got free access to airplanes, has friends that are pilots, and is dating a parachute instructor.

I just have an idea that I want to run by Carlos that might get us a large shipment in. Besides that, it would ruin that little life she's put together down there and I'd love to see her lose all that."

"Then we get to do her?"

Eddie grinned. "Yea. Then we both get to do her. In fact, I'll even let you go first."

Eddie reached down and pulled out the hunting knife from the scabbard inside his boot. He brought the blade up into the light and twisted it around letting the clean steel reflect light into his eyes.

"Then I'm going to gut the bitch."

About the Author

Soldier in the 60's, Rock&Roll Roadie in the 70's, Skydiving Instructor in the 80's, Pilot in the 90's, and Writer in the new millennium, Gregory P Robertson brings a wide and varied wealth of experience with him to his writing. Along the way, he found time to acquire an Electrical Engineering Degree, obtain Professional Engineering Certification in multiple states, and have a 27-year career with AT&T.

His past writing works include the nonfiction history of the Staunton Military Academy and the first volume of a collection of humorous memoirs entitled "Life As A Cadet – How To Find Humor With A Black Stripe Down Your Leg."

His first Novel was Southern Roadie, a military based thriller.

You can view his entire collection of writings at his website **www.gregoryprobertson.com**.

www.ingramcontent.com/pod-product-compliance
Lightning Source LLC
Chambersburg PA
CBHW022234020726
47496CB00004B/893

* 9 7 8 0 9 9 0 6 9 2 1 3 3 *